Home Signal
The Dominion Falls Series 6

Sarah Cass

Historical Romance
Romantic Suspense
Historical Western Romance

A Divine Roses Ink Book
Historical Romance
Romantic Suspense
Historical Western Romance

Copyright © 2013 Sarah Cass
First E-book Publication: February 2013
Second run publication: February 2023

Cover design by Sarah Cass
Edited by Megan Koenen
Proofread by Mary Terrani
All cover art and logo copyright © 2013 by Sarah Cass

PUBLISHER
Divine Roses Ink
http://www.divinerosesink.com

Other Books in
The Dominion Falls Series

Independent Brake
Changing Tracks
Derailed
Dark Territory
Green Eye
Runaway Train
Red Zone

Coming Soon in
The Dominion Falls Series

Dust Raiser
Chase the Red
Blizzard Lights
Dead Man's Switch
Bird Cage
A Highball Arrangement
Douse the Glim
Blood
Grave Digger
Bad Order

Books by Sarah Cass
The Tribe Series
The Tribe
The Wolf
The Chief
The Raven
The Lake Point Series
Santa, Maybe
Deep-Fried Sweethearts
Stalled Independence
Witch Way
A Thorough Thanksgiving
Eve's New Year
Heartstrings & Hockey Pucks
Luck of the Cowgirl
Stars, Stripes & Motorbikes
Free Falling
Love for Hire
Haunted Hearts
Stand Alone Novels
Masked Hearts
Leap

Dedication

To my family,
Who support me,
Even when they think it's weird.

Be proud. Be weird.
Be your unique selves.
Always

Table of Contents

Trigger Warning:

Rape.

If you are sensitive to the subject, feel free to skip Chapter 9. It is mentioned in subsequent chapters, but Chapter 9 is where the events takes place (fade to black, with lead-in.)

Protect your mental health, it's the most important thing.

You cannot run away from a weakness;
you must sometimes fight it out or perish.
And if that be so, why not now,
and where you stand?
-Robert Louis Stevenson

Jane stormed past Tom and the Marshal so quick, she reached the saloon first. However, before she could step foot inside, a wave of nausea overtook her hard.

She rushed into the alley to void her stomach. She'd eaten so little that day, in no time it was naught but dry heaves. A strong hand settled on her back, while low murmurs carried on not far away.

Rather than wait for the inevitable question, Jane spoke before Cole could. "Empty…the saloon."

"Lou?" The low murmuring had ceased at Tom's words.

Cole's hand left her back. She thought he'd gone to do as asked, but a damp kerchief was placed in her hand moments later. "Clean yourself."

"Miss Spencer." The Marshal's voice drew closer. "We can meet with them. You're not well."

"I'll be fine. Do as I ask, please Tom." Jane pressed the cool, damp fabric to her heated face. The worst had passed at least. She thought with some tea she'd be up to snuff.

"Tea?" Cole's hand rubbed her back.

She smiled into the kerchief that he'd guessed her thoughts. "Yes. I should be better once I've had some."

"I'll see you inside."

Before he could get far, she touched his arm. "Cole."

"Yeah?" He turned. In an instant, the concerned pucker of his brow melted into a grin. "There you are."

"Sorry?"

He tucked a finger under her chin. "You're ready to fight. Was worried I'd lose you again like after the fire."

"Simply needed a moment to collect myself."

"I figured." He kissed her forehead.

A stream of men filtered out of the saloon behind him. "Go. I'll be right behind."

"I'll have your tea in two shakes."

"I'll lock the doors behind me when I come in." Once he'd gone, she dabbed at her face with the wet cloth.

With the fire, and her near-constant state of illness she'd spent far too long wallowing. She knew the people that worked in the saloon, or at least she had.

It was time to face them all and figure out who was trying to ruin them.

She ran the cool cloth along her face and neck one more time, then headed into the saloon. She shut the large doors behind her, locking them tight.

The room was dim with the doors closed, but Tom was already lighting a few lanterns to fight the lost light. Cole approached with her tea, and she took it gratefully.

She turned her back on the staff still filtering into chairs to focus on drinking her tea and regathering her strength. It was time to fight it out or perish.

Sin goes in a disguise, and thence is welcome;
like Judas, it kisses and kills;
like Joab, it salutes and slays.
—George Swinnock

Every member of the Hangman's Inn staff sat in the saloon, including Sally who'd been released from the clinic that morning. The doors were closed, despite the mid-afternoon hour. Cole stood next to Tommy, who stood next to Marshal Lewis. All three remained silent as Jane finished the tea in her hand.

Jane set the empty teacup down, her hands on the bar for several minutes. Silence reigned through the customer-less room while she did whatever she needed to do. Cole noticed her back straighten, her shoulders pull back, and a calm slide down over her features.

Apparently, she felt composed again because she turned toward the staff gathered in the room. She walked up to Sally first, standing in front of her, holding her gaze silently. After a moment she shook her head, then took a step to the side to stand before Edgar.

As she held Edgar's gaze, Cole found himself holding his breath until she shook her head again and moved on. One by one she moved down the line, staring down every member of their staff until most of them squirmed in their seat.

In front of Larkspur, Jane lingered. A moment later she gripped the girls chin, turning it side to side. "I told you to stop with the opium, but that's hardly the crime here. We'll discuss it later."

Lewis leaned toward Tommy. "What's she doing?"

Cole grinned. "Taking control again. She's magnificent, ain't she?"

Tommy's lips twitched. "We sure this will work?"

"How good is she at getting the truth from you, Tom?"

"Good point," Tom acknowledged.

Jane paused again, this time in front of Violet. "What is it?"

Violet's hands twisted in her lap. "I…"

"Violet," Jane warned. "Tell me now."

"I told Wills." Deep red hues seeped into Violet's cheeks.

Jane folded her arms across her chest. "And?"

"He wants to do the right thing. I ain't been able to tell ya." Violet bit her lip. "I ain't sure what to do."

"We'll discuss it later. Thank you for telling me." Jane moved on to Cuddy. Then to Iris. For what seemed ages, Jane stared down the eldest whore until Iris tore her gaze away. Jane's fist clenched, but she moved onto the final two staff members.

Cole let out a breath of relief. Iris had been one of his whores for years, nearly as long as he'd been in Dominion Falls. She'd renewed her contract more willingly than any whore he'd ever had, and often. She was the last he suspected of betrayal.

Jane finished, but instead of returning to the bar, she returned to stand in front of Iris. "Why?"

Cole's whole body jerked back into tension. It couldn't be. Jane had to be playing a game to get someone else to confess. That had to be it.

"I thought we were a family." Jane frowned at Iris's scoff. "I thought—why would you do this? How could you help destroy us?"

"Jane." Cole moved forward to set his hands on her shoulders. "Why would you—"

"It was her. I can't believe I didn't see it sooner," Jane spoke with confidence, but anger colored her tone darker than he'd heard in a while.

Cole turned her to face him. She didn't shirk away. "You can't mean it."

"She helped hide Sally's real age, and encouraged her dissent. Sally told me that much herself." Jane lifted her chin, and the first waver appeared, but it was a tremble of her chin. Her next statement made it clear why. "She was the one sitting on that stranger's lap the evening he shot Mel."

"Lou," Tommy protested. "Bringing up Mel isn't right."

"Tell them." Jane leaned on the arms of Iris' chair, nose to nose with the whore. "Tell them I'm wrong, Iris. Go ahead. Hell, tell *me* I'm wrong. God knows I want to be."

Iris lifted her chin, not intimidated by Jane's stance or tone. "You know I can't."

"I am right," Jane reinforced the statement.

"Yes." Iris didn't blink when chaos broke loose. Staff and Tommy protested in a cacophony of yells.

Jane straightened from the chair. Oblivious to the chaos, she returned to the bar, leaning on it as she had before she'd started.

Cole's own anger threatened to blow out of proportion. He shouted across the room to silence everyone. "Get out. Everyone but Iris, get the hell out. I don't care where, but don't come back here for an hour."

Silence fell for a few minutes. The whole room clattered to life again as the staff rushed to accommodate his demand. Everyone streamed out the back door until it closed after Sally.

All that remained were Tommy, Lewis, and Cole himself. They all stared at Jane's back while she remained silent.

Cole cast a questioning glance Tommy's direction. If Jane wasn't going to speak, should they start the questioning?

Tom only gave him a subtle shake of his head.

"How much did he pay you?" Jane kept her back to the room, her knuckles white from her grip on the bar.

Iris chuckled. "More than you could dream of."

Jane lifted her head but didn't move any further. She didn't turn to face the woman across the bar, or any of them. "Was it just for the money?"

"No."

"Elaborate."

"Why should I?"

Cole snarled her way. "You'd damn well better answer or I'll dismiss the Marshal and deal with this the way Guy used to."

Iris paled slightly, then a pink heat returned to her cheeks. "You don't hit women."

"Never had a woman betray me like you did."

"She did," Iris sneered at Jane. "And got you turning away your own whores."

A low chuckle came from the direction of Jane, a cold sound with not a lick of humor. "Elaborate, Iris. Or I'll let Cole or Tommy, hell I'll let Graham. He didn't mind hitting women so much."

"Did you really think we all had no problem with the changes you were making?" Iris rose, only to sink back into the chair under Cole's dark look. She glared daggers at Jane's back. "Most of these girls had no false aspirations. They're whores. We're whores, and content to be so."

Tommy remained leaning casually on the bar, his brow creased. "If you didn't like the idea of becoming something other than a whore, why not leave?"

"Jane got me to help Lily and Ginger move on. Hell, she got me to let Daisy buy out her contract until I couldn't because of the damage to the saloon." Cole couldn't keep his lip from curling in disgust. "You were loyal. Coulda found you somewhere else."

"I signed my contract with you, Cole. Several times over. Most of the girls did—even when Graham came along. We didn't ask for her to come butting her nose in." Iris wrinkled her nose. "You gave her all the power, and we lost all the benefits."

For that, Jane finally turned. "You lost a good fuck once a week so you decided to ruin the entire business?"

Cole turned to Jane in surprise. She had to be pissed because she rarely got quite so vulgar.

"His skills are what got most of us here. And turned a lot of good girls into great whores," Iris spat. "Makes it worth sticking around with the bunch of weak-dicks around here."

Tommy's lips twitched toward amusement for the briefest of seconds before his gaze turned dark again. "Doesn't seem worth it."

"No it doesn't," Jane agreed. "Especially when it meant Mel got killed."

"He wasn't supposed to die." The first hint of emotion crept into Iris' features. Tears shimmered in her eyes, but they didn't seem genuine any longer. "That idiot was only supposed to cause trouble, not start shooting. I didn't want anyone to die."

"Well, he did. Was that worth the money?" Jane edged closer. "The fire—Tommy could have died. If it wasn't for Sally, he might have. You were content to leave him to suffer and burn."

"I didn't set no fire."

"I repeat, Thomas could have died. Were you the one that drugged him?"

Iris' nose wrinkled, her eyelids fluttering under Jane's continued scrutiny.

"You tried to kill Thomas."

"I just agreed to causing trouble."

"I thought you said you didn't want anyone to die." Jane's hand twitched toward where her holster usually hung. Seeing as she hadn't worn it, Cole felt a sense of relief. He had an odd feeling that she'd kill for her brother much as she'd once killed for Cole himself.

Iris straightened her back, chin raised in defiance. "He's no better than you. Whole lot of you think you're better than us. You wanna fix us when we don't want fixin'."

Jane turned her back on Iris, and Cole could immediately see why. Her anger had broken at the idea that this woman had tried to kill her brother. Grief lined her features as she took in her brother.

"Nobody forced anything on you," Cole spoke into Jane's silence. "You've all been free to leave if you wanted. We worked out deals for those wanting to leave."

"Kept hoping you'd finally give her up. See her for what she was. Thought maybe Graham would finally get through. He hated her much as we did."

"He didn't hate me, well." Jane's voice was steady again, and a flicker of a smile tickled her lips before the anger returned. "He thought he did. Turns out he really hated his wife, but that's neither here nor there."

Cole relaxed his hands from the tight clench he'd had them in since Iris' admission. He'd never hit a woman, but damn if he was close. After a deep breath, he thought he had enough control again. "So you agreed to cause trouble. Like the opium and lack of womb veils?"

"All of it. It was easy enough what with you and Graham fighting, and you and that bitch fighting." Iris' lip curled, but she scooted back in her chair when Cole took a step closer, his hands clenched into fists again. "Then I planned to take the money get the hell outta here."

Cole narrowed his eyes. "Then why are you still here?"

Iris pursed her lips. "I wasn't supposed to be, but Tommy found out the money was missing faster than I thought he would. I couldn't leave once he figured it out. I had to hope she'd have another one of her little fits and I'd manage to get out before you figured it out."

"Another of my 'little fits'?" Jane's jaw dropped.

"You don't got a clue anymore, all I gotta do is get you your tea and act all sweet and you're blind to it all." Iris smirked. "That bastard you got in there made things real easy for me."

Cole raced toward her for daring to call his kid a bastard but got yanked back. He fought against Tommy.

"Not yet," Tommy mumbled. "We're not done."

Jane herself was being held back by Lewis. After a few seconds, she stilled enough that Lewis relaxed his hold. She brushed her fingers over her hair to smooth it, but Cole noticed the hand was shaking. After she'd tugged her bodice straight, she cleared her throat.

Cole quietened marginally at Jane's renewed calm, but he knew anything could tip him back over into fury. Hands clenched, he didn't relax, but stilled enough that Tommy released him.

"I don't understand." Jane's voice was calm now but remained dark with barely contained anger. "I trusted you. I considered you and all of these girls family. I tried to—"

"I didn't become a whore to get a family!" Iris rose again, her face flushed, hair flying loose. "Family ain't nothing worth keeping around. And I certainly don't want to be your friend. Graham was right—the minute ya came around Cole weren't worth nothing. Not even a good time."

Cole raised a brow and muttered, "Good to know I'm worth something."

"If nowhere else, at least in the sack," Tommy murmured in agreement. Probably wrong to crack jokes right them, but it served the purpose to cool Cole's anger enough that he didn't feel quite so ready to snap.

Jane cast a glare at them broth before turning her wrath to Iris. "Then why seek out my friendship? You were the one that came to me, that helped me get established with the girls. They wouldn't have ever listened to me if it wasn't for you."

"I was tryin' to figure out your game with Cole. Thought I could turn it on ya and get Cole back. I didn't want no madam, neither did the girls." Iris set her hands on her hips. "When ya started actin' like one instead of just lending an ear I realized my mistake."

Jane pinched the bridge of her nose. She looked a little green, but Cole thought it might be the shock instead of the baby. "Then when Gus Warren started coming around six months ago."

"I was already lookin' to leave or cause trouble. His questions got me thinkin' he was after something too, so we worked out a deal." Iris shrugged. "I wasn't gonna have to do nothin' but cause a little trouble, he was gonna do the rest."

"Trouble—like sending notice to Marshal Lewis that he'd find something interesting here." Jane shook her head. Behind her, Lewis frowned. "You're the one that told Warren about Clara, then?"

"Ya mean you."

"No," Lewis said in a dark tone. "She means Clara."

Cole would have been relieved at his statement, especially after the talk he'd just had with Jane, but given the circumstances.

Iris laughed. "Right. Of course. She got ya on a leash, too."

Jane swayed slightly, but Cole didn't dare go near her. She leaned on the bar, relieving Cole's immediate concern. "Where's the money, Iris?"

"Gone."

"Gone—*where*."

"Went out on this morning's train. Was getting picked up in Denver. Don't know what they were doin' with it. I was gonna pick up my money when I got there and take off elsewheres."

"How much did he offer you?"

"Eight thousand." Iris looked mighty pleased with herself. "That's why I didn't care none about giving you a few measly bits after the fire."

Jane stared at the floor for some time. Her finger tapped on the bar in a cadence like Alma's had a tendency to. "Who was it?"

"I only ever talked to Warren." Iris folded her arms across her chest. "He didn't tell me who he was taking orders from, and I didn't care. So long as you was gone finally."

"By all accounts you would be gone, too."

"Well, after two years of suffering, Cole had to suffer too. Watchin' ya swing again shoulda done it."

Cole was blinded with fury again, his forward motion stopped only with a tackle by Tommy. He fought Tom off and rose, glaring at his brother-in-law.

Jane eyed him calmly from across the bar. She offered him the smallest smile of understanding. "I'm not swinging, Cole. Her threats, Warren's threats, they came to nothing."

Her calm tone was all that settled him again. He glared at Iris. "I kept ya on because of loyalty alone. Not skill or profit. Shoulda tossed ya out years ago."

"Shoulda," Iris agreed. "Wouldn't have had to see ya become a worthless pillock."

Jane held her gaze on Cole's for several long minutes. Cole remained still, unwilling to get quite up in arms again. That didn't stop him from keeping his fist clenched, ready to fight if he needed to. Seemingly satisfied he wasn't going to act, Jane turned her attention back to Iris. "Is there anyone else involved?"

Silence.

Cole waited for Jane to make a move. He knew if he did, it would be more action than threat. Instead, he nodded to Tom.

"Tell us, Iris." Tom leaned on the table in front of him. "I don't want to do this the hard way, but I will. I'm sure the marshal has a few telegrams to send.

Lewis' brow rose at the suggestion. Still, the man actually nodded. "I will need to see if we can get the money intercepted. I've got a good description of Warren to send along."

Iris startled at that. She sank back into her chair, skin pale again. "Marshal. Ya can't."

"Who else is involved?" Normally Tommy had a note of humor in everything he did. Every bit of that humor disappeared into a dark, threatening glare that made Iris quail under it. "You breached our trust, and we don't take kindly to that. You insulted our family, and we really hate that. You stole, and trust me, I'll see to it you get a good neck-stretching for it yourself if you don't cooperate. You've got one chance here. Who else is involved?"

"D—Dahlia was, but she got too strung out and Cole sent her packin'. After that I got Lark helpin' a bit. She was annoyed with Jane's yellin' for a little opium."

"And?"

"I—I don't know. All I know is Warren was snoopin' around. He coulda talked to anyone. He was offerin' money like he had plenty to spend." Iris began to fidget under Tommy's fury. "I do know Violet's wrong. Wills left town yesterday. He was dressed in his Sunday best and only had one small satchel."

"Wills?" Jane's surprise jolted her into speech again. "I've never had a problem with him. He's always been exceedingly friendly to me. Why would he be involved?"

"His problem was with me," Cole muttered. Years had passed since the incident. He had no idea Wills would take it so far. "Caught him cheating about five years back and turned the tables on him. Took every last cent he had. It was a good haul and he got stuck here in town. Knew he ain't ever forgiven me, and he spent the past four years trying to win it back. Didn't realize he'd go that far."

"And here was his chance to get it, plus more for doing little else but screw a few whores." Jane stormed away from the scene, upstairs toward their room. Oh yeah, this was gonna be ugly.

Tommy stared up at the room like he wanted to go after her as much as Cole did.

Cole himself stood stock still until the door slammed. On the one hand he knew he needed to let her blow off steam before he tried to help—on the other, he wanted to make sure she was all right.

Tommy turned back to Iris. "Let's get you to jail. That should give you plenty of time to think about all that money you won't be spending."

Cole kept his gaze on the door to his and Jane's room. When Tommy brushed past him, Cole startled back to what was happening in the room. Tommy led Iris toward the doors of the Inn, and his grip must have been fierce because she didn't fight him a lick. Cole turned back to the marshal. "What's Iris looking at for punishment?"

"Not sure Tom's threat'll hold much water unless he pulls strings," Lewis admitted. "Right now, we'll hold her until we get more. Maybe she'll remember more information once she's good and bored."

Cole took a deep breath. "Thank you, marshal. I'd best get—Alma."

Leanne led Alma inside through the door Tom had just opened to take Iris out. Her bright smile faltered as she took in the group. Her gaze landed on Tommy last. There was a flicker of alarm on her features before she nodded to him. Without a word, she ushered Alma all the way through the room. She cast a sideways glance at Cole on her way past.

Tommy gritted his teeth, giving Iris' arm a good yank on the way out.

Marshal Lewis nodded. "I'll leave you to your family. After I've helped Mr. Young, I'll go see about sending those telegrams. Talk to you shortly, Mr. Mitchell."

Cole didn't acknowledge him, just waited until he'd left the Inn, closing the doors behind him. Cole moved to the doors to lock them. When he turned back to the empty saloon floor, he took a shaky breath. After so many days being closed because of the fire, it was odd to see it empty again. He hated it, especially knowing why.

Soon enough the staff would return and the doors would open. Until then, he had to check on Jane. He stormed through the saloon, taking the stairs two at a time.

On his way to their room, he heard Jane's voice in Alma's room. "But at the time their finances run short as it chances, and then I feel very sad, very."

Leanne laughed. "O'Tuama! You boast yourself handy at selling wine and bright brandy, but that fact is the liquor makes everyone sicker, I tell you this I your good friend Andy."

Cole pushed open the door, surprised to find Jane laughing and smiling with Alma. Something was off about the whole scene. When Jane began another harmless limerick, she didn't look at Leanne at all, and had even gone so far as to turn her body away from the woman. He narrowed his eyes, but as he opened his mouth to speak, Jane interrupted him.

"Cole is here, which means it is time for supper. Good thing, too because I'm rather starving, aren't you Alma?" Jane rose when Alma nodded. She maintained her eerie smile, and barely looked at him at all. "You had quite an afternoon. I'm sure Cole is looking forward to hearing all about it. Aren't you, Cole?"

Cole could only nod when Jane finally faced him. No bit of friendliness or playfulness met him. Somehow he managed to smile when Alma turned his way. "Yeah. 'Course I am. Looking forward to it."

Jane brushed past him without a word. When he tried to touch her arm, she pulled it out of his reach. Silent, she made her way downstairs, only stopping when she got to the middle of the empty saloon. She spun on him, her brows furrowed.

Cole braced for battle over him locking the doors—but the fight never came. Jane clamped her mouth shut and strode to the doors.

Alma followed Jane, and Cole kept pace with hers. With the doors unlocked, Cole led Alma on ahead of the other two women in hopes Leanne could have some impact. Instead Leanne caught up to him and Alma. He frowned her way, but she only shook her head.

"I know when I'm not wanted, Cole." Leanne peeked over her shoulder. "What the hell happened? She's…"

"I'll tell ya in a bit," Cole muttered when they reached Cora's. Already there sat a table full of friends and family, so he headed their way. He exchanged the usual pleasantries and held out chairs for Alma and Leanne. When Jane caught up to the table, he did the same for her. He eyed her quietly as she sat. Jane exchanged hellos, but said nothing beyond the realm of basic decorum.

He ignored the questioning looks, almost relieved when everyone seemed willing to pass it off to her pregnancy. Conversation rallied around the table after a few minutes, but Cole didn't participate. For once, neither did Jane unless she was called upon, and even then her answers were short and to the point.

Halfway through supper, she pushed aside her plate.

Cole rose when she did. "Jane?"

"I can't eat another bite," she said by way of explanation. When she lifted her eyes to his, the coldness lingered in them. "I'm going back for more tea. Is that a problem?"

He grabbed her hand. "Jane."

"Release me. Now."

He dropped his hold on her, anger and concern crashing together into a sickening heavy weight in his belly. As she stormed off, he sank back into his chair. The lump in his stomach had effectively killed his appetite for food and conversation.

A few minutes later Tommy joined the table in a similar sullen silence. Leanne leaned in to butter up Tommy with her best smile. Within minutes he'd shared what had happened at the Inn. The table fell silent around him.

Before any questions could come his way, Cole rose. "Tom. Would you mind walking Alma back when she's done? I'd best check on Jane."

Tommy gave him a short nod. While Cole headed to the door, the conversation around the table picked up again.

Cole stalked down the street toward the Inn. No friendly exchanges as Jane had taught him, he didn't even dare make eye contact. The doors to the Inn were wide open, the lamps lit. He assumed the staff had returned and had opened. Inside he found Jane by herself behind the bar, and he stopped up short at the sight.

Jane slammed a beer down in front of Hammy. No smiles, no making the man blush, at least not in the good way. She moved down the line. When Rose moved across the bar with one of the men, Jane took immediate notice.

She waved them over and without a hint of her usual humor or platitudes, spoke with them over the bar. Cole couldn't believe his eyes when she took the money from the man before she waved them toward the room. She'd done a lot in the past few years, but the whore money she'd always had one of the menfolk take.

While she poured more drinks, he slipped behind the bar. "Jane. What in blazes are you doing?"

"What does it look like? We have a business to run. It isn't shut down yet, and until it is I'm making it far more efficient and trying to get back some of the money we lost. Don't worry. Your cut is in my left bosom, everything else on my right." She set her hands on her hips. "Did you want to check?"

"Jane!"

"Do you know a safer place?"

"Come on." He grabbed her wrist. "We gotta talk."

"There's not a chance in *hell* I'm leaving this place unmanned."

"Then use Edgar," he snapped.

"No." She twisted her wrist free of his grasp. Another drink was poured and money exchanged.

He sighed, glancing at Hammy. The man stared miserably into his beer. All around the saloon, the usual ruckus was muted and quiet. No one appeared particularly happy, even while drinking and gambling. This was not how his saloon was, definitely never since Jane started taking an active role in the business.

Everything was wrong. Somehow he had to make it right. He walked up behind Jane, setting a hand on the bar on either side of her. He leaned in close. "This ain't you. Let's go talk."

"I'm not interested in comfort right now." Jane shrugged him off. "If you're looking for that, there's a bar full of whores. I tossed Larkspur out on her barely clad ass, but I'm certain we can—"

Cole spun her around so fast, she turned a little green. "You're not seriously suggesting I screw a whore right now, are you?"

"Well, I'm busy."

"Tell me you ain't really saying that."

"I'm the one that's half deaf, Cole—not you. Now if you want comfort, you either screw me here in front of everyone, find company on the floor, or go upstairs and get real friendly with your own hand. I have work to do."

He scooped her up fast. Her shriek left his ear ringing. The urge to toss her over his shoulder when she fought him tooth and nail was incredibly strong, but he held off. Knowing he'd never make it upstairs with the fight she was putting up, he glanced at Hammy. "Open the icehouse for me—now!"

Hammy flew to his feet. He ducked under Jane's swinging legs to get into the storeroom. By the time Cole got in there, he had the icehouse door open, and he'd pressed himself against the wall while Cole carried the flailing Jane.

On their way through the room, Jane's fight knocked bottles and cans from the shelves. She hit Cole and did her damnedest to break free. Somehow he managed to keep her right where she was. He shouted to Hammy over her screams. "Make sure no one comes near—not until I let ya know we're good. No eavesdropping or I'll cut you off completely."

Wide-eyed, Hammy only nodded as he shut the door behind them.

"Let me go!" Jane stumbled when Cole did just that. "Let me out."

Cole caught her the second she raced for the door. She slapped him hard and tried to make a break for it again. He caught her around the waist, cursing when her nails dug into his wrist. "Snap out of it, you crazy bitch!"

"Let me go. Let me get back to work."

"You just suggested I screw a whore. I ain't letting you go nowhere."

Her fight weakened. Tears shimmered in her eyes as she fought. Then she pushed off him, her back to him. "Detachment. I need detachment."

"What?"

"I'm no better. I'm such an idiot. I was wrong. I'm not better."

"Jane!"

She turned toward him. Though she blinked rapidly, tears slipped down her cheeks. "Let me go."

"No."

"Please."

"I ain't ever letting you go."

The second he stepped closer, she sagged. All fight drained from her in a heartbeat. Her head dropped to his chest. "I'm no better than Clara."

"Yeah you are."

"I'm blind. Ignorant."

"Stubborn. Hot-tempered."

"Cole," She chastised quietly. Her arms wrapped around his waist. "How could I let her fool me like that?"

"You didn't *let* her fool you. This ain't the same."

"Yes it is! I wanted this to work. I was so wrapped up in what *I* was feeling for you, about everything, that I let my ability to observe and get to know people totally disappear. I should have known. I should have seen it."

"But you didn't. Don't mean you need to give up on everything and everyone." He tucked his finger under her chin. "That ain't you."

"I can't trust myself to trust them."

"There's no way everyone is always gonna be honest as you are. Question is, are you just gonna give up on everyone? Even me?"

"I thought she was my friend. I cared for her like family."

"You've gotta trust yourself."

"How?"

"Do ya love me?"

"Yes."

He wiped a tear from her cheek. The smile he wore at her immediate response couldn't be stopped. "I trust you."

"Maybe you shouldn't."

"Too late."

"I don't know if I—"

He cut her off with a kiss. Every second she melted into him more until her body sagged against his. He scooped her up in his arms. With her in his lap, he sat on a block of ice.

"You're a brute." She nestled into his shoulder.

"Yeah."

"I love you."

"Love you too. Don't you dare ever try to pawn me off on a whore again."

"You're lucky you didn't take me up on it."

"Who needs a whore? I got a looney bitch right here on my lap."

"Toady."

"Damn straight."

We learn not in the school, but in life.
—Seneca

Jane reveled in Cole's warmth, mostly because her back was freezing cold. She shivered down to her toes. "We shouldn't have done that."

"How's that?"

She chuckled low. "Because my back is cold."

"But you feel better." Cole propped himself on his elbows. A playful grin curved his handsome features. "At least a little bit. Right?"

"A bit—you dunderhead."

He immediately began to tickle her. Pinned as she was, she could barely fight him off.

"Cole! Stop!

He captured her lips, the tickling fading into more insistent touches. Immediately her body responded, arching into his. Once she was flat on the block of ice again, his kisses trailed along her neck. "Thought your back was cold."

"Freezing. You're going to have to warm me up."

"I'd suggest a bath…"

"Mmmm," she hummed along with her libido at the very idea.

"Let's see to it."

"We can't." Regret tinged her actions as she pushed him back. Disappointment over her lingering libido made her groan. "We have to work."

"Jane."

"Please. I must fight. I don't have to fight you—but I have to fight."

"There's no way we're gonna get back that kind of money in two days. You know that." He stood to his full height, adjusting his trousers rather than look at her.

"I know."

"We've maybe got three days since Cutler is in town. We can't do it."

"I said I know—but I won't lie down and take it." For the first time in hours, playfulness crept from where she'd stuffed it in her distress. She nabbed the hint of joy to gobble up like a starving woman. She tugged on his tie. "Unless of course, you are the one giving it to me."

He groaned deep, cupping her face in his hands. "You really don't play fair."

"I know. I'm cruel. However, I need tea. We need to work. Until we have this business forcibly taken from our hands, we fight for it. It's our home."

"Not if you don't—"

"I won't risk the baby," she interrupted with a guess at his concern. "But that means you're going to have to work in my place. We can't let things ride, we have to—"

"I think ya broke Hammy's heart."

Tears welled so fast she had trouble blinking them away. Far too often in the past few months she'd taken her frustrations out on the dear sweet man. "I'm a horrid person for the way I treat him."

"Nah."

"Yes. I need to stop letting the nicest man on the planet suffer my tempers."

"You let me suffer them."

"You are not the nicest person on the planet."

"I ain't?" His lips hovered near hers. "You sure?"

"Oh, you are very naughty. Naughty can't be nice…well, it can."

He chuckled low. "Let me remind you."

"No. I need to get up. The ice is melting through my petticoats."

Cole helped her to her feet. After she'd gotten her clothes straightened, he tugged her close. "If we're gonna work, we're gonna do it the way we always have. I know you think you can't trust yourself—but you never did wrong by this place. Plus, we got potential investors that trust how you handle business, you can't go changing that now."

"Easier said than done."

"Put Edgar back behind the bar. Shower Hammy with his free beers. If you wanna ride the girls harder, that's your business."

"How did I end up the madam?"

"I used to handle 'em a different way. Know you don't want me doing that." He held her arms pinned behind her back so she couldn't smack him for it. A stern furrow set in his brow. "The customers don't just come for the booze and gambling—they come because you always got a way with them. Don't lose that—don't lose who you are because of this mess. That crazy woman out there tonight ain't the one I married."

She couldn't help the grin that formed through his speech. Never in all her time around Cole had she heard such an eloquent and long-winded speech. "This must be important to you."

"Why?"

"You are using so many words."

He released his hold on his arms. A finger chucked her under the chin as he chuckled. "I already used actions. Want me to go back?"

"I wouldn't mind, but we have a business to run."

"And you need tea."

"I really do."

"Then get your ass out there and do what you do best."

"Best?"

"All right. Third best."

She laughed low. "Third, hm?"

"I think you know what one and two are."

"Making up, and fighting."

"Damn straight."

She turned for the door, but he wasn't done yet. A pinch through her skirts caused her to yelp and jump. She cast a glare over her shoulder at him. When she threw open the door she found Hammy hovering at the door to the storeroom.

Cole kissed her neck. "Go make him feel better. He's crazy about ya, always has been—won't take nothing."

One glance around the storeroom told her the mess she'd made had been cleaned up, likely by Hammy himself. When Hammy turned at her footsteps, she rushed over to the old man. Throwing her arms around his neck, she placed a warm kiss to his grizzled cheek. "Oh, Mr. Hamm. Please forgive me."

"Aw, Lady Jane."

"I was no lady tonight. You accept far too much grief from me. I don't deserve the kindness you always show me."

Cole cleared his throat. "What do you say, Jane?"

"I say tonight he drinks free." Jane stepped back, but kept Hammy's hands clasped in her own. "To make up for my boorish behavior."

"Ya don't gotta do that." Hammy shuffled his feet. A gap-toothed grin broke across his features. "But I sure am much obliged for the offer."

"I insist." Jane couldn't have been more thrilled to see the man smiling. She vowed there and then to never take her anger out on him again. He was the last to deserve such a treatment. "Go on now. I'm going to make my tea, but Cole will make sure Edgar knows your drinks are on the house."

Cole squeezed her arm gently. After a gentle kiss to her cheek he slipped out of the room behind Hammy.

Jane turned her attention to making her tea. With the pot set on to boil, she reached for the tea. A clearing throat pulled her from her business. In the doorway stood Sally. A bandage remained on her cheek, neck, and left arm, but otherwise she was healing well. "Sally. How are you feeling tonight?"

"Real good. Everyone's being real nice."

"But?"

"Can I ask ya somethin'?"

Jane gestured to some crates. She sat on one as Sally made her way over. Jane faced her full on. "What is it? Feel free to ask me anything. I'll try my best to be honest."

"How do you do that? Be so honest all the time?"

"I've seen the consequences of being the opposite. You end up like Iris is now. There's been so much pain and deception, and it could have been avoided with honesty. It isn't always easy to be honest. Sometimes you can even hurt people you care about, but when you tell the truth—you never have to remember your lies."

"Iris was real nice to me. She took care of me."

"I know. She helped you hide the truth for a whole year."

"I…" Sally's cheeks darkened. She ducked her head rather than face Jane. She picked at a loose thread on her overskirt.

Jane felt another surge of warmth for the young girl. Her life had been turned upside down in such a short time, twice in recent weeks. Jane tucked a lock of hair behind Sally's ear, exposing the bandage on her neck. "It is difficult when someone we care about hurts us. Most of the time you find yourself unwilling to believe they could do such a thing. You doubt they could ever be capable of inflicting so much pain."

"Did she set the fire?"

"I don't believe so, but I think she was aware of it happening. She knew Tommy was upstairs. She's the one that fixed it somehow so he couldn't wake up."

"She told me Tommy was still inside. I—"

The whistle of the teapot startled Jane. She rushed to the pot, wiping tears that had escaped. While she poured the water for her tea, she fought down the renewed pain and doubts Iris' actions had caused. She cleared her throat. "I have some sweet orange tea on the shelf, Sally. Would you like some?"

"Yes, please," Sally said in a meek voice. She remained silent while Jane prepared their drinks. When Jane handed her the tea, Sally's hands shook so it rattled a moment before she got it to her lap. "I'm afraid you'll think that I was helping."

"Helping Iris? No, Sally. You were being troublesome, but I think your dislike for me was more akin to rebellion."

"Isn't that what Iris…"

"No. Iris was hellbent on revenge. Perhaps she encouraged your rebellion, but I severely doubt that the young lady that risked her own life to help save Tom is quite capable of the amount of anger Iris has displayed."

"She said you were selfish."

"Oh, but I am."

Sally's cup stopped halfway to her lips. "You admit it?"

"Of course. I am selfish, most especially when it comes to Cole." She smiled at Sally's giggle. The girls joy pushed away some of Jane's lingering doubt and anger. She didn't dare say she felt maternal to this young woman, but protective for certain. "The beasts of burden you bore are nothing compared to what you'll find some day, Sally. Trust me, when that happens, you'll be every bit as selfish as I am."

"Beasts of burden?"

"Asses. The men that pay for entertainment are primarily asses."

"I ain't ever heard it put like that."

"Don't let Iris' point of view mar your own, Sally. She might have loved that life, and some of the other girls might, too. That is their lot, their choice. How did *you* feel about pleasuring those men for money?"

"I—well, sometimes it wasn't so bad."

Jane hid her smile behind her cup. "Sometimes?"

"There were one or two gentleman that were nice and kindly. Maybe even enjoyable. Mr. Wilder was…"

"Ah yes. I've heard talk about Mr. Wilder. I understand he is rather generous—and not just monetarily." Jane allowed her chuckle free now. "Besides him, most of these men don't know which way is up and couldn't find their way out of their own pants without a map, much less know what feels good to a woman."

Sally's laughter burst from its seams. "That's exactly how it seems."

Jane took another sip of tea. "Being a whore doesn't make you any less of a woman. I've never thought that of any of Cole's girls. I've found many of them to be smart and funny. That is to say, until the past six months or so when the trouble started."

"You're friends with that one from Denver. The one that used to work here. Iris talked about her. Said she was Cole's pet for a while."

"Pet?"

"Yeah."

"Interesting. They usually refer to them as his favorite." Jane pondered that a moment. Perhaps Iris had known Leanne wasn't servicing customers back then. As a whore, she'd be more likely to notice than anyone else Cole had to deal with.

"I thought it strange. She didn't like her at all. Said he kept her from working as much, didn't let her sleep with the other whores or nothing."

Jane chuckled low at that. Subterfuge was not Cole's strong suit. She imagined back then it had been even more the case. Especially when it came to his raw feelings about his family. "Leanne is…unique. And yes, she is very much my friend."

"And Daisy."

"We're attempting friendship. It was a long road for us, mostly because she was Cole's favorite until I came along."

Jane sighed, thinking back over her past with Daisy. "All of that aside, you should know that you get considerably less pleasure from being a woman having to deal with bumbling fools and degenerates in place of figuring out what it is you truly enjoy about the act and being able to ask for it since you are the one seeking pleasure, rather than being the one that is paid to deliver it."

Sally's mouth hung open a moment. "You actually ask?"

"No. I don't ask. I demand." Jane grinned against her teacup. "You will one day too. You will meet a man that excites you, stimulates you, and makes you bold enough to demand. Until then, you'll have to wait, I guess."

"I never gave you my answer."

"No, you haven't as of yet. I told you there is no rush."

"What would the rules be if I remained?"

"Your education is first." When Sally immediately tensed, Jane raised her hand to stem any protest. "After we spoke in the clinic I got to thinking that perhaps it would be difficult for you to attend school here where you've been known as Pansy. While I'm certain at least five of the children would be kind to you, it would still be difficult."

Sally nodded. "They know what I've done here."

"I would be willing to tutor you but make no mistake— it would be no easier than attending school. I would expect you to work." Jane set her cup down to focus on the girl. When Sally met her gaze, she nodded. "As your final test I'd want you learned enough to earn a second-class teaching certificate."

Sally gasped. "I…I couldn't…"

"I'm not saying you would be required to be a teacher, but I want you capable." Jane set a reassuring hand on Sally's.

"That would be a test only—not a career decision. After that, the choice is yours. When you are eighteen if you decide you still wish to be a whore, I'll find you an appropriate place where you'd be safe and in a better class of company."

Sally chewed her lip thoughtfully. "What else?"

"You'll be expected to work as a chambermaid for the Inn."

"I'd have to clean piss pots?"

"And make beds, and take food to the guests—all things I do myself. You would be paid for your time; it would not be slave labor. Lastly, I would like you to contact your mother."

"I can't!"

"You do not have to tell her where you are. I would even allow you to send the letter to my family in New York and have it mailed from there, but she should know you're alive. A mother needs to know."

"I—I'd have to think about that one."

"Fair enough."

"Cole's all right with it?"

"Yes."

Sally traced the edge of her teacup with her finger. After a few minutes she lifted her hand to brush it along her bandage. "Even if I wanted to, I might not be able to work again looking the way I do after the fire."

"Like I said at the clinic, that's a hurdle we'd cross when you're eighteen. If you want to move to another position doing something else, I'll do whatever I can to help you."

"Why?"

"Because it's too easy to get lost when you run away. You've had that happen once already in your life, and I believe you deserve better. I think all the girls here deserve better. If they don't want better, I won't force them. It's never been all or nothing for any of them."

Tommy's large form filled the doorway. "Janey?"

Sally lit up at Tom's voice.

Jane chuckled softly at Sally's reaction. The girl clearly cared for her brother if nothing else yet. "Yes, Thomas?"

"Lewis got some news. They were able to intercept the money in Denver—it was still in the mail bag. Had a lead on Warren, but he made himself scarce before they could detain him." Tommy's face beamed in happiness none of them had had an hour prior. "We got our money back, at least. It's being brought back on tomorrow's train."

"Thank goodness." Jane sagged as the tension flew from her body. "It's about time something went right."

"My buddy Joe's coming with the money," Tommy added.

"Joe. The Pink?" Jane's confusion carried into her voice. Something about Tommy's friend having the same name as Krenshaw's Pink unnerved her. "I…"

"I trust him, Jane." Tommy seemed to read her doubt. "He was on his way here anyway."

"He was?"

"Yeah. I asked him for help with the Warren matter. Figured there was no better way to bring the money back than guarded by a Pink."

"Good idea," she hedged. After a moment, she shook off the doubt. Of all the people she'd lost faith in, Tommy wasn't one of them. He'd never given her a reason. She turned her attention back to Sally. "It's about time for me to go meet Alma and read her the story I promised. Why don't you take another few days to think about it and let me know when you're ready?"

"Thanks, Jane." Sally smiled warmer than she had yet. The fear she'd been clinging to since the fire seemed to have faded. "I'll let you know soon as I decide."

Jane stood to pour her another cup before heading toward the door. She squeezed Tom's hand as she passed. Cole headed right toward her the second she emerged. He yanked her into a deep kiss that she gave into easily.

He rested his forehead against hers. "We ain't dead yet."

"No. We aren't."

Half a truth is often a great lie.
-Benjamin Franklin

Jane wiped down the glasses she'd cleaned. She took great care in order to not make any noise as she set them away. The guests weren't her concern when it came to noise. What she didn't want to disturb was Alma's playing on the piano. Beside her sat Cole, listening intently.

Something akin to an actual conversation flowed between the pair amidst the notes. Jane was loathed to disturb the peaceful moment. To that end, the doors to the Inn were open, but only for access to the hotel and fresh air. The 'saloon closed' sign hung in place and would remain so until after lunch.

A movement by the doors pulled her attention from the piano. In the doorway stood the enigma of all her brothers, Nick. She held her fingers to her lips, but waved him in. When he sat across from her, she offered a smile. "Drink?"

"Bourbon," he spoke quiet as her. As usual, not even his goatee trembled with his words. While the unusually still nature of Nick could be disturbing to most, Jane passed it off as another way he masked himself.

Jane poured his drink, then returned to cleaning glasses. Nick turned to study the pair at the piano. From the time her brothers had come into her life, her relationship with Nick had been the shakiest. The last months with his presence in Dominion Falls had helped her finally make strides with the brother most angry toward Clara.

He turned back around, removing his bowler which he dropped on the bar. "Glad to see you're getting good use from the piano."

"We are now, although it wasn't instantly welcome. I'm pleased it's here now for Alma." Jane leaned on the bar. "When you sent the piano your letter indicated humor, not struggles. Have you and your wife truly parted ways?"

Nick's sharp eyes lit on her. The goatee twitched in his silence. Finally, he took a long drink of his bourbon. "Tommy's got a big mouth."

She refreshed his glass. "Why didn't you tell us?"

"What could you have done?"

Rather than speak, she circled the bar to wrap her arms tight around his neck. After a full minute, his shoulders sagged and he wrapped his arm around her waist. His cheek rested on her shoulder. She sighed deeply. "I'm terribly sorry."

"I don't blame her. I am quite particular. I'm not easy to live with."

"Exactly what Thomas said." Jane cupped his cheeks in her hands. "You are a good man, and a good brother. I'm still sorry. Particular or not, two people living together is a difficult concept without compromise."

"I don't compromise."

"Yes you do. You compromised for me." She squeezed his hand. "Come. Walk with me to the train. Tell me if Tom's suggestion you might remain in Dominion Falls is true."

Nick only hesitated long enough to polish off his bourbon. He grabbed his hat, offering his arm. "I have been considering it. Although, I have my hesitations."

"Such as?"

"The amount of chaos you bring into the life of everyone close to you."

"You could use a little chaos." She bumped his hip. "Or a lot."

"I've had enough chaos to last a lifetime, more than."

Jane suspected he was thinking of the war. The somber note that fell between them reflected as much. "Many men that were in the war can say the same. Some of them give up and let themselves never be the same. You don't seem the type to give up. You are a Young, and from what I've seen, all Young's are too annoyingly logical and stubborn for such things."

"A compliment and an insult wrapped into one." He patted her hand. "Another thing the Young's are talented at."

"Subterfuge, logic, words, and pure stubbornness. Am I missing anything?"

"Humor, of course."

"That applies to most. I do still wonder if you are capable." Jane did her best to hide her smile. "Heavens, I've only ever seen you crack one, maybe two smiles the entire time I've known you—then again, you do hide your mouth. How do you eat?"

"You're going to pester the life out of me if I stay here."

"Not at all. I'm going to pester the life *into* you." She turned toward him, hands on her hips. "I worry about you when you're far away and know you could ignore my letters if you wished. When you are here, I can be certain you hear everything I need to say."

"Perhaps I should return to New York."

"I think you should stay right here."

"Will you let me be if I say I'm considering it?"

"Perhaps."

"I am considering it, honestly." He offered his arm again. "Now tell me how your meeting with the investors went this morning?"

Jane perked up at his question. The morning had been spent going over any remaining questions the potential investors had. In the days since their initial meeting, there'd been several questions to answer. "I think it went very well. We won't know for certain for some time. We'll be contacted once they're back in their offices and have decided. For now, we must wait."

"And your money is arriving today?"

"On this train. Thomas said Joe was doing more digging in Denver last night, but got on the train this morning. Maybe he'll have more information as to who Warren really is—at least we can hope he does."

"You said you thought Underwood was not as trustworthy as Cutler believed. Tommy said he had the same feeling."

"I have nothing to base it on—just a feeling he's slimy."

"You sound less certain than you did a few days ago."

"I'm finding it difficult to trust my gut at the moment. I was so very wrong about Iris—maybe I'm wrong about this guy."

Nick hummed, an annoyingly skeptical sound. "Tommy said you had a good talk with Sally last night."

The change in subject threw her off balance. "What?"

"You accepted that she wasn't helping Iris."

She frowned as she realized how it hadn't truly been a change in subject. "In full admission—it was difficult. I want to believe her. She's so young, and despite her previous occupation, still rather innocent. I want to believe that Iris was the only one carrying around such bitterness."

"Have you talked with the others? Really talked with them?"

"I haven't had the time, and I only seem to be able to gather the energy to be confident in myself in short bursts."

"'Trust in the instinct to the end, though you can render no reason'."

"Emerson."

Nick set his hand on hers where it lay on his arm. He gave it a gentle squeeze. "Your instincts have been pretty spot on since you came to Dominion Falls. We all make mistakes—not one person is perfect. You're going to make mistakes."

"I always make mistakes. Reading people is not usually one of them." She sighed. "I have to admit this whole situation has shaken my confidence to its core. I'm questioning much of the trust I've placed."

"Would you be a tyrant?" There was a hint of laughter in his eyes when she turned to him in confusion. "Aeschylus."

"'In every tyrant's heart there springs in the end this poison, that he cannot trust a friend'."

"I really do hate you sometimes."

She laughed heartily. "Look at that. There is humor in there. How about this one? 'He who believes in nobody knows that he himself is not to be trusted'."

He narrowed his eyes.

"Auerbach."

"Jane."

"'It is better to suffer wrong than to do it, and happier to be sometimes cheated than not to trust'."

"I know that one." Nick snapped his fingers. A moment later his hand dropped. "It's…"

"Samuel Johnson," she supplied. "'I have great faith in fools. My friends call it self-confidence'."

"That one's easy. I've heard it from Clara."

"Yes?"

After a long pause, he muttered, "Damn."

"Poe. Let's see. What else?"

"Jane?"

"Yes?"

"Do shut up."

"I don't think I can. This is too much fun. Michael always said you hated my memory for verse. Let me see, there has to be one you do know." She pursed her lips as she thought. When the quote came to her, she brightened. "'Self-trust is the first secret of success'."

"You didn't have to go back to Emerson for me to get one right."

"Apparently I did."

The foreign sound of his laughter joined with hers. "My memory for words was never good. You and Charlie had the lock on it over all of us, but I was worst. You're cruel to tease me with it now."

"'Memory is the mother of all wisdom'. Aeschylus."

"Then you cannot be too wise—you can't even remember your real name."

She smacked his arm in mock anger. "Now who's being cruel? You should realize that joke is losing all humor. It's about time to put it to bed and leave it there."

"About time means it still has some life."

Her protest cut off at a series of yells and whoops. They both turned to find three horses tearing down the road toward the tracks. Leanne raced between Tommy and Mike at top speed. Jane laughed as the trio tore past them and over the tracks out of town.

She glanced toward Nick. "You should join them. It wouldn't kill you to have some fun. I know Leanne is quite beautiful, and she's an absolute joy. Maybe she can figure out a way to make you truly smile."

"I don't know what you're talking about."

"The three of you boys have been drooling over her since she stepped off the train. Michael could well ruin his chance with Daisy at this rate. You, my dear Nicholas, are freshly divorced and it wouldn't kill you to have fun. I think Tom's the only one with an actual chance—that is if he weren't such a total ass."

"I—" A sharp whistle drew their attention again as the trio tore around the corner. Leanne reached out toward Nick, her horse barely slowing.

"Go." Jane pushed him. "Remember how to have fun."

When he stepped forward and caught Leanne's hand, leaping onto the back of her horse easily, Jane laughed. She waved at them all as they departed. "Oh, Leanne. You really are dead set on making those boys look like idiots."

"And she's doing a good job of it." David's voice startled her out of her musings.

She spun to hug him. "David!"

He returned the hug, chuckling low. "It's good to see you, too."

"Where is Lee?"

"I'm on duty, so she's in some big secret meeting with Cora."

"Must be about her dress." Jane hooked her arm with his. "A few more weeks until you enter the land of wedded bliss again. I do hope you'll have more luck this time."

"I intend to." He fell into step with her toward the depot a short distance off. "Jesse is excited as all get out, especially since Daisy says he should be able to use a crutch to walk him down the aisle."

"Walk? So soon?"

"Like his Ma, he is."

She half-glared at him. "I thought he was having so much fun in the wagon you got him so he could get to school. Just yesterday I saw Isaac and Cindy racing around town pulling the wagon with Jesse and Lizzie holding on for dear life."

"He does—but he wants to walk down that aisle 'like a man' is how he put it to me. Apparently our son is ready to be grown up."

"That's too bad. He's going to stay little forever."

"You know, there are some things you *can't* control."

She pouted. "But I really, really want to."

"Too bad."

"Rules really are horrible. Sally's right."

David snorted. "Sorry to disappoint you, but we can't stop him from growing up."

"We'll see."

"Lewis says your money is arriving today."

"It is. I intend to get it back in hand as soon as possible." She clasped her hands behind her back and tried to appear more innocent than she felt. "Are you heading to the depot for your usual lawful presence during the disembarking and unloading? Or is it awful presence? I can never remember."

"You aren't funny."

"Of course I am. I'm anything that I say I am. I am pregnant and if you don't agree with me, I'm liable to dissolve into tears or throw up on you."

"Or both?"

"That is the most likely scenario of all."

"How are you feeling these days?"

She stepped onto the platform with him, debating her best answer. Her actual nausea was likely the core of his question, so she focused on that. "My nausea is mostly under control. As long as I'm drinking the tea regularly and getting rest, I'm able to function."

"Good to hear." He nudged her. "Are you ever going to see about getting that louse to marry you?"

"Why in heavens would I do that?" The secret elopement still made every question on the subject bring a smile to her face. She wondered if she'd ever tire of circumventing the questions with truthful, if purposely vague, answers.

David quirked a brow, poking her stomach.

She set her hand where he'd poked. "You and I are raising a child together and we are hardly married. We don't even live together."

"True, but will you try to raise a child in the saloon?"

"It's an Inn now, and God-willing the investors will pull through so we'll have an actual living space that's separate from the Inn while still attached."

"You really think you can get it done that quick?"

"I have the construction schedule worked out. Barring a horrendous winter and with a hard push in spring we could very well be done in time." She dropped her hand from the barely noticeable bump on her abdomen. "It is my home and has been for a long time. It will be the child's home as well. We'll find a way to make it work."

"I still can't imagine Cole as a pa."

Jane had to bite her tongue to keep from stating that Cole was a pa three times over compared to David. No one knew of his first child, only a few people knew for certain Cindy was his daughter, and no one knew he'd adopted Alma so many years ago.

"Sorry. It's hard to picture."

"You don't need to apologize. I do wonder why you believe it's so tough to imagine. He's always been good with Cora's children, not to mention you've seen yourself how good he is with Jesse. Of course he's been great with Cindy and Lizzie as well. He might occasionally be particularly uncouth, but he's a good man."

"With a dark side."

"We all have one."

"I suppose we do."

She turned her attention to the train as passengers began to disembark. At that moment she realized she had no idea what the man she was looking for looked like. "Tom was supposed to be here to introduce his friend, but I suppose he's too wrapped up in the game to make a proper appearance."

"Game?"

"The game of trying to win the heart of the lovely Madam, Leanne. I'm quite sure Mike is going to ruin his chance with Daisy if he keeps this up. As for Nick? Well, I don't mind if he plays. That man needs to learn how to smile with regular frequency."

David chuckled. "What does Leanne think of this game?"

"She finds it great fun, of course. In the end she'll take none of them to her bed, but she'll let them try."

"I doubt they mind."

"Only a male mind would be so childish."

"Only a female mind would think to play with them."

"True." She tilted her head as a taller gentleman stepped off the train. He wore a nice suit, had a well-trimmed beard, but his shoes were scuffed. The man bore an air of confidence, and scanned the depot with the slyness of a fox on the hunt. Even as her gut said the man had to be Joe, it also twisted with a taste of disgust. "That may well be him."

"You think so?"

"Perhaps."

"Sorry I'm late." Tom hopped onto the platform. "Lost track of time."

"Hard to keep track when your brain is in your pants," Jane muttered.

David chuckled low, not caring when Tom frowned at him.

"Jane, come meet Joe." He led her toward the man she'd been eying. "Joe."

Joe held out his hand. "Tommy, you bastard! How'd you get mixed up in this kind of mess in this place?"

"I told you, Janey's keen on getting her nose mixed into trouble." Tom shook Joe's hand heartily. He clapped him on the shoulder for good measure. "Glad you could head this way and help us out."

"Had nothing better to do. My last assignment ended a couple weeks ago. I told them I needed a break, so I'm not due back until after Christmas." Joe turned his attentions to Jane. "There is no way this stunning woman could be Jane."

"There is every way," Jane corrected him. Even as she shook his outstretched hand, she had to dig deep to resist the urge to yank her own away. There had to be a reason Tom trusted him, even though she found it hard. Something about him brought up a feeling she was certain wasn't hers, but Clara's, and it wasn't pleasant. "I assure you, that's who I am."

"Nah." Joe clapped Tom on the shoulder. "Tommy, there's no way this lovely woman could be related to your ugly mug."

Tom laughed. "No wonder you need a break—if you can't even see the stunning similarity between us."

Jane arched her eyebrow at her brother. "Wit alone."

"Miss Spencer." Joe bowed his head. "Or may I call you Jane?"

"I have not decided yet." Jane couldn't bring herself to smile at Joe's bark of laughter.

Joe scooped her hand in his again, kissing the back of it. "Well, a beauty such as yours demands respect, so I will submit to the propriety of Miss Spencer until told otherwise."

"Don't worry, Jane. He's harmless. He thinks he has endless charm."

"'Flattery is the worst and falsest way of showing our esteem'. Billings." Jane clasped her hands behind her back to prevent any further gushing over her appendages. She really wanted to wash her hands of the feel of him. "I prefer sincerity. Now what is the procedure to procure my funds and depart?"

Joe clapsed his hand over his heart. "Accept my sincerest apologies. I had thought you had a sense of humor like Tommy."

"I rather do." Jane straightened at the backhanded insult. The nagging emotion from the back of her mind stretched its way into a headache. "However, I do not believe you do."

Tommy nudged her with his elbow. "Be nice. I promise he isn't as bad as he acts."

"Time will tell, Tom." She set her hands on her hips, focused on Joe. "I must thank you for returning our funds to us swiftly. In keeping with that behavior, I do hope you'll hand them to me now. Perhaps another time you might prove you are not such a boor."

Joe stepped closer. "Perhaps we should choose a place away from the crowd?"

Jane turned on her heel to wend her way through the crowd. Before she could take a step, her skirts shifted. A firm hand groped her ass. She whipped back around in a heartbeat. The heel of her hand slammed into his chin, and she kneed him hard in the groin.

"Jane!" Tom lurched forward when Joe hit the boards of the platform.

She ignored Tom, bending over the man she'd felled. Without a second glance to the satchel he carried, for it was too obvious to hold the money, she looked over his person. She yanked open his jacket to reveal a leather pouch secured to his shoulders like her holster. She ripped it open and pulled out the wad of money inside. "Idiot."

As his eyes blinked open, she stepped over him to leave the platform. David rushed up, mumbling something about escorting her. Before she could reply, Joe started laughing. She turned in surprise.

"Damn. She really is related to you." Joe accepted Tom's assistance to his feet. Still, he didn't resume his full height, remaining doubled over. "Definitely passed the test."

"Excuse me?" Jane stormed forward.

"We met before." Joe smirked. "I was testing the waters. I wanted to see how different you were."

She turned her ire on Tom.

Tom raised his hands in surrender. "Don't look at me. I didn't tell him to do anything. I had no idea he'd pull a stunt like this."

"You really don't remember." Joe finally managed to stand straight again. "Because you used to like me."

Jane wrinkled her nose. "I don't right now."

"I think I got that message."

"Your cock certainly did."

I have never seen an ass who talked like a human being, but I have met many human beings who talked like asses.
-Heinrich Heine

The day the money had been stolen, Jane and Cole had moved the safe into their room. No money would enter or leave it without Jane, Cole, or Tommy to do so. They'd even taken the step to change the combination.

Jane locked the money in the safe, relieved to know it was more secure now. A knock on the door pulled her to her feet. The world spun as she rose to fast. "Damn."

Once everything stopped turning, she opened the door. On the other side stood Sally. Jane smiled in welcome. "Sally."

"You looked a little sick when you came in. I brought you some tea." Sally held up the tray. "Hope you don't mind."

"Not at all. Thank you. I was going to make some before I headed downstairs. You saved me the time." Jane gestured to the table. "Why don't you join me?"

Sally hesitated on the threshold. She glanced over her shoulder. "Um. Are you sure?"

Jane chuckled softly. For years, no one had been allowed in Cole's room. Many of the whores still held onto the rule.

Since Sally could potentially become family, she saw no reason for such thoughts. "Of course I am. I keep some extra tea in the room, including the orange tea you like."

"I—thank you." Sally followed Jane to the table. As she began to pour the water, she cleared her throat. "Who was that guy that came in with Tommy?"

"His name is Joe." Jane took her seat. She tapped the handle of her teacup with a nail. The man crawled under her skin in the worst way. "You know those beasts of burden we spoke of the other day? I have the feeling he is a very large example of one."

"Tommy seems to like him."

"Doesn't make him less of an idiot—it just means he's probably not all bad."

"Are you saying I should avoid him?"

"I certainly plan to." Jane sipped her tea until it was halfway gone, and her stomach settled to a tolerable level. "Thank you for bringing this for me. I really needed to have some before Alma and I head to the library."

"You're taking Alma?"

"Yes. Cole needs to work here, and I need work over there. At the library I can read to Alma or let her look through the books on her own."

"Would you mind if I came too?"

"What?" Her cup dropped to the saucer. She hadn't expected Sally to ask. She smiled, setting her hand on Sally's before the girl worried. "Of course you can. I certainly don't mind the company. I've read most of the books in the library."

"I ain't read a book in a long time," Sally admitted quietly. "I never much cared for reading."

"It's not for everyone. So much so that some adults still don't know how to read, nor do they care to learn." Jane eyed Sally when the girl flushed. Sally avoided her gaze carefully. "Sally? What is it?"

"I know how to read. I mean I…I…can."

Jane let the silence linger. She set aside her tea. "You said your grades weren't good."

"I did fine in arithmetic. Numbers are no problem for me."

"Cole's the same way. I need paper for true number running, he does it all in his head. What about everything else?"

"I don't know why. I read the books and stuff; it just doesn't stick. Only thing I was ever good at was the numbers."

"That's why you aren't thrilled with my insistence that you get your education?" Jane squeezed Sally's hand. "Learning isn't easy for everyone. We can figure out a way to make it work."

"Ma said I was stupid. There's no excuse."

"I don't believe you are stupid," Jane insisted. "We'll figure out what the problem is and try to fix it. Every issue has a solution, you only have to find it."

"You really think so?"

"I'm certain of it. Do you think you're willing to stick around long enough to find out?"

Sally chewed her lip for a minute. "I think so. I mean, I'd like to try. I like it here, 'specially now that I'm not entertainin'."

"I know the feeling." Jane polished off the last of her tea. They were running out of time before they had to leave.

"Sometimes a place feels right, and you aren't willing to leave—no matter the cost of staying."

"Jane," Alma's quiet voice interrupted them. Right on time, as always. The young woman shuffled her feet as she glanced at them, then back at the ceiling. "It's three o'clock."

"So it is, Alma." Jane smoothed her skirts as she rose. "I guess that means you're ready to head to the library since I said we'd leave at three. If it's all right with you, Sally is going to come along with us."

Alma nodded, her fingers tapping the edge of her book. "We're still reading."

"Yes. We are still reading as planned." Jane glanced at Sally. "Shall we?"

Sally rose, smoothing her own skirts. "I think I'm ready."

Jane ushered them out so she could lock the door behind them. Loud laughter from the saloon prohibited any conversation. Jane leaned toward Sally. "Why don't you and Alma make quick of it. The noise disturbs her. I'll be right behind you."

Sally took the suggestion and hied toward the doors.

"Bonny Jane and sometimes Jane the curst, but Jane, the prettiest Jane in Christendom," Joe called from the table he sat at with Cole and Tommy.

Jane wanted nothing more to ignore the man, but impulse made her stop. "Are you truly brutalizing Shakespeare in such a way?"

"Taming of the Shrew," Tommy said in a not-so-subtle aside to Cole.

"Myself am moved to woo thee for my wife," Joe continued. The grin he wore wasn't fazed by the toothpick he chewed on.

Jane had the strangest urge to shove the toothpick to the back of his throat. The sick knot in her stomach would not disappear, and his teasing didn't help. Instinct alone pushed her to return fire with fire. "Asses are made to bear, and so are you."

"Women are made to bear, and so are you."

Jane turned her full focus on Cole to stem her urge to hit the man again. "We're going to the library. You men enjoy your afternoon."

"Come, come you wasp," Joe called as she moved to the doors. "I' faith, you are too angry."

Jane glared his way. Her teeth gritted as she spoke again, "Beware my sting."

"I'd drop it," Tommy hedged. Clearly he got Jane's tone even if Joe didn't. "She's not in the mood for play there, Joe."

"Not to mention you are no Petruchio, and I sure as hell am *not* Katherine." Jane spun on her hell and stormed toward the door.

Outside Sally and Alma waited on the porch. Sally kept a quiet conversation with Alma, talking about the clouds.

"Jane," Cole called. He stepped onto the porch, touching her elbow.

Jane sighed at the renewed interruption. She handed Sally the keys. "Go unlock the library. We cannot continue to delay Alma."

Cole's brow furrowed. "Sorry."

"It's fine." She turned to face him. "What?"

"You all right?"

"Highly annoyed, but I'm fine."

"I ain't keen on Shakespeare."

"You're only keen on the most indecent books filled with smut." Jane relaxed enough to smile.

"Be lying if I denied it." He studied her. "So what was that?"

"It's a play within a play. Essentially Petruchio marries a strong, independent woman. Through the course of the play he breaks her down into a proper, well-behaved wife who is happy to be as such." Jane folded her arms across her chest. "I do not happen to appreciate the insinuation in any fashion. Now, I must go read to Alma as promised. I won't delay her schedule further."

Cole brushed a finger along her jawline. "You don't usually mind a little teasing, and he's just using words."

"He's a little too familiar with his teasing. I happen to not like it, not one bit. But you go, enjoy yourself." She stormed off to the library without another word.

Necessity dispenseth with decorum.
—Thomas Carlyle

Cole left Jane to her own devices to allow her time to calm down. A few hours later, he stepped onto the porch to meet them for supper. There was no immediate sign of Jane, but Sally walked with Alma down the street toward Cora's. The two spoke quietly together, wrapped into some discussion that seemed to keep Alma distracted from the heightened crowds in the street.

He took a chance on finding Jane at the library. As he approached, Jane stepped outside. She turned her back to lock the door.

He stepped onto the porch, keeping his distance until sure of her mood. "Hey."

She turned her back to the door. A warm smile lit her features. "Hey yourself."

"Feeling better?"

"Why don't you tell me?"

He didn't need to be asked twice. In a long stride he closed the distance between them to crush his lips to hers. He pressed his body into her until she was pinned to the door. Her soft moan satisfied him to her mood. With a low chuckle, he pulled back from the kiss. "You feel awful damn good to me."

She sighed, a soft pout on her lips. "If Alma wasn't waiting on us, and we didn't have so much going on at the saloon tonight, I'd let you find out how good I feel right now."

He trailed his fingers lightly down her chest. "We don't got no time?"

"As much as I would enjoy spending five minutes to help relieve whatever tension you might have, I already altered Alma's plans twice today. I shouldn't do so again."

"When do I get you all to myself again?"

"Hmmm. That's a tough one. Technically—never. I am pregnant, after all."

"Oh, you're funny. *Real* funny."

She slipped under his arm and took off down the street. Her laughter carried behind her as she scooted away from him.

Glad to see her in better spirits, he could only join her laughter as he jogged to catch up with her.

"I did have to be honest," she said when he caught up.

"You planning on working tonight?"

"For a while, yes. So are you—the high-in poker game is tonight. Michael directed several of his guests our way for it. The game should bring in some good money for us and the Inn. I'm beginning to see more and more why you want gambling to replace the whores." Her fingers laced with his. "And since you'll be dealing with the big money table tonight, I will need to be paying attention to the poor saps that can only deal into the nickel ante."

"Joe's getting in on the high game." Cole didn't miss the way she tensed beside him. "Gonna have to keep an eye on him. Think he's got a hell of a poker face."

"And fast hands," she muttered.

He wanted to ask more, but they'd arrived at Cora's. Jane wasted no time diving into conversation. Cole didn't bother trying to keep her focus. Though she might feel better, the mere mention of Joe had left her tense and in need of distraction. There was something more she hadn't told him, he figured she would when she was ready.

In no time, Cole found himself distracted as well. Leanne wrapped him into a vibrant conversation with Nick and Daisy. His sister truly had learned well how to distract, and disarm, men and women alike. Even Daisy, jealous as she was of Leanne's flirtation with Mike had been laughing and joining in with relish.

Once his supper was over, Cole turned to say something to Jane, but found Tom's ugly mug instead of her. "Where the hell'd Jane go? And when did you get here?"

"Been here five minutes—you've been too busy arguing with Leanne and missed Jane telling you she was heading back." Tommy chuckled. "I get that Leanne draws attention rather thoroughly, but you might not make it so obvious to Jane."

Leanne snorted. "I'm sure she doesn't mind."

Cole laughed as well. Jane knew she had nothing to fear with Leanne. For the moment, at least, Tom acted as though he still didn't know why to the general public. For which Cole was infinitely grateful.

"And you have yet to explain that." Tom pointed his fork at Leanne. "She is usually ready to hurt anyone that intrudes on her territory."

Cole slapped his brother-in-law's shoulder, grateful the man played the game well knowing what he knew about the marriage and Leanne. It was no wonder at how the man had been a Pink. "Jane knows she ain't got nothing to worry about. I'd best head back, though. Gotta get the table set up."

"I'll be back soon." Tom saluted with his fork. "I offered to take Leanne for a stroll, but she's going to come back for a drink at The Hangman's Inn after."

Cole made his goodbyes quick so he could head back to the Inn. If Jane had already been gone five minutes, she would get impatient with him if he dawdled too long. As soon as he stepped into the Inn he caught a whiff of her perfume over the smoke and sweat. She breezed right past him, a tray full of drinks and empties balancing on her hand. Nothing could stop her grin as she bustled through the saloon.

He leaned back against the wall to enjoy the familiar sight. She looked more like her old self than she had in a while as she skirted among the tables. With every step she greeted familiar faces, cracked jokes, and swatted hands. Some of the men were newer and didn't know better, but some that made passes were familiar faces that did it in play.

Cole couldn't help but notice she avoided the table where Joe sat as much as possible. The man's request for a drink despite the whore in his lap sent Jane his way. Cole's eyes narrowed as Joe didn't bother to conceal his too intimate touch, and the man's laughter at Jane's slap and smart retort unnerved Cole further.

His lip curled as he began to understand Jane's annoyance with the newcomer. While most men took her reminders, or orders, to leave their hands off her as she was not for sale to heart. Joe didn't seem to care. The man appeared to take it as a personal challenge. One Cole would see to correcting at his earliest opportunity.

Cole shoved off the wall at a gesture from Jane. He went to the table she'd indicated, where he'd be leading the poker game. The moment he got there, his mood lightened at a familiar touch. Her fingers danced along his shoulder, then down his arm muscle as she set a drink in front of him.

Her breath brushed his ear. "House drinks coffee. I know it's difficult for you, but I ask you don't taunt the players, even when the house is up. No girls for the high boys until they've folded. It's far too easy to hide cheats with the women."

"I made the rules, remember?" He tugged her skirt to pull her attention away from the table set up. "How many times are you gonna repeat them to me?"

She ran her fingers through his hair. A smirk grew as she slipped them down his cheek until she gripped his chin. "Until you get them through your thick skull. You used to break your own rules all the time for the fun of it. I know these boys are paying good money, but they're paying for the game. If they want to diddle a girl, they can cash in and go to a room."

"What if the dealer wants to?" He took his chance to grope under her skirts. She didn't slap him away, at least not physically.

"The dealer will have to wait until the table is clear and the house has its money. Patience will get him great rewards."

"You sure about that?"

"Have I ever deceived you about the value of a reward?"

"Never."

"Then stay where you are and get ready." She squeezed his shoulder. "Edgar is cashing in three of your players now. Oh, and eyes on the game—you can't be watching the floor. Or me."

"Why did I agree to this again?"

"Because I promised you something special." She leaned down to kiss his cheek, but her hand dropped into his lap. Her fingers teased along his length.

He groaned at the touch. The second she pulled away, he snarled. Before he could gather his wits enough to even grab her hand, she'd slipped away into the crowd.

Just then the players arrived at the table, so he could only glare at her departing back. A few minutes later, the table was full and the game began. Once the game was running, it didn't take much to keep his focus on the game as directed. The men were all good players and he had to keep a tight rein on the game, and his focus on the action.

Unfortunately he found occasional distraction by way of Joe regularly demanding Jane's attention for drinks. Because of this she arrived at the table about every fifteen minutes. Cole's tension rose as every time she came by Joe made a comment or a physical pass at Jane.

After a couple hours of the game, Cole had had enough. He knew Jane preferred to deal with grabby men herself, but he was about tired of waiting for her to handle it with this guy.

As the table took a break to stretch their legs, Cole leaned toward Joe. Cole spoke quiet under the din but kept a dark threat in his tone. "Jane ain't merchandise. Touch her again and you're outta the game."

Joe chuckled. "Never said she was merchandise. Her and I, we go way back."

"Don't matter none what you were when she was Clara. She's Jane now. I don't like no one touching what's mine. Do it again and you're out."

"Yours?"

"Yeah. Mine."

"Clara—I mean, Jane—tied to one man?" Joe finally turned his attention away from Jane to Cole. "You?"

"Damn straight."

"Well, that is new. She always had two or three on the line."

"Not this time."

"Huh."

In jealousy there is more self-love than love.
—Francois de la Rochefoucault

Cole's hands slid down her sides to her hips. His voice rumbled low right behind her ear. "House is cleaned up."

Jane bit her lip against the excitement he'd stirred. The second she set down the glass she'd been cleaning, he tugged her against him. "We're still not closed."

"No." He nipped her neck, setting her nerves on fire. Her sigh of response had him chuckling warm against her neck. "That a problem?"

She noted the handful of men in the saloon. Only one or two at the bar, but several were watching them, including the damnable Joe. That was enough to steel her resolve. She turned to face Cole, determined to end it before he got started. "Impatient?"

"Damn straight. We could use the icehouse again."

"No, thank you. I don't want another cold back."

The familiar heat in his eyes sparked higher. Inch by inch he backed her against the bar. His body pressed into hers until they couldn't have slipped a playing card between them. "I'd be willing to suffer it."

She giggled despite her intentions to cool him down. The fabric of her skirts brushed her legs. Bit by bit they shifted right where his hand lay on her thigh. The man was lifting her skirts in front of the whole bar? She hadn't seen him this possessive in a long time. "Are you really so impatient? Or are you laying claim to me?"

"Both."

"I see."

"How long is it just for you?" His intention was made clear as his fingers made their mark, slipping through her folds skillfully.

A shudder ran through her against her will, and the words to push him away got lost in the kiss he planted. Her fingers buried in his hair as his lips trailed along her neck. His skilled fingers teased along her sensitive flesh, drawing a whimper from her. Every protest over their audience flew from her head, but she acknowledged them by burying her face in his shoulder to hide her features.

He murmured against her ear, "How long?"

"One—one hundred and fifteen seconds unless…oh!" Her hand clenched against his neck at his insistent touch.

"Unless," his warm voice rumbled against her. She bit her lip to keep from exclaiming over just what his demanding touch was doing to her. Every move urged her forward, consumed her until she would have sworn nothing else existed but them, and his thrusting, taunting fingers.

"Jesus, you're…" She whimpered against his neck.

"Yes?"

She clung tight as shudders she wanted to keep hidden ripped through her body. Determined to make it look like no more than an intimate embrace, her nails dug into his neck. Breathless now, she wanted to curse him over his blasé treatment of the situation, but the pleasure wouldn't let her at the moment. With one last whimper, her body relaxed against him.

His teasing fingers pulled away and fabric slipped slow down her legs. He kept her tight against him, their embrace not changing. "How long was that."

She couldn't touch on fury over what he'd just done, but anger wove its way through her until her lax body tightened in tension. She pushed him back. "I don't appreciate being used."

"At all?"

"I can handle myself." Her own word choice caught her off-guard. The warm tremble that still coursed through her bolstered her amusement at the double meaning. Still, she managed to smack him in the chest. "You're a brute, a possessive ruffian, a swine—and it was twenty-three seconds. A new record."

"I don't like your old friend."

"I don't like him either." The mention of Joe soured her enjoyment of moments ago. "As to that, stop trying to prove yourself better. You win easy. I don't remember him, and I don't care to. Nor do I care what he remembers. I've got all I need in twenty-three seconds with some very skilled fingers. Don't act like a child."

His protest was interrupted by a voice down the bar. "Janey. Can I get another whiskey down here?"

"Sure thing, Mack." Jane moved to the shelf to grab the whiskey.

Cole set his hand on her waist. "You really leaving it like that?"

"Suffer. If you had done that out of pure desire for me, perhaps you'd get five minutes in the storeroom. However."

Whiskey in hand, she went to move but found herself blocked. He set his hands on either side of her, leaning into her. She shook her head. "You decided to show off and while I appreciate the, um—gesture—you're going to have to wait for yours."

She pushed back against him to give herself room to move. Down the bar she filled the three glasses pushed toward her, including Macks. When she walked back over to Cole, she frowned at the dark expression on his features. "I know you're not that upset that I turned you down—not knowing what's coming later. What's eating you?"

"Why didn't you set him straight?" His voice was low, and the lingering noise level in the saloon made it tough to hear. She imagined that was by design as the man was across the room with his own bottle of scotch. With every sip, the man watched their interaction closely despite his conversation with Tom.

"I've hit him, kneed him in his jollies, and swatted away his every attempt with words as well as my hand. What clearer message could I send? He doesn't seem to care much when I tell him to keep his hands off."

"You ain't done nothing tonight but smack his hand away and talk smart."

"As I do with every man that walks in our doors. He most stubbornly refuses to listen."

"There's more."

She lowered her gaze at that. He wasn't wrong. There was a deep-seated something that went far deeper to parts of her truly unknown. "Not here."

"I'm holding you to that."

"Of course." She leaned into him, wrapping his tie around her fingers. She turned their act playful again, unwilling to let Joe get a sniff of anything more serious. "You are who I'm going upstairs with. I won't give him the satisfaction of getting me to hit him again. He sees it as a game. I think he's the muck beneath the muck of the hot springs. A man with absolutely no hope in heaven of touching me like you did a few minutes ago."

"I still say—"

"Lou!" Tommy's voice boomed through the saloon.

Jane glared his direction. "What?"

"Come here." Tommy waved. "Cole, you too."

"Game's over, so I get whiskey now, right?" Cole frowned. "Gonna need it if you really want me to behave."

"Bring a full bottle, two glasses, oh yes—and trust me."

"I got no problem trusting you."

Jane crossed the floor, stopping long enough to tell Edgar to head behind the bar. At the table, she intentionally took the seat furthest from Joe. All her attention went to Tommy, and remained there.

The second Cole joined them, Tommy leaned forward. "We've been talking about Warren. You know I told you it was familiar. Joe knows his real name, and now that we have it, I can tell you for sure he's tied to Underwood."

That got Jane's attention. "Really? How so?"

"We all have fake names," Joe spoke instead of Tom. "Pretty standard practice that makes it easier when you're ready to leave and move onto the next job. Tommy tells me you got experience with that."

Jane glared at Tom for the indiscretion about her past.

A warm hand settled on her knee. Cole's voice was casual. "All of you, Tom?"

Tommy features darkened under Jane's continued glare. "We don't always use them, just on certain jobs. Some guys prefer to use them all the time, like Warren."

"I'd say I was surprised he used the name for this job, but I'm not." Joe chuckled. "The man doesn't have much imagination to begin with. I was looking over some of his info when Tommy mentioned him. He was good for certain jobs, but not creative."

"Why didn't you recognize him?" Jane studied Tommy.

"Never worked with the guy. I didn't cross paths with every Pinkerton that ever was, Jane. Only really know about five. We aren't exactly a friendly bunch." Tom shrugged. "Especially those of us with more specialized talents."

Cole leaned forward, skating over the comment Jane wanted to question Tommy more on. Luckily he did, though. For his question was more directed to their current situation. "So what is Warren's connection to Underwood?"

"Cousins." Joe leaned back in his chair. "Believe it or not, it's that cut and dry."

"Wait. All of this has been Underwood?" Cole glanced at Jane. "Why?"

"He said he wanted to branch out when we met him." Jane rubbed her temple at a sudden headache. The combination of Joe's presence and the influx of information had her on edge. "Then his plan is to get us to go under. What are his finances like?"

"For a minor partner, they're substantial. Looks like he's been building them up for a while, looking for a prime target to take the plunge." Tommy pointed to the papers in front of him. "Dominion Falls has been generating buzz since the train got to town, and the rate of growth is increasing all the time."

"And we have a prime location right in the heart of town." Jane turned to Cole. "We go under, they need to sell the place to pay back the investors—he could easily snatch this place up in a bidding war. Giving him prime land to sell at a profit, or to make whatever he wanted."

Joe tapped the arms of his chair. "Thing, is, we can get Warren. With his real name, it's no problem to find him. There's no proof he set fire to this place, though."

"Fraud, but again, we'd need the burden of proof that he's out to harm us." Jane's frown deepened. "That's great. We finally have the information, but there's nothing much we can do about it."

"Shouldn't we let Cutler know his partner's out for blood?" Cole's arm circled her shoulders, the warmth easing some of her tension. "It don't seem right to just cut our losses."

"We could tell him what we know." Jane shook her head, feeling hopeless again. "Without proof it's our word against a man he's worked with for years."

Tommy's gaze drifted, a calculating look behind his eyes. "How long are they staying in town?"

"A few more days." Jane bit her lip. "Cutler has been marvelous facilitating all of this for us. I'd hate to see him or his business damaged by all of this."

"Protecting his interests would be important to him," Tommy muttered.

"The investors he brought are all leaving two days from now, Cutler the day after."

"Give us a couple days to figure something out, Jane. Cole's right. We can't cut our losses and leave this guy to do it again." Tommy's distant gaze brightened. He nudged her leg. "We've got to make sure your one sure-fire investor stays solvent. He doesn't need his partner double-crossing him."

"Thank you, Thomas." Jane rose to leave, then hesitated. "Will you help me with something in back? Cole can get the riff-raff kicked out so we can close and retire for the evening."

Tommy hopped to his feet. "Sure thing. I'll be back in a minute."

Jane squeezed Cole's shoulder. After a second, she leaned in close. Making sure her lips brushed his ear, she whispered, "Shouldn't take more than a few minutes, and then we'll finish our discussion."

Cole winked. "I'm holding you to that."

"Good." In the storeroom Jane automatically poured the water for her tea while she waited for Tom to arrive.

"All right." Tom closed the door behind him. He leaned against the shelf. "What's your question?"

"You know what it is. What is the deal with that cretin out there?"

"No deal. You and he had a fling years ago." Tommy held up his hand at her protest. "Correction, he and Clara had a fling. When we were working together, he came out with me to visit you. Guess you both kept it up off and on for a couple of years until you disappeared on us."

"I cannot begin to imagine I would be interested in him."

"He's acting up. Jealous. I wouldn't worry too much." Tommy's shrug did little to reassure her. "That *Taming of the*

Shrew bit was something you did often in jest. He kept saying he'd get you to settle down like Petruchio did."

"Not even marriage would make me a Katherine. I don't like him at all."

"I've gathered as much."

"I…" Jane steeled herself for the next question. Tommy must have sensed her nerves because he straightened. "You knew Clara's past like no other. The things she did, had done to her…"

"He's never done anything before to make me question him."

"She's crawling in my brain." Jane put her hand to her head. "Nearly frantic."

"You're remembering?"

"No."

"You sure?"

"Thomas." Jane blew out a breath. "Every time I look at him, I feel like she's there, and not in a good way."

"Clara gave me no indication one way or the other," Tom spoke much gentler now. "She always seemed happy to hear news about him, even asked on occasion…"

"Asked what?"

"What he was up to."

"Maybe where he was? Perhaps seeing if she had reason for worry?" Jane met his gaze. "Maybe that was because, like you said, she'd become good at hiding it."

"I was around them on that first visit. I would have caught something, I'm sure of it." Tom stepped closer. He pulled her into a hug. "It's been a few years since I've seen him—but he's pretty harmless. All talk, no action."

Her stomach still turned, but his surety calmed her riled nerves a bit. The protective length of his tight hug eased them more. "If you say so. Don't get me wrong, I'm pleased he's assisted us in this matter, but I don't care for him. I've dealt with my share of pigs in this town—and he is obscene."

"I'm sure he'll back off. I'll talk to him."

"Thank you. He appears to have no desire to listen to me, and I'd rather not have Cole breaking a Pink's face in. We've had enough trouble to last us a while."

He kissed her forehead. "I agree."

"Tom?" Another thought occurred to her. One she hadn't addressed with him yet.

"What?"

"One other thing." Jane stepped back to eye him. "I know you said Pink's use fake names, which means it's entirely possible that I'm overthinking things."

"You always do, but that doesn't always mean you're wrong." He propped a foot on a nearby crate. "Lay it on me."

"Krenshaw."

"The late or current?"

"Jackson." She leaned against a shelf of liquor. "He had a Pinkerton in his pocket. I know because he was happy to brag about it."

"I've heard."

"He called him Joe when he bragged about him to me."

Tommy's brow furrowed. "It couldn't have been Joe. He would have reached out to me the second he knew it was Clara the man was after."

"Would he?" Jane leveled a hard gaze at him. "You all thrive on secrecy."

"He would have." Tom's voice was firm, but she noticed he focused awful hard on the icehouse door instead of her. "I hadn't told him I'd found you again, so he would have."

"You can't guarantee that."

"No," he admitted. "I'll do a little digging myself. This time on him. Would that make you feel better?"

"Immensely."

"Consider it done."

"Thank you. Can you do me one more favor?"

Tommy folded his arms across his chest. "You're lucky you're my favorite sister."

"I'm your only sister."

"Exactly."

She chuckled softly. "Fair enough. I just—until my nerves are eased, I don't want Joe in on our plans, whatever they come to be. I know you trust him, but I can't yet. He hasn't proven himself trustworthy."

"Your instinct can be flawed at times." He stuck a finger over her lips to shut her up. "But that's usually when you go plotting to make yourself bait. That isn't the case this time, I'm assuming."

She shook her head to confirm.

"Fine. I agree. Now drink your tea and go be indecent with your man somewhere other than behind the bar in a saloon full of people."

Jane made a vain attempt to appear embarrassed. "Not much excitement otherwise."

"Somehow I think you'll manage."

"We'll do our best."

Tom shoved her back. "Terrible."

"Always." Once he'd left the storeroom, she sighed deeply. Maybe Tom would have the effect he thought he would. If nothing else, she had to push back the visceral reaction. The man had helped them, whether she liked him or not.

The door to the storeroom opened again, and Cole walked up with a grin. "All clear." His arms wrapped around her waist from behind as he placed a kiss on her neck.

"Are you as ready to retire as I am?"

"You bet."

She poured the rest of the hot water into a ceramic tea pot on the tray. When she moved to grab the tray, he took it from her grasp. Rather than argue she was capable of carrying a tray, she waved him forward and followed him out of the room and upstairs.

The silence lingered after they'd returned to the room. She poured a cup of tea and glanced his direction when he bent to remove his boots. "Sally has decided to stay."

Cole straightened. "Really?"

"Yes. I'll be helping her with her schooling, and we'll have to add our plans to include a space for her should the investors come through."

"You already got that added in, don't you?"

"No," She hedged. At his laugh, she shrugged. "Not on paper."

He pushed his boots under the bed, still laughing. "In your head."

"I suppose I was thinking about it." She crossed the room and knelt on the bed, straddling him. His hands went to her waist and she ran her fingers through his hair. "I'm sure we can find the room."

"You keep taking in strays, we aren't gonna have enough room to house guests that'll actually pay."

She leaned into him and grinned. "I don't take in all the strays. I let Katherine take care of some of them."

He dropped back onto the bed and rolled them until she was underneath him. "Stop taking in strays."

"Stop agreeing if it vexes you so."

"You vex me."

"I thought you liked that."

His lips hovered near hers, teasing and taunting as the heat of his body encompassed hers. "I might."

"What could convince you?"

"If you shut up."

"That's hardly vexing. It's the opposite. So that still wouldn't make you like—"

His lips covered hers, pulling her too deep into the kiss to allow argument.

When he released her from the kiss, she was left breathless. A slow grin formed and she arched into him. "I guess there are other ways to vex you."

"Prove it."

"Yes sir."

*What we are today comes from our thoughts of yesterday, and our present thoughts build our life of tomorrow:
our life is the creation of our mind.
—Buddha*

Cole remained on the bed while Jane moved about the room. Despite their relaxing night, she'd woken up tenser than ever. Her morning illness lasted longer than usual. When she made her tea, her hands shook like crazy.

He would have offered to help, but knew she'd bite his head off—or even his cock based on her level of tension. While she drank her first cup, he rolled onto his back.

"Sorry," she muttered.

"For what?" Relieved to have her talking, he got himself to sitting. Relaxed against the headboard, he studied her. "You haven't done anything."

"I've made you afraid to help me."

"Not afraid. Smart enough to leave you to alone while you worked through it."

"Smart enough to lie through your teeth." She smiled a genuine smile, but it faded in a heartbeat. After another sip of tea, she rose. The walk across the room to his side kept splitting her robe open to reveal the creamy, white length of leg.

He adjusted the sheet to cover his body's immediate reaction. Now was not the time, given her recent illness and his naughtiness of the night before.

Jane never missed a trick, though. Her brows rose, and she looked pointedly at the sheet. "Behave."

"That's why I covered it." He winked. "Now tell me what in blazes has you madder than hell after last night? Was it your twenty-three seconds?"

Her lips pursed at the implication, but she shook her head. "I still don't appreciate being used, but no."

He set his hand on hers. "What is it?"

"Everything. Nothing. That idiot in my head."

"Clara?" His interest piqued. Very rarely did he get worried he'd lose Jane, but the idea that Clara would return always concerned him. Especially when Jane talked about her like she was near. "What do you mean she's in your head? Are you remembering?"

"At least you have the decency to sound panicked rather than excited."

"Who the hell—"

"My brothers, for one." Jane set her hand on his chest, and the action instantly cooled his racing nerves. "She isn't coming back. Even if I remember, she died years ago."

"You don't know that."

"I do. Her letters told me so." She leaned in to brush her lips across his. "No, this has little to do with her returning, or my memories returning it's more…emotions that aren't mine."

Cole tugged her closer until they sat hip-to-hip. "How so?"

"I don't know how to describe it, exactly. An instinctual reaction that doesn't belong to me. Like when it comes to my brothers. No, that doesn't work either because I adore them as much as she did, I think. Perhaps more."

"Jane."

She chewed her lip. "When David came into my life."

"Not my favorite way to start."

"Says the man that pushed me to talk to him in the first place." Finally, a genuine smile lighted on him. She leaned across him; her right hand next to his hip. Her gaze held his. "I didn't feel the same way she did, I never did, but emotional instinct told me to trust him. I liked him genuinely first because of her, I think."

"What's this got to do with anything?"

"Joe."

Tension shoved its way back through his muscles until his jaw locked.

"Sexy as your smolder is, stop that." Her fingers danced along the lines of tension in his jaw. "It's the opposite with him that it was with David."

He relaxed under her touch despite his better judgment. "Can't yell at me for being tense when you've been tense since you jumped out of bed."

"Fair enough. Believe me, I did not plan to wake up this way. Not after last night." She blew out a gust of air. "It's been bothering me. Something about him sets of this feeling of…discomfiture. No, I'd go further to say disgust."

"Tommy says he trusts him."

"He also said Joe was one of Clara's suitors."

"Willing or unwilling?"

"Tom says willing."

Cole narrowed his eyes, not missing the way she grimaced. "You don't believe it."

"I trust Tom." She rose from the bed. The nervous flutter returned to her hands as she paced the length of the room. "I've always trusted Thomas."

"You aren't Clara," Cole reminded her. "You don't suffer fools like she did."

"I know."

"Jane." As he'd hoped, she stilled at his tone. "You ain't her."

"I feel like bugs are crawling under my skin when he directs his attentions my way." She tucked a lock of curls behind her ear.

"Then don't trust him."

"I told Thomas not to reveal our plans to get Underwood, once we make them of course."

"Good start."

She returned to his side, her features calmer. "You don't think I'm overreacting."

"Nope. In fact, I think you should start carrying your Remington again."

"Oh, that's hardly a proper attire for a woman of business." She glanced at the nightstand where she kept it.

"You took it to Denver, and that was a pleasure trip."

"I don't feel safe on trains."

"Don't know why. Just because you were pushed from one, shot on another, and had one blown up under your feet."

A soft chuckle filled the room. Her eyes sparkled when she turned her gaze back on him. "Fair enough. I don't know, I haven't worn it regularly since the Renegade attacks stopped."

"It's not forever, but if ya don't feel safe, it'll help."

"That's true." She turned to lean against the headboard beside him. Her head nestled against his shoulder. The long stretch of her leg hooked over his raised knee. "I feel safe here, too."

"You're always telling me we can't live on sex alone. I wouldn't mind trying, though."

"We can't. There is also much to do." Her deep sigh brushed along his chest.

"What now?"

"Nothing."

"Liar."

"Nothing different." Her fingers danced along his stomach, though her far-off look indicated more distraction than intention.

"Maybe ya need distraction."

"I'd need more tea for that. Also, we're supposed to meet Thomas at nine."

"Thought we only needed five minutes."

"Main problem with that is you can never restrict yourself to five minutes." She pulled out of his arms too fast for him to pin her down. Her laughter carried her across the room.

"You don't play fair."

"Neither do you." She indicated to the sheet that could no longer hide his excitement.

"Come back to bed."

"We have plans."

"Screw our plans."

"I'd rather screw you."

"There's my woman."

*Happiness is not the absence of problems,
but the ability to deal with them.
-Charles de Montesquieu*

Jane buckled her holster under her bust. The holster still fit as well as the day Kilmurry had made it for her. She caught Cole's gaze in the mirror. "Happy?"

"Are you?"

"I feel safer, anyhow."

"Didn't answer my question." His hands slipped around her waist, tugging her back against him. "Happy?"

"I'd be happier if we were spending all day in bed together." She chuckled low at his quiet rumble of approval. "However, we have things to do."

"Damn responsibilities."

"I do rather agree." She patted his hands. "You go on. Meet the train. We're not meeting with Thomas until three where we'll have tea and plot the downfall of Underwood."

"We don't got much time for that."

"We'll manage. We have a little time, at least." She tilted her head to meet his kiss. "Now go or you'll be late. I won't be far behind."

"Yes, ma'am." He kissed her soundly once more before leaving the room.

She shook her head, still laughing under her breath. His staunch belief that she wasn't crazy had eased her nerves interminably. Though she still had the uncomfortable sensation of Clara creeping around in her mind, at least Cole didn't think her fears were unfounded.

She slipped from their room without another worry allowed to cross her mind. However, soon as she locked the door she made a surreptitious check of the floor.

Though she felt far more secure with her weapon on her person, she didn't care for an unnecessary encounter with Joe. Not, at least, until she was certain she had her own wits about her and not Clara's unrestrained wits.

After all, it would do Jane no good to act a fool without a spine. It seemed Joe was the type that needed a far clearer picture of who she was and what she wouldn't tolerate.

When she descended the stairs she spotted Sally behind the bar pouring a drink for Hammy. She crossed the floor, smiling at their new ward. "Sally? What are you doing?"

"Chauncey had to run to the necessary. Hammy showed up, so I thought I'd get him situated." Sally set down Hammy's beer.

"Kind of you to step in to help out. Thank you." Jane wrapped an arm around Hammy's shoulders. "You're rather early today, Mr. Hamm. I know we open the bar early now that we're a hotel, but you still don't usually come by so early."

"We finished with a project." Hammy wiped foam from his lip with his sleeve. "I came in for a refresher before we start on the next one. Told the men to not come back until after lunch."

"I see. What's up next on your roster?" Jane turned to face him. "Are you still building over on Second?"

"Aye. The Kilmurry's are next."

"Really? Mrs. Kilmurry said it would likely be spring." Jane's gaze followed Sally as she moved down the bar to fill more drinks.

"Daugherty's delayed the theater, so I had an opening. Figured we'd start early on the Kilmurry's. They got shop space, but it ain't what they want."

"I'm sure they're thrilled with the acceleration. I'll leave you to your refresher. Sally Ann."

Sally moved back to where Jane stood. "Yes?"

"Why don't you take the afternoon off? I'm working on something with Cole and Thomas after a bit, and Katherine is minding the library."

"What about Alma?"

Jane was touched that Sally thought about the young woman. "I believe Leanne is taking her on a picnic. You're welcome to join them, or make your time your own."

"Really? Thanks."

"No need to thank me. You're a free young woman now, with the exception of a few rules." Jane patted the young woman's hand. "If you need some money to grab a meal—"

"I got my own." Sally straightened. "Leftover from before, and since you've been paying me, too."

"All right, then. Enjoy your time." Jane stepped outside into the bright sunlit day. Unfortunately, she spotted Joe heading for the Inn. She diverted her gaze rather than return his wave.

"Bonny Jane." Joe's voice slithered down her spine until she thought she might shiver from the feel of it.

"Do not start." Jane turned to face him dead on.

"I'm only playing. Clara and—"

"Let me stop you right there." Jane was satisfied with his mouth shutting at her words. "I don't much care what you and Clara did or didn't do, willingly or otherwise. I have no interest in any of it, nor in you. I appreciate the assistance you gave in returning our funds, but I am not going to participate in whatever game you are trying to play."

"Now, Jane." He stepped closer. "You haven't given me a chance to charm you."

"Your charms do not interest me in the slightest." She held her ground even as the stirring of life in her mind told her to run. "All that interests me is when you will depart our company, nothing else."

The fear in her brain spiked when his playful smirk turned cold, a light of something in his eyes. In an instant it was gone, replaced with a pleasant smile. "Fair enough."

She was spared further conversation when a wagon pulled to a stop in front of the Inn. Jane turned her attention to the folks on the wagon seat.

The pair was unfamiliar to her. A young man she guessed to be about eighteen, and a handsome woman, built strong and rather sure. She eyed the sign above the doors before lowering her gaze to Jane.

Jane's shoulders relaxed when Joe departed the porch to head inside. She offered a smile and nodded to the stranger. "Good afternoon. Might I help you with something?"

"Afternoon. The blacksmith directed us here. We were looking for a horse for my young'un here." The boy groaned at the term. The woman cut him a look. "You're a spring chicken, boy. Stop complaining."

Jane grinned when the words were delivered with the warm smile of a mother instead of harsh tones. "You're in the right place. Cole is an expert hand at breaking and training horses. He should be back shortly. I'm Jane Spencer, by the way. Co-owner of this establishment. We haven't met yet."

The woman hopped out of the wagon, and as she circled around Jane noted that her apparent skirt was actually parted in the middle like pants. She dusted her hands on her skirt, then extended one toward Jane. "Names Laura Edwards. This here is my oldest boy, Matthew Coleman."

Jane didn't question the distinction between names, merely shook Laura's hand heartily. "Ah yes. You bought land north of the settlement, yes? For a ranch?"

"That we did. Matthew and I are here to get things started with some hands. We need the fences built before the boys can bring up the cattle. My husband's still in Texas with the young ones, Bonnie and Stephen."

Jane extended her hand to Matthew, but the young man's attention had settled behind her. His distraction was absolute enough that Jane glanced to see what caused it.

Sally walked toward the door, her gaze focused on her reticule as she dug through it. She paused in the doorway a moment, her head lifting as if she felt the stare of the young man. A flush pinked her cheeks, a smile flittering across her lips before she turned and darted down the street.

Jane turned back to the pair, noting Matthew's gaze had followed Sally's departure. She offered Laura a conspiratorial smile, then cleared her throat. "Well, then I guess we can expect more trail runs soon."

"Soon as we can get up and running," Laura confirmed. She smacked Matthew across the stomach. "Matthew. Where are your manners?"

Matthew jumped at the reprimand. A sheepish smile crossed his features. "Sorry."

Jane took his now extended hand. "Good to meet you, Matthew. That young woman was my ward, Sally. If you were wondering."

"I, um—" Matthew rubbed the back of his neck. "What about the horse?"

Jane did her best to school her laughter. "Of course. Cole should be along soon, but I'm happy to show you what he has ready. Unless you're wanting something he still needs to properly train."

"No. Matthew's ride didn't survive the trip. He needs something that'll do good work now." Laura fell into step beside Jane with Matthew trailing behind them. "He had Sawyer long as I've known him. Took it hard."

Matthew grumbled a bit behind them.

Jane chuckled softly at his quiet complaint. "I can imagine. I don't know what will happen if I were to ever lose Tempest. She's a wonderful horse."

"Sawyer was the best." Matthew paused at the corral fence beside the two women.

"Those three are ready for sale. I wouldn't recommend the brown, he's more a farm horse. The paint and the chestnut would be better, I believe." Jane gestured to the three in a smaller enclosure outside the training corral.

Matthew moved closer to where the horses were. Before he'd hit the fence, the chestnut lifted its head and walked forward to meet him. At a click of Matthew's tongue, the horse nickered and shook out its mane.

Jane smiled at the interaction. "I think the chestnut likes him."

"Sure seems so." Laura laughed softly. "Not that it's a surprise. Matthew's got a knack."

"I know the feeling." Jane glanced over at approaching footsteps. "Speaking of having a knack. Laura, I'd like you to meet Cole Mitchell. He's the one that trains and sells these beasts around here. Cole, this is Laura Edwards. Her and her boy Matthew are building that ranch north of town."

"That so? Good to meet you." Cole shook Laura's hand. "What's your boy doing?"

"Looking for a horse, though it seems he's found one." Jane leaned up for a kiss. "I'll leave you to the negotiations. I'll see you at three."

"Three." He winked, then stepped toward where Matthew stood with the chestnut.

"It was lovely to meet you. I hope we'll see more of you and your family once they're all here." Jane shook Laura's hand again before making her leave.

She would post a letter, then perhaps take a ride before the meeting. A ride might clear her head for the upcoming task of figuring out how to get to Underwood.

The hair on the back of her neck rose, and her stomach tightened. A sensation like someone watched her. She spun around, searching the streets, but spotted nothing.

Shaking it off, she dismissed it as imagination and nerves. Still, her stomach churned enough she thought she might get a tea before heading out on her ride.

We believe no evil until the evil's done.
—Jean de La Fontaine

Jane climbed the steps to Cora's restaurant slower than necessary. The day before they'd developed a plan to get some information out of Underwood before he left. Through much discussion, they'd settled on one, and Thomas had immediately left afterward to see it would be played out the very next day. She, for one, was not looking forward to her part in it. It involved lies and deception, but Tom had pointed out that she should know firsthand that sometimes you needed lies to catch a liar.

Against the distaste for the event, she managed to make it inside the restaurant to seek out Leanne. She sat across the restaurant near the table where Cutler and Underwood sat. Unwilling to waste any further time on nerves, she headed right for her friend. Without ceremony, she interrupted the conversation Leanne was having with Cora. "You need to stop."

"Excuse us," Leanne said with politeness to Cora. When the woman departed, Leanne narrowed her eyes at Jane. "Excuse me?"

"Your games. Leave the Young boys alone."

"What games? I'm having a good time, and they most certainly aren't complaining."

"Because you're too busy leading them along." Jane leaned on the chair toward Leanne. "They deserve *far* better than a bored madam trying to bide her time until her train arrives. Leave them all *alone*."

"No." Leanne rose to face Jane dead on. "They're *big* boys, Jane. Rather enjoyably so. They can make their own decisions."

"They're also men being led around by a whiff of rotten dessert."

"Rotten?"

"Just because it costs more doesn't make it any less so."

"You're a fine one to talk." Leanne's lips curled in a sneer. "I've heard plenty about the great many boys you led around before you decided to take up residence in that den of iniquity yourself."

"I was never a whore."

"Just because they *don't* pay for it, doesn't make it less true."

Jane narrowed her eyes, doing her best to keep her laughter contained at the gasps of shock around them. When they'd practiced their arguments at the Sage Brush Hotel, they'd been doubled over in laughter. After all, Leanne's manipulations had managed to get Mike and Daisy officially courting, Nick smiling more, and Tom was smitten.

Unfortunately, or rather fortunately, they had the attention of Underwood. That fact alone helped Jane keep her laughter pushed down. She set her hands on the table to get nose to nose with Leanne. "Leave them the hell alone. Go back to your room and diddle yourself until your train gets here. You go near them again and I will see to it you regret it. I won't break up another fist fight between them."

"Oh, please don't." That morning the first step of the subterfuge had been set in place, and Leanne had been the gleeful audience between the three brothers. Jane had interceded—far more carefully than she had when Cole had fought Al. Leanne winked. "You do know that the winner gets the spoils."

"Shouldn't it be the loser gets the spoiled meat?"

"You would know."

"Get your things out of the Sage Brush Hotel. Stay away from Michael. Stay away from Nick and Thomas as well. Or else I will—"

"Jane! Leanne!" Katherine rushed toward them. Her features were pale as she looked between them. Unfortunately, they'd had to keep most of the town out of the loop to be safe. Poor Kat had no idea it was all deception. "What in heavens name is going on?"

"Jane's jealous." Leanne adjusted her skirts, then tugged her bodice side to side to bump her bosom until the bulged from the device plump and round. "She misses being able to play and is trying to make me stop. However, I'm getting far too much satisfaction from the deal. Those boys are a dandy distraction from my boredoms."

Kat blinked several times, her brow twisted in confusion. "What?"

Jane laughed, making sure it was more cold than humor. "You really are a stupid whore. Trust me, you will regret this."

"Jane!" Kat clutched Jane's arm. "You don't mean that."

Leanne rolled her eyes, hand on hip as she glared at Jane. "I never regret—it wastes far too much time. Time that could be spent in far more enjoyable pursuits. Speaking of which,

I'm due for a ride with Tom. He promised to make it a wild one, and then after I'm meeting Mike for a nice relaxing soak in the watering hole. You do remember how I enjoyed that, don't you? Best of all, after that Nick has asked for an intimate picnic. I'm all aquiver with anticipation for that."

Jane kept her jaw clenched as Leanne brushed past her to flounce out of the store. With Leanne gone, Jane had to closer her eyes and take a few deep breaths. She hoped it appeared that she was trying to contain anger rather than laughter over the ridiculousness of the whole thing. The only bad part was that Kat believed any of it. Jane wanted nothing more than to tell her friend the truth, but when Kat set her hand on Jane's arm, she yanked it away. "Not now, Katherine."

"Jane." Kat blocked Jane's attempt at an exit. "Would you mind explaining to me what in heavens just happened? This makes no sense"

"I explained to Leanne that she needs to stop playing with the Young boys. She's not listening. I'm going to see that she pays for such an error in judgment." Jane rushed around Kat to get out the building fast before any further questions could arise.

Right as se hit the bottom step Leanne and Tom rode past on Faro. Jane set her hands on her hips, glaring at the departing pair. Honestly, she was a little jealous that they were using Faro, after all that was the horse she and Cole had first rode together on.

A short distance away, Cole eyed her in silence. Near him Alma sat with Cindy and Lizzie. The group had gathered on the porch of what had been the town's church before they'd built the new one in the meadow. Norman was nearest her, trying to wrangle the group of boys in some sort of order to divide out the fishing poles between them.

Jesse, Isaac, and Arthur were not making it easy on him. Each of the boys were having more fun laughing and mock-fighting. Never mind Jesse's arm was in a sling and his good arm was being used to hold a crutch, he was giving as good as any of them.

David leaned against the building, chuckling behind his hand as Norman battled with the boys.

Jane remained still when Cole crossed the street to stand before her. "You're all going to head out now I take it?"

Cole nodded, his gaze drifting toward where Leanne and Tom had disappeared. "Everything all right?"

"As well as can be expected." Jane used the vague reply as the safest way to say all had gone as planned. "Really gets my goat he's acting an ass using our horse."

"You're mad they're on Faro?"

"First time you tried to get your jollies being close to me was on that horse."

He chuckled low. "You enjoyed it much as I did."

"Perhaps." She sighed, turning her attention back to the chaos in front of the building he'd come from. "It appears as though your boys' day is going to be half girls. Tell David to not let Jesse boss them around too much. He likes to think he's older, and it makes him feel big since he's still healing."

"He's a boy." He nudged her gently. "We'll keep an eye on him. Hope the girls don't get bored with fishing."

"The girls are total tomboys. As for Alma, I think she just likes hanging out with you, and those children. Plus, fishing is a nice, quiet activity which is good for her." She set her hand on his chest, attempting a stern expression. An expression made more difficult by Norman's increasing frustration. "You be nice to Norman. No old man comments. And be nice to David. There's only a couple of weeks left until he's tied into the restraint of marriage."

"Well then what *can* I do? You're taking all the fun out of it."

"You'll have plenty of fun later." Jane leaned into him. "Promise."

"Evil woman."

"Is the Inn all set?"

"Edgar's got the place until two. After that Seth takes over, and then Tommy after supper. You staying at the library today?"

"Yes. Ms. Pine is bringing in a group of children for a school outing."

"How is it you got them kids outta school for today?"

Jane shrugged. "Easy. Jesse is well ahead of his class, and I had him write a report on the history of Dominion Falls to show he wasn't missing anything. Isaac and the girls did the same. Arthur is already taking his exams to get his teaching certificate, and also head of his class, plus he impressed Ms. Pine with his experiment on electricity."

"What you're saying is all the kids you're helping are ahead?"

She didn't bother to hide her smile, evens she skirted the question. "I bribed Cora and Kat with the wisdom of this being a special occasion since the next two weekends are completely full of wedding activities—and David is not about to have a stag party no matter how hard you try. Plus, Alma is only in town for a little while longer."

"You're slick."

"Anyhow. Ms. Pine is bringing the children by for their outing on the history of the town in preparation for Founder's Day. I've received a full briefing on the history of the library from Mrs. Daugherty herself."

"Did Lil mention the fire they had?"

Jane sighed at the mention of the town setting books on fire. "Yes. She told me the reverend before Reverend Green took exception to some of the books, and there were quite a number of books lost in the fire that was set after his sermon. I won't be telling about it in a way that will mention anyone involved, so no one will be painted in bad light."

"If anyone can spin a story and still be honest, it's you."

"Damn straight."

"D-damn straight," Alma's quiet voice said from behind Cole. She'd walked up without Jane even noticing.

Cole laughed, despite Jane's horror. "Guess we need to watch our language. Don't think Ms. Wellman's gonna appreciate that."

"I guess you're right." Jane smiled at Alma. "Have fun today, Alma. Repeat all of Cole's bad words, let's see if that makes him stop."

Cole narrowed his eyes at her wink. When she started to move away, he grabbed her and dipped her into a deep kiss before plopping her upright again. "Remember that for later."

"Don't think I won't." She swept close enough to him that her skirts hid the way she teased his length. "And you remember that."

"Damn."

Laughing, she darted away before he could grab her again. Once in the library, she got straight to work. Books were set away, the shelves dusted, and the windows wiped down. With the knowledge that children were coming by, she removed her gun from its holster to slip into her top drawer. She put the holster in with it.

No longer did she feel entirely safe with it off, but at least it was right in reach. Besides, children didn't need her walking around with a Remington on her side as she spoke about the history of the town and library. By the time she got everything settled to her satisfaction, Sally arrived.

For an hour they worked together over a book. Jane tested her as they went page by page. As Sally read a passage aloud, Jane sat back in her seat. "Good. Now tell me what you read."

"I..." Sally frowned down at the page. "This is hopeless."

"It isn't hopeless at all. We're figuring this out. It may not seem like it, but we've learned quite a bit today."

"Like what?"

"Like reading straight doesn't do you any good at all." Jane pulled the book toward herself. "You can't stare at a page and digest the information. Reading aloud helps, but hearing someone else read to you seems to be the best solution."

"I can't always have someone reading to me. And what about those tests? I won't pass if I can't figure out how to read normal."

"This is day one, Sally. We need time. I promise we'll figure this out." Jane squeezed Sally's hand at the girl's doubtful frown. "You aren't dumb. You learn in a different way than most. We all learn differently, honestly. Alma does, Tommy, Cole, me. We all learned what we did in different ways. All we need to do is figure out your way."

"I hope you're right."

"Give me more than one hour to figure it out, hm? Patience is not my strong suit either, but I believe we're both going to have to practice it."

The concern that creased Sally's brow eased. "I guess so. I'd best get out of your hair, I can hear the kids coming."

"I hear them, too. When Horace gets in, please tell him to expect me around five. After I'm done here, I will eat supper before I head back home."

"When are the boys due back?"

"All I know is they said before sunset. With that lot, we'll see if they even make sunset."

Sally grabbed the book and got to her feet. "I'll tell Seth. Can I take this with me?"

"Of course." Jane followed her out to the porch. She waved at the incoming group of schoolchildren, and ushered them into the library along with their teacher, Ms. Pine. The next hour was occupied with story-telling and questions, and Jane was happy for the distraction.

After the last child had been ushered out the door, she cleaned again. A few townspeople came through, but otherwise she read to fill her time. Also to occupy her mind after the argument with Leanne. With a sigh, she dropped her cheek to her hand and tried to focus on her book.

"Jane?" The now annoyingly familiar rumble of Joe set her nerves on edge.

She glanced at the drawer on her left, half-tempted to draw the weapon immediately. Shoving the instinct aside, she managed to force a smile. "Joe. What can I do for you this afternoon?"

"Saw that fight with Leanne this morning." His tone indicated surprise, which meant Tommy had kept his promise to not fill Joe in on their plan. Joe moved slow along the wall, scanning book spines. "I wanted to check on you."

Jane closed her book to buy time. Inwardly, she tried to remind herself that he'd been very well behaved, rather quite absent since she'd spoken to him the day before. She rose to her feet, trying to push aside the intrusive bubble of emotions that were only partially hers. "I'm doing fine. You had no need to check on me. I have plenty of people that do that on a regular basis."

"We were friends once, you know. More than, actually."

"I told you quite clearly. You were friends with Clara, not me." Jane's hands fluttered on their way back to the desk. His insinuation didn't miss her notice, but her gun was just a whisper away. "I don't much care for you."

"Too bad. We had a lot of fun." He pulled a book from the shelf. On his way to the desk, he flipped through it casually. "I still find it hard to believe you've settled down with one man. Even now as 'Jane' you hardly seem the type."

Her hands clenched convulsively. "It's hardly any of your business what my life is now. While I appreciate the assistance you've given us in our business matters, I do not consider you a friend as Thomas does. My personal life is off limits to you."

"Don't even want to try to be friends?"

"No."

"'The lady doth protest too much, methinks'."

"'O, but she'll keep her word'." She unclenched her hand as he came to stand before the desk, eyes still focused on the book in his hand. With subtle movements, she edged toward the drawer. "I do have work to do."

"Of course you do." He thumped the book closed. It dropped onto the desk before her.

One glance at the title, *Dangerous Liaisons*, made her heart stop. She lunged for the drawer, but he clicked his tongue before she got it open. She lifted her gaze to see the barrel of a gun already pointed at her.

"Now, now, Clara. Don't be rash."

Jane's hand was half in her drawer, but she didn't expect she'd be a quick enough draw to even get her hand on the gun before he fired. She froze in place, trying to form words, any words.

He shook his hand. "Come around the desk, Clara. Leave it where it is, and I won't shoot."

She should scream, run, do anything really. Nothing would listen to her command for a full minute as they both stood there in a gross painting of fear and malice. Then, she listened to him and pulled her hand free of the drawer. Still, she didn't close it. Perhaps she'd get another chance if she let him think he was in control again.

Slowly, she skirted around the desk. With him not moving, the gun ended up right against her chest. She swallowed hard against the lump in her throat. "Don't do anything stupid. Cole and Thomas will kill you."

A smile broke his features. "Come now, Clara. We're just having fun like we always do."

The second he slipped the weapon back in his holster, she bolted for the door with a shriek. He caught her around the waist, and kicked the door closed on the way around.

She fought against him hard, kicking down on his foot, and throwing her head back. He managed to catch her by the face and shoved it back against the shelves with pure brute force. The room spun around her as she dropped to the floor.

She pressed a hand to the back of her head where she'd hit. Damp moisture met her fingers. When she pulled them free, they were red with blood. Her thoughts were fuzzy from the impact.

Vaguely, she heard the lock click. The room settled into semi-darkness as he pulled the shades closed. His footsteps approached too fast for her to scramble away, much less for her gun.

He grabbed her by the chin and hauled her to her feet. "Let's try this again. No one is watching. Tell me how you missed me, Clara."

Disgust roiled in her stomach. She wrinkled her nose as he leaned in close, his breath brushing her ear.

"Tell me."

"I'm not her, and she didn't miss you either." Jane spit in his face when he withdrew to glare at her.

One solid punch to her ribs made her gasp. In that moment, she thought of the baby. Her gaze fell on the desk. If she could just get there.

She didn't have a chance to plan. He grabbed her hair in a tight grip. Her head arched back as he tugged it toward him.

His fierce gaze held a fire of lust she'd seen too often in men's eyes making him seem almost crazy. "Don't think about it. A little rough was always your way, but gun play isn't part of the deal, my little pet."

Revulsion slid down her spine, threatening to empty her stomach contents on him. She twisted out of his grasp, crying out as the motion not only tugged on the wound on her head, but ripped several hairs out. She rushed away from the desk in hopes of distracting him.

When he grabbed her right arm, she swung around and punched him solid in the nose with her left. The grip on her arm relaxed enough that she freed herself. She made it all the way to the desk before he caught up again.

Another punch came to her kidneys before he slammed her hard into the edge of the desk. Pain shot across her abdomen before it tightened. No. No, she couldn't…she'd sworn.

When he grabbed her hair again, she didn't fight. Unable to contain them, tears streamed down her face. If she fought, he could kill her baby. He might not know about it, but it could still happen. She couldn't let it happen. Any of it.

"Let's try one more time. Tell me how much you missed me. Better yet, show me."

Her options faded into the darkened room. It was her or the baby.

In the end, it wasn't a choice at all.

Not to be provoked is best; but if moved,
never correct until the fume is spent; for every
stroke our fury strikes is sure to
hit ourselves last.
-William Penn

The day of fishing had gone better than Cole expected. He didn't know whether to be annoyed or amused by the fact that he and David had managed to get along and have a good time. He had no doubt Jane would find it amusing.

He got Alma situated with Sally, then went to find Jane. He'd been surprised to not find her in the bar on his return. Since she'd not been down there, he went to their room. When he opened the door, he found her brushing her wet hair, fresh from a bath. Frustration tugged his amusement away. "You trying to ruin my night?"

She kept brushing her hair in even, methodical strokes. No laughter bubbled out of her as expected. No flicker of emotion at all. Stroke by stroke, her hand drew her brush through her long hair. She hardly seemed to notice when it snarled on a thick curl. "Whatever do you mean?"

"Taking a bath without me?" He strode over to her side to place a kiss on her neck. When he set his hands on her hips, she didn't soften against him like she always did. "Jane?"

"Sorry." When she met his gaze in the mirror, he could plainly see torment she tried to hide. "This wasn't a bath for pleasure."

"Jane?" Every lick of his amusement faded. Something was wrong, and it made his insides squirm. He set his hands on her shoulders to try to offer some comfort. Tears shimmered at the corners of her eyes, and she uncharacteristically shrugged his hands away.

She darted away from him. When she pulled out a simple chore dress from behind the curtain, he knew without a doubt something was wrong.

Concern lodged in a firm nodule in his throat. "What happened?"

She set the dress on the bed, then bent to get some shoes. Even though she tried to duck away, he saw her wince. "I'm going to get dressed. Once I am, I will need you to take me to the clinic straight away."

The clinic? Panic seeped into his heart, pounding in his ears. "*Jane.*"

Finally, she turned to face him. The robe slipped from her shoulders to puddle on the floor. Jaw set, she met his gaze before she lowered her eyes.

Cole could see dark bruises blossoming on her ribs and stomach. When she turned for her chemise, there was another at the small of her back. Fists clenched, he ground his teeth together. Words weren't coming, not that he'd know what to say. His gut told him what had happened, but he had to hear it. Or maybe he didn't.

"I had a visit at the library today." Her voice was eerily calm, though her hand shook when she set it over the bruise on her ribs. The chemise cascaded over her head, covering the evidence of brutality.

"Who?"

"Joe."

"I'll kill the bastard."

She stepped into the dress, still strangely calm. No, not calm. Dead.

"I had my gun, but I had it in the drawer because of the students. He got his faster than I got mine. After that, and a few convincing points on his part," her hand settled on the bruise on her abdomen, "it was either succumb or risk our child."

Cole's whole body shook with rage. He couldn't speak. Part of him wanted to go shoot the man's cock off, but the rest of him had to make sure she was okay.

"In the end, I chose to do what I had to in order to protect our child as best I could. It may have been too late by the time he slammed me into the desk." She turned away, her fingers climbing the buttons along her spine. "I need to make sure my choice didn't put our child at risk anyway."

"Jane!" Cole burst out in shock.

The deadened expression on her face cracked under his brutal yell. "Don't. Please. Not now. I can't do this right now."

"He raped—"

"*Not* now!" Her breath came in ragged gasps. "I need to go to the clinic. Are you going to help me there, or shall I find someone else that can escort me?"

He rushed over to reach for her arm, but the bruises he'd seen there stopped him. "Jane."

"Don't make me say it again," her voice trembled. "I'll have Mr. Hamm take me to the clinic, then. He was kind enough to escort me home from the library."

Cole blinked in shock when she sat to pull on her boots. He bent to try to help, but she shoved him off. The thoughts racing in his head battled as strong as his emotions.

She said nothing further, finishing the last button before walking to the vanity. With one simple, practiced movement she twisted her hair into a knot and pinned it fast. She headed for the door. "I will be at the clinic. When I return we can discuss what happened."

All the air in the room seemed to be sucked out when she left. Cole dropped to his knees. It couldn't be real. He hadn't seen what he'd seen. Heard what she'd said. He struggled to get himself together for her, but didn't know how. He didn't understand how she could be so calm.

He flew to his feet to race after her, but right outside the room he ran into Tommy. With a snarl, he grabbed the man's shirt and threw him into the wall. "*Bastard*!"

Tommy gripped Cole's wrists. "What the hell is your problem?"

"Not now Cole," Jane yelled from downstairs.

Cole dropped his grip on Tommy's shirt to tear down the stairs for her. He gulped for air when she left the saloon on Hammy's arm cool as can be.

Tommy stormed down the steps behind him. "What the *hell* is going on? I thought we agreed to the plan."

Cole spun on him, but the dozens of eyes on them gave him pause. He stormed into the storeroom. The second Tommy followed him, Cole got in his face. With a quiet, threatening tone he spoke, "You said he was *harmless*. You told Jane he was all bark no bite"

Tommy didn't back down from the challenge in Cole's stance. "Who?"

"Joe." In that instant, all Cole's anger faded into nothing. He sagged against a nearby shelf, unable to keep his knees from buckling. He grabbed his head as the realization spun through his head again. "No. It ain't possible. Not Jane. *Not her.*"

Tommy didn't react when Cole shoved him out of the way and tore out of the Inn. Cole raced to the clinic at top speed, but when he burst inside, Tommy was tackling him. They hit the wall, and Cole tried to shove him off.

Tom grabbed his arm and held him back. "Hey."

Cole whipped around to take a swing at him. "I gotta get in there."

"You don't burst in. You don't know what they're doing."

"I'll tell ya what they're doing! They're making sure the baby's okay because that bastard friend of yours." Cole clenched his jaw. "He paid her a visit—when she was alone."

Tom's face went slack. "He went to talk to her?"

"Talking don't bruise people. She told me she had to succumb to save the baby. What the hell does that mean to you?"

All the emotions plaguing Cole twisted and darkened his friends face.

"Thank you, Mr. Hamm," Jane's soft voice filtered out of an open door before it closed again.

Hammy turned, stopping short when he spotted the two men. His ruddy features paled, and he took a step back. After he'd cleared his throat, he managed to speak. "She asked me to bring her here. That all right?"

Cole managed a stiff nod. Of all people, he knew Hammy'd never hurt her. "Thank you. How is she?"

"Actin' strange." Hammy frowned. "Not bein' mean or nothing. But she ain't talkin', or smilin'. Just starin'."

Cole flinched at the words. His stomach did a sickening flop. "Thanks. Get on back to the saloon. Rest of the night it's on the house. Wait. She said—she said you took her home from the library today."

Tom sat on the edge of the desk real casual-like, but his fists clenched when he folded his arms across his chest. "What happened, Hammy?"

"I was headin' to the saloon after workin' out at the Carter farm today. When I walked past the library, she was strugglin' with the lock. She was cryin' and all." Hammy looked at the floor. His hat twisted in his hands. "I don't like seein' Lady Jane cry none. I thought she was hurt. She said she weren't hurt so bad, but she'd like me to walk her home, even though it ain't that far. She was shakin' and cryin'. I couldn't say no."

Tommy's jaw clenched. "You see anyone else?"

Hammy shook his head. "No."

"Thank you." Tommy nodded. "Beer's free all week."

Both men remained silent as Hammy left the clinic.

Cole turned toward the wall, pressing his hands into the wood as his chest constricted. Try as he might, he couldn't erase the image of her back in their room. Every bit of her was fighting to be strong, but she was failing. He shook his head. "No. This ain't happening. It ain't."

"It *is* happening," Tommy snarled. "And I'm going to *kill* that son of a bitch."

"Get in line." Charlie closed the exam room door behind him. When Cole stormed forward, Charlie stepped in his path. He held up his hands to stop him. "Wait. She doesn't want you in there if you're flying off the handle."

"I don't care!" Cole contemplated throwing Charlie out of the way.

"She's the one that was attacked!" Charlie dared to shove him back. "We're all pissed, every one of us, but what *she* wants is key right now."

"He raped her." Cole's anger snapped at the words, his shoulders drooped under their weight.

"Yes," Charlie confirmed. "She's got a nasty bump on the back of her head. It's no longer bleeding, but she's going to be sore for a while. The bruises on her torso and arms should heal normally."

A wave of bile rose in Cole's throat. "What about the baby?"

"Everything still looks all right. She said—" Charlie's voice caught. He took a shaky breath, but still had to clear his throat before he could continue. "If she'd fought him further, he would have beaten her more. He'd already punched her twice and thrown her into the desk. She knew then how much risk the baby could be in. She wasn't willing to lose another child, so she let him do what he wanted."

By the time he finished, Cole was gasping for air. "She didn't have to."

"She thinks she did!" Charlie stood toe to toe with him. "If you want to see her, you need to get yourself together.

She'll kick you right back out of that room you go in like this."

Cole grabbed him by the collar. "When it's Millie in there *then* you can tell me how to act!" He shoved the doctor aside and burst into the room.

Jane's back was to the door. She fiddled with the edge of the exam table, her back straight with tension. With each step he took, her chin lifted a little more. When he hesitated right behind her, she spoke quietly, "Revulsion? Or fear?"

"You don't revolt me. How can you ask that?"

"I chose this course. I may not have been willing, but I could have fought more than I did. Does that disgust you?"

His jaw clenched. "You had no choice."

"I could have fought."

"You didn't want the baby hurt."

"I disgust myself." Her voice cracked. With a shaky breath, her head dropped to her chest. Shaky hands smoothed over her skirt. "I need another bath. I need to—I need another bath now."

He stopped her when she tried to move around him. Her wide blue eyes lifted in surprise. When he pulled her against him, she flung her arms around his waist and held on tight. Her sob broke his heart right in two. He whispered, "Oh, Jane."

"I know you're angry." She hiccupped between sobs. "I know you're going to kill him, but I can't hear it right now. Take me home. I'll be safe there. I can try to get clean there. I need to get clean. I have to get clean. I need to—"

"Shhh." He smoothed his hand over her still-damp hair. Every time he brushed over the bump from the hit to her head, she winced. All his fury flew away at her tears. He only wanted to do all he could to help her. "We'll get you home. You need Kathy and Leanne?"

"Yes. When you leave I will. Right now, I need you."

He scooped her up to carry her. When she fought against him, he frowned. "Jane."

"Let me walk. I can't be weak. Let me walk."

Setting her down, he brushed his fingers along her cheek. When she turned her gaze upward, he searched her eyes. "You know you don't gotta prove nothing."

"I don't want people to know. I will walk on my own." She shook her head. "I don't care how scandalous I've been, there are some things that don't need to be spread far and wide by the gossips of this town."

Every inch of him hated letting her walk when he wanted nothing more than to hold her, but he knew what she said made sense. "You do what you need to do."

"Thank you. You will do what you need to do soon. I need you first, please. Just until I'm home. I need you. I need you."

He didn't hesitate to hold her close when she collapsed against him. His heart had stopped beating it constricted so tight. "You got me, long as you need me," as he said the words, they felt empty and weak compared to what was happening.

She sniffled against him. Her arms squeezed tight around him once more before she straightened. When he fumbled to fish the handkerchief out of his vest, a hint of a smile peeked through before it faded as fast. She wiped at her tears.

The moment they left the room, Tom was there. "Lou…"

"Find him." For the moment, she'd managed to put strength in her voice, but she leaned against Cole too heavily for him to think it was more than bluster. "Cole will only be able to keep it together so long. When you find out where he's headed, come get Cole. He'll be ready."

"All right." Tommy's jaw clenched. He didn't meet either of their eyes.

"Pinkerton's are the best at deception. You told me yourself. He told us himself. Stop blaming your sorry ass, I don't have time for it." She turned her attention to Charlie. "Please go get Kat and Leanne for me."

"All right." Charlie nodded. "Anything else?"

"No. And no one else, either. I don't want anyone else to know." Jane trembled in his arms but stood tall. "Not Michael. Not David. Not Daisy."

"Jane." Charlie's brow furrowed. "You're due for an appointment tomorrow."

"I do not have to remove my bodice. I will wear long sleeves. Bruises fade—and you said there was no true damage to my ribs, and the baby suffered no damage. She does not need to know. No one does." Jane had a death grip on Cole's hand. "It's bad enough the two of you know. I don't want pity."

Charlie frowned deeper but nodded. "Fine."

Jane slipped from Cole's grasp to walk back to the Inn.

Cole jogged after her, wrapping his arm around his waist as they entered the saloon. They cut right through the floor with little of Jane's usual banter, right back to the bath house. Once inside, Jane still didn't give in to whatever emotions she was covering.

He filled the tub for her so she could undress. By the time he'd finished, she'd only managed to remove her shoes. She just sat on the stool, one shoe still in hand, staring blindly at it.

Cole gingerly pulled the shoe from her hand. He slipped his hand into hers. With a gentle tug, she rose to her feet. He unbuttoned the buttons for her, slipping it down over her shoulders to the floor. With just her chemise on now, he hesitated. Her hands rested on his chest, and he closed his eyes against the wave of emotion.

"Your touch is safe. It has to be safe." A soft whimper reached his ears. Her head dropped to his chest. "Unless…"

"I ain't disgusted. I'm furious."

The weight of her head left his chest. When he opened his eyes, she was pulling the chemise up herself. He set his hands over hers until she released her hold on the muslin to lift her arms.

After he'd set aside the garment, he rested his hand on the bruise along her abdomen. The one that had made her give in. His jaw clenched against the rage rising inside.

She set her hand on his forearm. "Go."

"I ain't leaving you."

"You stick around, you'll lose hold of the anger. You need it."

He framed her face with his hands. "You need me."

"Yes."

His gut twisted tight. The heart he thought had stopped beating raced before plummeting to the floor. Leaving wasn't right, but neither was staying. Not when the bastard thought he'd gotten away with it.

"Help me into the tub, then go. Tom will be here soon. Katherine and Leanne will be here to help me. When you've taken care of him, when you come back, then you can be here for me. I'm not alone, and I am not going to break."

He let out a long, shaky breath, fighting with his warring instincts. With a gentle touch, he brushed his thumb across her lips. "Can I?"

"Please," she whispered.

He brushed his lips across hers. She tensed under him enough to make him hesitate. Then her lips softened under his and they lingered in the soft kiss. Pulling back after mere moments, he exhaled a blast of emotion. He scooped her up gently to carry her to the tub.

As he set her in the water, she held on around his neck until she was almost fully submerged. Her soft sob against his neck wasn't missed by him. He sank to his knees next to the tub.

He pressed his forehead to hers, holding her gaze. "What can I do?"

"Forgive me."

"Nothing to forgive. You did nothing wrong."

"I love you. I'm so sorry. I'm so sorry. I'm so…"

He pulled her to him. "You didn't do this."

"I'm so sorry. I love you."

"Love you too."

"Forgive me…"

Whilst shame keeps its watch,
virtue is not wholly extinguished in the heart.
—Edmund Burke

Kat crossed the street quick as she could. The task of getting the excited girls to bed, and soothing Norman's annoyance at her requested departure had taken longer than she'd hoped. Charlie had indicated some level of urgency in his request she go see Jane.

The intensity of Charlie's appeal had Kat on edge. Her pressing questions had resulted in a stonewall response. The idea that Jane herself had to tell the story worried Kat even more.

As she stepped onto the Inn's porch, a horse tore around the corner. Leanne brought the horse to a stop and leaped down. She threw the reins over the hitching post. "Kat. What's going on?"

"What are you doing here?" After the scene in Cora's earlier, Kat couldn't imagine why Leanne would come by.

Leanne shrugged. "I have no idea. Charlie sent Hammy to the Sage Brush to get me. He said Jane needed to see me, and it was urgent."

"I got the same message from Charlie himself." Kat furrowed her brow. "I thought you and she were fighting, though."

"It was all an act. We're trying to get Underwood to see me as a potential help to him, or at least a bedmate."

"Did it work?"

"Sure did." Leanne slung her loose golden waves over her shoulder. "What do you think I was doing when Hammy arrived?"

"I'd be too afraid to ask—if I didn't know you better, of course."

"Of course." Leanne sighed. "I had him in the spring, taking a little dip. I made sure to bring along a tincture of absinthe. Right about now he likely believes our relaxing dip has gone much further than it ever could."

"Clever."

"I've learned a few tricks in my time."

"If it was going so well, did Hammy's arrival ruin your plans?"

Cole appeared in the doorway, interrupting the line of questioning. Hollow, haunted eyes stared at them both. He didn't speak a word, though he opened his mouth a few times as if he was going to. Kat had never seen him like that, even when him and Jane were split.

Kat found herself a total loss for words, and the panic of Charlie's visit hit her hard again. She found herself stuck between wanting to comfort him and needing to demand answers.

Leanne didn't hesitate like Kat did. She grabbed his arm. "Cole? What is it? What's wrong?"

"She needs ya." Cole coughed when the words came out rough. "She's in the bath house now. Go on."

"No. She needs you," Kat objected. If anything happened, she knew without a doubt the person Jane always needed was Cole. "It's always you she needs. Why us?"

"I got things to do." He shrugged off Leanne's hand. He stormed through the saloon, taking the stairs two at a time. By the time they got halfway through the saloon he'd gotten to his room and headed back out with a rifle slung over his shoulder, and a hat pulled low over his eyes.

Leanne looked as confused as Kat felt but took a shaky breath. "Guess we'd best see what's going on, then."

Kat tried to ignore the turning of her stomach. She rushed through the saloon with Leanne. After a quick tap on the door, she stepped inside. "Jane?"

Jane sat in the middle of the tub; knees pulled to her chest. She stared at the far wall with no emotion on her features. "I need more water. Hot water. Hot, hot water."

"All right." Kat frowned when she realized Leanne hadn't joined them yet. She grabbed the nearest bucket from the stove to fulfill Jane's request. "What happened?"

Silence echoed back from the tub. When Kat carried the water over, Jane didn't move a muscle. The steaming water sloshed into the tub, but Jane didn't even flinch when it hit her skin. Kat reached out to touch Jane's shoulder.

Jane shrugged her shoulder away, but otherwise didn't move.

"What can I do?" Kat leaned on the edge of the tub.

"More water." A tear slipped down Jane's cheek.

Kat refilled the bucket to replace it on the stove. She grabbed the next steaming bucket to carry back. "Here you go."

The door opened, then closed again with a solid snap. The lock clicked louder into the silence. Jane flinched, her eyes closing as she released a breath.

Leanne grabbed a stool to place beside the tub. When she sat, facing Jane, she smiled. "Not that I mind being witness to your bath, but is it wise with the plan?"

Jane still didn't move, her eyes still closed. "I was right about Joe."

"He's an idiot. I know. I see the creep vibe too, but—"

Kat knelt beside the tub when Jane finally turned to face them. The same haunted, dark pain echoed in her eyes that had been in Cole's. Kat gasped, clasping her hands over her mouth as it dawned on her. "Oh, no."

Leanne moved off the stool, kneeling directly in front of Jane. "He got you?"

Jane's brow twitched a moment before she turned away again. "Would you get my back please? Really scrub."

Leanne grabbed the sponge but glanced at Kat. "Jane."

"My back."

"I'll be the judge, and I'll be the jury,"
said cunning old fury: "I'll try the whole
cause and condemn you to death."
—Lewis Carroll

Cole shoved his rifle in the saddle's holster. Faro stomped and edged forward like he sensed Cole's urgency.

Cole hopped into the saddle and edged the horse forward while Tom got on Brag.

With a shaky breath, Cole glanced toward the Inn. The small window near the ceiling of the bath house still shimmered with candlelight. He imagined it would remain that way for most of the night. He wanted more than anything to be the one in there helping Jane. There was something he had to do first.

Tommy finished adjusted his own rifle's holster before he sat up straight. "Bastard left his stuff at the boarding house. Told Rosenszweig he was heading out on horseback and to forward it all to his home in Ohio."

"Jane said," Cole choked on the words before he could finish them. His fist twisted the reins around. "He told her we couldn't touch him. She told him we'd kill him."

"She was right." Tom turned his horse north. "Let's move. They said he headed north out of town. We'll start there and figure out where he turned around. We only have about three hours of decent light left to track him, maybe four if he went west."

Cole spurred Faro forward. The pair of them raced out of town at a breakneck pace. They circled wide around the Edwards ranch and kept on toward the distant tree line.

After an hour of riding, they finally reached the treed foothills. Cole pulled Faro to a halt, waiting for Tommy to catch up. "Let's split up here and look for a trail."

Tom nudged his horse east, while Cole moved west. Within fifteen minutes Cole heard a sharp whistle from Tom. He turned the opposite direction, racing to catch up with Tom.

For almost two hours they managed to follow the trail. After heading north for several miles, Joe had veered east and went all the way into the mountains where he turned south again.

Cole cursed inwardly as the trail led them through the foothills to the east of town. They were close enough to see the glimmers of candlelight from windows and streetlamps. Knowing the bastard had passed right on by home while they'd wasted over two hours going north first burned him up into a rage again.

They curved back up through the foothills toward the nearby mountains where the trail turned north again. Tom slowed his horse half an hour later and turned to pull the lantern off the saddle. "It's getting too dark to see the trail without this. I'm sure he's still ahead of us, but if we get close, the lantern will give us away."

"Think we'll catch him?" Cole urged Faro into place next to Tom as the lantern flickered to life. The trees around them cast wild shadows in the flickering light. "He's got hours on us."

"I don't think he's running too fast." Tom lowered the lamp so the light flickered near the forest floor. He scanned the area for signs of the trail. "Cocky bastard probably thinks good old Clara will stick to pattern."

Cole's lip curled. "What do ya mean by that?"

Tom straightened in his saddle. He studied Cole for a minute before he leaned on his pommel. "Did Jane tell you what I knew about my naïve, foolish, stubborn sister and her time in Utah?"

Cole shook his head, wracking his brain. She'd ranted and raved about Clara enough, but his memory wasn't like hers. "I've heard lots of complaints."

"Michael, and Clara's letters, made mention of the men she kept company with. She didn't bother to mention that not all of them were by choice."

Cole's mind went numb for a minute. "Clara bragged to Michael. I remember Jane saying that. Bragged about the men."

"I tried to help, but she didn't want it. That's why she ran to Utah in the first place, because I took care of cocksucker number one. One of her students that thought he'd teach her a lesson." A mix of fury and pain swept across his friends face before it hardened into stone. "She packed herself up and moved to Utah. I tried to help her there, and at first I could tell, she was a terrible liar. Then she got good. I couldn't tell all the time."

Cole closed his eyes against the red fury that blinded him. "Joe?"

"If my guess is right, this isn't the first time. I'm pissed as hell at myself for not seeing it back then—and not trusting her instinct now." Tom rubbed his hand over his face. "Like Jane said, we're trained for deception and guile."

"Clara never told you about him, then."

"She also never had a man whenever he saw her. Not a steady one. He never went to visit when David was in her life." Tom clicked his tongue at his horse. They moved along the path again. "I'm guessing the reason he ran is he's not one hundred percent certain she wouldn't tell you, or me, this time."

"So he's on the move, but not so fast."

"Exactly."

Cole guided Faro around over the railroad tracks. They both slipped out of their saddles to search for the trail again.

They walked slow along the tracks on either side, searching for signs Joe had passed that way.

Halfway up the mountain, and another hour wasted, Cole spotted a broken branch. With a little more digging and the helpful light of the moon, spotted a real trail inside the tree line. "Found it."

"Good. We'll have to camp for a few hours to rest the horses once those clouds roll in and the moon's no longer any use to us." Tom stood next to him, staring into the woods. "Going on the bet he's going to camp, too. We'll head out again at first light. I'm sure it won't be long before we find him by daylight."

"I'm guessing you know, but we do this, we ain't doing it by the book. There ain't no law I care about out here."

"Damn straight."

"Plenty of men get lost in these hills."

"You're not getting an argument from me, Cole. I'm used to jobs like this. No law. Biggest question is, who gets the bullet?"

"I do."

Tommy nodded. "Just so long as I get to see him suffer first. Bastard double-crossed me to get to her."

"No law."

"No law."

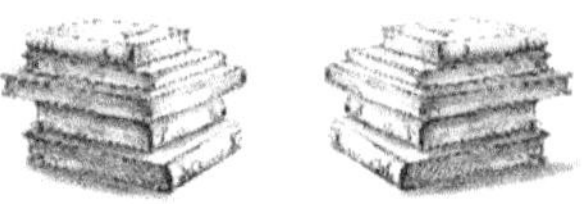

*Fools, through false shame,
conceal their wounds.
-Horace*

Jane's hands shook too hard to button her dress. Near the door, Leanne and Kat stood in whispered conversation. Each hushed word grated on Jane's raw nerves. "Stop whispering about me like I'm not in the room."

Leanne and Kat both had the decency to appear repentant. Kat attempted a smile that fell apart immediately. "Sorry."

"We aren't sure what to do." Leanne walked forward. Her hands settled on Jane's shoulders, a frown appearing when Jane fumbled with another button. "Why are we here? You're not letting us do anything to help. You definitely don't want a fuss."

"I can't be alone right now." Jane lowered her gaze at the crack in her voice. She dropped her hands from the buttons when she failed for a third time to put a button through its hole. "I—Cole can't be here. He has to—he has— I needed you both. You're the only ones I could tell that wouldn't—you wouldn't—I—I can't be alone."

The second Leanne buttoned Jane's dress, Katherine wrapped Jane in the tightest hug. "Then you won't be. Tell us how to help."

Jane wanted nothing more than to crack right there and then. To break apart into dust to be swept away in the storm raging through her. For years she'd fought to be different than Clara, but at the moment she was beginning to understand. After she'd wiped her tears, she took a bracing breath. "First, I need some tea. After that, I want company, and diversion."

"I'll prepare your tea," Leanne offered. "You and Kat head on upstairs and I'll follow right behind."

Jane squeezed Leanne's outstretched hand. "Thank you."

Kat wrapped her arm around Jane's waist. Together they walked to the stairs. The saloon bustled with activity, but blessedly no one noticed them, or if they did, they remained quiet. Kat didn't speak at all on the way upstairs or even once they were in the room.

While Jane put her boots away, Kat turned down the bed. Jane climbed in it gratefully, letting her sore body sink into the soft bed. "Talk to me about Lizzie and Cindy. Did they have fun fishing today? What did Norman think?"

Kat clenched her fists. "What? I can't pretend like this isn't happening, Jane. How can you?"

"If you can't, you need to leave." Tears burned Jane's eyes, but she refused to waver. When Cole returned, maybe she could let herself break. "The only way I can make it through is to redirect my energy. I can't spend hours dissecting what happened. I made a choice—a choice that sickens me to my core, but I would make it again."

"It wasn't a choice!"

"It was. I chose my baby knowing full well what would happen if I stopped fighting. Once I made that decision, I didn't fight him at all."

"It wasn't a choice."

The tears she'd been holding back for hours erupted in a loud sob. Jane buried her face in her hands, her whole body trembled uncontrollably.

Kat's arms encompassed her. The invitation was all she required to unleash her emotions. She'd invited her friends because she needed them. Grief, anger, and a good helping of self-loathing piled into a churning of emotions so intense she was soon gasping for air.

The addition of Leanne's hand running gently through her hair helped bring her back to a semblance of calm. Still the tears would not cease. Jane wiped at them with a fierce swipe. She hiccuped and dropped her forehead to the knees she'd pulled close to her chest. "I feel so stupid."

"You aren't stupid," Leanne murmured. The mattress shifted as she sat behind Jane. "If you were, you never would have suspected he was no good. He got you in an impossible situation without even realizing it, and he had you trapped beyond what he could have dreamt of."

Kat sat in front of Jane, her hand settled on Jane's knee. "You protected that baby."

This time the welling of tears was accompanied by a wave of nausea. The whole scene in the library replayed in her mind. Jane heaved off the bed toward the bucket, which she made thorough use of.

"Guess I was too late with the tea," Leanne whispered.

"No, sweetie." Kat sighed. "That's pure revulsion."

When Jane managed to return to the bed, Leanne immediately handed her a cup of tea and a cool, damp towel. "Darling, you are exhausted. You should rest. It'll be hours before they get back, maybe longer."

"I can't sleep." Jane sniveled, but drank down the tea with no argument. Somehow she suspected this time it wouldn't be able to fully cure the nausea that plagued her. Every time Joe's face flashed in her head, she was certain she'd vomit again.

"You've got to." Leanne continued to rub her back in a soothing, gentle motion. "I'm trying to stay on Cole's good side for a change, and he'd just kill me if I let you stay up all night."

Kat held her hand. "Listen to her, please."

"I'll try, but I'm not making any promises." Jane sniffed. "You shouldn't stay too long, Katherine. Norman will ask too many questions as it is. If you're here too much longer, there will be an inquisition."

"I can handle Norman. Don't you worry about that." Kat gave her hand a squeeze. "Do you need anything?"

"I need Cole home safe." Fear panged through her heart. Jane knew Cole had to go, and that Tom knew what he was doing, but she also knew Joe was a slimy bastard.

"We know." Leanne tugged Jane until she lay against her pillows. "I'll stay right here with you. We'll wait and worry together. If you happen to sleep, all the better."

"You need to get back to the hotel." Jane's mind raced for something else to grasp onto. Anything but what it kept circling back to. "Underwood."

"Underwood is in happy land right now. Mike agreed to make certain he was taken care of. I'm letting him sip on my absinthe, so never you worry."

"Everything will be taken care of," Kat said quietly. "You wanted distraction, so talk. Until you fall asleep, just talk."

Fresh tears sparked in Jane's eyes. Shame filled her at the first thought that popped into her head. "I'm starting to understand why Clara wished to forget."

Man finds nothing so intolerable as to be in a state of complete rest, without passions, without occupation, without diversion, without effort. Then he feels his nullity, loneliness, inadequacy, dependence, helplessness, emptiness.
-Blaise Pascal

Jane sat alone in the quiet saloon, though she didn't fail to notice the kind old man out on the porch. Given the time of day, it was too early for him to be waiting on the saloon to open. The untouched tray of food before her turned her stomach. Kat had been kind enough to bring the food by two hours previous, but Jane could not eat. Her stomach was too upset, even after several cups of tea.

She knew it was more than the pregnancy. The events of the previous day, and Cole's continuing absence had her on edge. Until Joe, Cole's had been the only touch she'd ever known, and she was more than happy with that; but now a slimy revolting sensation lingered on her flesh.

Jane flew to her feet and tried to catch her breath. Early that morning she'd sent Leanne away. While she'd needed her friends during the long night, there were things that needed to be done. Jane didn't want to risk their attempts to get information out of Underwood. Nor did she want to change her life and make anyone aware of what had happened.

She pressed her hands to her face, wishing it would rid her of the headache. For that matter, ridding herself of every other ache and pain that brought her mind right back to the library.

Bile rose so fast, she almost lost it on the floor. She gripped the edge of the bar, taking deep breaths until it subsided.

"Lady Jane?"

Jane opened her eyes at Hammy's voice. She breathed out another calming breath.

"Are you all right, Lady Jane?"

"I'm fine, Mr. Hamm. Feeling a bit poorly this morning."

"Still?"

"Always anymore, it seems." She managed to straighten. When she turned, Hammy remained hovering by the doors. "Come in, Mr. Hamm. I know we're not open, but I'd rather you hover over me inside than out."

"I ain't hoverin'." Hammy shuffled into the saloon at her request.

"You are." Jane went to his side, hooking her arm through his. "You are kind to be so worried. I wish you wouldn't. I've made it through a hanging, after all. Feeling poorly isn't going to kill me. Why don't I get you a beer for your kindness?"

"Much obliged." Hammy sat in the seat she guided him to. He remained quiet while she poured his beer. After a sip, he sighed. "Sure you ain't hurt, Lady Jane?"

"Just a bump on the head."

"Won't make you forget again, will it?"

"I would never forget you, Mr. Hamm." Jane kissed his cheek gently. She hopped into the seat beside him. To be honest, she was grateful for the distraction of his company. All her emotions were so jumbled they came and went like tides on the shore.

One part of her was determined to not be like Clara, but she felt like she was failing. She thought she'd be stronger than this, but all she wanted to do was disappear.

A few minutes later, she'd dive right back into a furious vile temper which would leave her certain she wouldn't let it bother her, for she was more angry than distraught.

The moment she leveled out, the fear would return. The real fear Joe would walk in the door again was something she thought should be minimal, especially considering the weapon she had secured on her person again. Even so, she couldn't stop her occasional glance toward the door.

"Lookin' for someone?" Hammy glanced to the door, then back at Jane. "Cole?"

"Yes. I had hoped he'd be back by now."

"Where'd he go, anyhow?"

"He had something to do." Jane kept her answer intentionally vague. Her stomach churned again, threatening to boil over. She held her handkerchief to her mouth. Right then what she wanted most was Cole and Tommy home safe. Whether they had or hadn't killed Joe was of no consequence to her now. She just needed them home safe.

"Lady Jane?" Hammy's hand settled on her shoulder.

Jane wiped at tears she hadn't realized she'd shed. "Damn it. Sorry."

"Jane?" Sally jumped backward at Jane's yelp. "I'm sorry. I thought you heard me come downstairs."

"It's all right. I'm jumpy as all get out this morning." Jane exhaled slowly. She had to get herself together before she had the whole town gossiping. "Sorry I startled you."

"I'm sorry, too." Sally's brow wrinkled. "Are you all right?"

"Yes." Jane knew she said it fast, but it didn't matter. She was getting tired of the question, honestly. "Tired. I don't sleep well when Cole isn't there."

Sally plucked an apple from Jane's tray. "Where did he go anyway?"

"He and Tommy took off on what's probably some damn goose chase. A wild boar, or the like." Jane spun her teacup on the bar.

"Sure it was wild?" Hammy polished off his beer. "Petey let his hogs go to sod when he started dippin' in his own moonshine."

"Valid point, Mr. Hamm." Jane sighed.

"They'll probably shoot each other before they get the boar, or hog. Whatever it is they're after." Sally giggled, which led to Hammy laughing as well. Even Jane managed a smile at the implication. After she'd taken a huge bite of the apple, Sally spoke around the food in her mouth. "I hope you don't mind. I offered to take Alma to the swimming hole at Mike's place. It's so hot, I thought she'd like to cool off."

"That's an excellent idea, Sally. I appreciate it. I won't be opening the library today, so why don't you both make a day of it? Eat a picnic there if you'd like." Jane pulled the reticule off her belt to hand to Sally. "I'll have Violet do the chamber pots today for you."

"They're already done." Sally accepted the purse, tying it to her own belt. "Got them done first thing. Changed the sheets, too."

Jane sighed. "Thank you, Sally."

"Hey, Janey!" Graham pounded on the door frame as he strode into the Inn. "You'll never guess where I've been."

Sally excused herself. Jane waved her off willingly. Sally was not a fan of Graham, and Jane wouldn't fight that.

Jane squeezed Hammy's shoulder, turning her attention back to the large man striding toward her. "I couldn't begin to imagine, Graham. These days you're in too good a mood for me to even begin to contemplate the sort of things you'd be up to."

"Keep that up and I won't tell you." Graham waved a beefy finger in her face.

"Then, please. Do tell." At this point Jane would take anything that would suffice for distraction. Considering how excited Graham was, maybe he had something.

"I've been out at Tuck Crumbie's claim." Graham dropped into the seat next to Hammy, then paused. "Hammy. What are you doing here?"

"Just checkin' on Lady Jane." Hammy polished off his beer. "I'll get out of your hair."

Jane set her hand on Hammy's. "Thank you, Mr. Hamm. Please, go about your day as you normally would. I'm well taken care of."

Hammy glanced toward the stairs when Sally and Alma headed down them. "You're gonna be alone."

"Graham is here right now, and I'll head to Cora's for lunch. You can stop worrying about me." Jane urged Hammy to the door. "I promise, I'll be fine."

Hammy didn't look too happy about leaving, but he did. Jane let out a long breath, hoping Hammy hadn't raised too many suspicions in Graham.

"Your hair," Graham said randomly.

Jane turned around, confused. "What?"

"You don't got it up. You never wear it down unless Cole asks you to."

"I hit my head yesterday. I think Mr. Hamm is worried I'll forget everything again, elsewise he wouldn't be hovering." Hit her head was an understatement. The knot on the back of her head had made even braiding it uncomfortable, so she'd left it loose for the morning. "I'll put it up before business. Now what did you want with me?"

"Oh, right. I've been out at Tuck Crumbie's claim. You know Tuck, right?"

Jane took the stool beside him. "I certainly do. I had no idea he had a claim. Unlike most of the others that kept a hold of their small claims, he's not once been in here trading gold."

"That's 'cause Tuck never found a lick of gold or silver on his claim. No one expected him to." Graham waved his hand toward the north. "It was a small-ass claim. Wooded, hardly room for a shack so he wasn't living there. None of us could figure out why he kept going out there to come back with nothing."

"Is there a point to all of this, Graham?"

"Tuck's sick. Real sick, says your brother. Gonna die pretty soon."

"How fascinatingly morbid."

"No, that isn't the best part!"

She had to work to keep a smile contained. "I didn't realize it was good, by any measure."

"Sure it is. He told me he wants to unload his claim, but didn't know what to ask for it. I mean, there isn't gold there. Too rocky to make a livable claim of." He leaned in. The man practically twitched in his eagerness. "But it does got something else you might be interested in. I made him swear to let me talk to you first before your brother got wind of it."

"What is so exciting about this claim, Graham?"

"A hot spring."

"What?" Unbelievably, a stir of excitement rippled through her. Such a thing could be a huge draw, not just for the hotel, but the town in general. "Are you certain it's there? Is it usable?"

"It sure is. He kept it real hidden and secret. Said it's not easy to get to, and it sure isn't. You'd have to clean it up and make a good trail. If you want it, I bet we can talk Tuck into a real solid price for you. I'll even knock some off his burial for it."

"Graham Cooke, I never thought I'd see the day I said this." She leaned in to kiss his cheek. "You are an angel. I need to see it today. Now. If it's viable, I need to show Cutler."

"No problem. Get Cole and we'll go."

"Neither Cole nor Thomas is here. It'll have to be me." Jane got off her stool, thrilled for the distraction and excitement to keep her from pacing the floors waiting. "I have no time to waste. Cutler will be leaving in a couple of days."

"Then let's move."

*If an injury has been done to a man
it should be so severe that his vengeance
need not be feared.
—Niccolo Machiavelli*

Cole edged through the trees quiet as possible. Tommy had gone on ahead to scout out Joe's location. Once again the man had circled back south. After half a day's ride, they were nearing the south lip of the valley.

Twice they'd had to turn tail and find shelter as Joe had doubled back as if to check if he was being followed. Fortunately, Tommy was better at hiding his trail than Joe; and Cole had learned a few tricks from Kelly on several hunting excursions and occasional manhunts.

An hour before they'd left the horses behind for fear of detection. They were getting closer every time they had to stop. Cole was worried about Jane, but he had to focus on the task at hand.

Soon they'd have the bastard. And the bastard would find his frontier justice.

Tommy held up a hand to stop Cole's movement. Cole immediately went on alert, searching the trees for any sign of the man they were chasing. He spotted the hat just above the trees about a mile off, and glanced at his brother-in-law.

Tom nodded slow and steady.

"Can you knock him down from here?" Cole barely finished the question as Tommy raised his rifle.

"Should be able to. I just need a good, clear shot."

Cole let his gaze drift back off in the distance. It was a beautiful, bright day filled with warmth Cole couldn't feel. Right down to his gut a chill rolled through him.

He shook it off best he could, studying the hat in the distance. The play of light and shadow through the trees made it seem as though it was moving, but he couldn't tell for sure.

Hair rose on the back of his neck and he drew himself taller. The hat wasn't moving. Just he lifted his hand to stop Tommy shooting, the gun fired.

The crack echoed through the trees. A horse screamed in the distance.

"Horse is—" Tommy was cut off by a bullet whizzing by a moment before they heard the shot.

Both men got low to sprint through the trees toward where the shot had come from. Tom skirted wide out of Cole's vision likely to get around the bastard.

Cole leaned back against a tree for cover as another crack of gunfire rented the air. He leaned around the tree, aiming for where the gunfire had come from.

Another round hit the tree near him. He didn't wait, he immediately fired another round. So did Tom by the sound of another crack of gunfire nearly simultaneous with his.

This time Cole heard a satisfying grunt of pain and the crackle of breaking branches afterward. He raced forward, coming upon the man moments before Tom.

Cole leveled his gun at the man's head.

"What the hell are you doing?" Joe gripped his leg where the bullet had struck. "Trying to kill me?"

"You know me better. If I wanted you dead, you would be." Tom kept his rifle leveled at the man. "Don't worry, there is a plan for that."

"Are you insane?"

"No, but you might be." Tommy glared at his former friend darkly. "You rat bastard. You double crossed me to get to Jane."

Joe scoffed. "What in blazes are you talking about?"

Tom had nearly lost his cool, rushing forward to shove the gun right in Joe's face. "You *raped* her."

To those words Joe dared laugh. "It wasn't rape. It was rough, sure, but it wasn't rape. That's how she likes it."

Cole couldn't help himself, his gun fired almost of its own volition. The bullet hit the man's shoulder, dangerously close to the jugular.

Joe cursed loudly, clutching at the fresh wound

Weapon freshly cocked, Cole leveled it at the man's head. "Wanna try again? I told you not to touch her."

His attention now on Cole, he glared at the man through his hissing grunts of pain. "You really think Clara's yours? She's likely got a good couple—"

"She's *mine*. You dumb bastard. She's carrying my kid."

His brow quirked, Joe managed to chuckle. "Well…"

"You find that amusing?" Tommy's rifle moved so fast, it was a blur. Another round hit Joe in the undamaged leg. "Raping a pregnant woman?"

"Aww…fu—"

"Shut the hell up!" Cole narrowed his eyes, drawing back the hammer on his revolver. "Guess there's a lot you don't know. You told her we couldn't touch ya."

"You can't kill me." The words came out in guttural grunts as Joe's hands went between his wounds trying to stem the flow. "I've got powerful—"

"Lots of people disappear out here. Happens all the time and there's no one the wiser."

Tommy grimaced his way into a smirk. That's when Cole noticed the stain spreading across the man's shirt and even soaking his vest.

Cole turned away when Tommy cut him a look. "He's right. I've seen lots of men disappear over my years here."

"Bodies are easy to get rid of," Tommy pointed out. A small strain had entered his voice. Subtle, but definitely present. "You're not following a well-traversed path. Makes it that much easier. You forget, I've got the same connections you do. Even if something does come to someone's attention—although I got no idea who'd miss your sorry ass."

"You won't get away with—"

Cole's fired his weapon. The gunfire echoed through the trees before blessed silence fell.

"About time. I was tired of listening to his bull."

*What's gone and what's past help
should be past grief.
—William Shakespeare*

Jane paced the length of the Inn's porch before she sat on the bench. The second she sat another horse came into view and she was on her feet again. All day she'd battled the clock and her fears.

One minute everything was happening too fast for her to handle, and in the next time itself seemed to stop. When it did all her emotions magnified into chaos.

Graham's tip about the hot spring had been an underestimate. Turned out there wasn't one, but three small pools of steaming hot water on the claim.

The ride to the claim wasn't long, and it seemed to be an extra attraction they could include with the hotel. Soon as she'd seen the land, she'd used Nick to negotiate with Tuck for a selling price along with a contract buying his silence. Her two biggest problems now were coming up with the rest of the money and finding someone willing to squat on the land to guard the springs.

She'd hesitated to tell Cutler only because Underwood would learn of the development, but in the end she'd told him. On his encouragement, she'd sent telegrams to the potential investors to alert them to the impending additional bonus to The Hangman's Inn.

While she'd never stoop to calling their hotel a health spa like Michael had, the hot springs had a draw even for the wealthy patrons of the Sage Brush Hotel. The purported health benefits being touted by a doctor in Buena Vista had drawn enough people to that small town. Perhaps this could draw more people to their Inn, and they could charge a menial fee for townsfolk, and a larger fee to Michael's patrons. For a brief, shining couple of hours she'd found hope to cling to once again.

After the distraction of such events, she'd tried to force herself to behave 'normal' as possible. She'd spent time with Alma and Sally, though not in the library per usual. She knew she'd have to reopen the library eventually, but that would be a task for another day when Cole was home and safe. Once she had spent time reading with Alma and Sally, she'd gone to see Daisy as she'd been scheduled. True to his word, Charlie hadn't told her a thing, for she didn't check any of Jane's bruises, or even give her an offhand look.

All the distractions in the world hadn't ended her near constant state of nausea. She'd been unable to eat much of anything all day but had kept down her tea. While she'd joined Sally, Alma, and most of her brothers for suppertime, she had been forced to push food around her plate rather than try to stomach it.

Charlie stopped her after to inquire how she was going. Blessedly, he'd been kind and extremely brief in his inquiry. For this, above all her previous injuries and illnesses, he seemed determined to allow her what she needed within reason.

The sun now hung low over the western mountain ridge, casting deep shadows down the streets. Lamplighters skirted along the street through the crowds, climbing to light the lamps quick as possible. One paused in front of the Inn to light the lamp there before moving off down the cross street.

Jane searched the lengths of the adjoining street for any sign of Tom or Cole. The lack of familiar horse or rider left her hands shaking. She resumed her pacing in the increasing darkness. When she turned, Leanne stood at the opposite end of the porch, hands on her hips. A frown so similar to Cole's tugged Leanne's lips downward. "Jane, please sit. I can tell from here you're exhausted. Have you slept at all?"

Jane turned her gaze back along the street. "No. I can't sleep. I can't. Not until they're home safe. And you shouldn't be here."

"I did a bad thing, but I had to get Underwood handled."

"A bad thing?"

"I visited little China today. Grabbed some opium."

"Leanne!" The shock pulled Jane from her constant search.

"Underwood is a man of many vices. I figured he wouldn't turn down some opium, and I was correct. He has apparently had it before and enjoys it quite a lot. I'm sure he still thinks I'm there with him." Leanne set her hand on Jane's arm. "I belong here with my friend. Plus, I wanted to see if Tom had come back."

Jane might have dismissed Leanne's arguments if but for two reasons. For one, Jane really wanted the company of someone who wouldn't question her mood. One that understood without needing to probe deeper. Her nerves had reached a breaking point, and she knew it. Also, she could tell by the slight crack in Leanne's voice that she was truly concerned about Tom. "Where are they? Why haven't they come back yet? Did he…"

"They'll be here." Leanne soothed, her own voice shaky. "They will, they have to. Now sit, please. You sacrificed yourself for that baby—so you'd better sit and try to relax before you hurt it all on your own."

Jane's heart clenched at the admonition. Leanne had been nothing but kind in her scolding, but Jane's heart hurt anyhow. "You're right. I'm sorry. I just—where is he?"

Leanne hushed her gently. She sat beside her on the bench, running her hands along the curls still tumbling down Jane's back. "He'll be here. Cole and Tom are big boys, they can handle this. There's no way Cole's not coming back here to you."

"I know," Jane whispered, all the while praying for it to be true.

"Janey!" The friendly voice interrupted her emotions' attempt to escape into terror once again. Jeb Conley's big grin greeted her as he hopped onto the porch.

Jane plastered on the most sincerely bright smile she could manage. Mr. Conley was a high roller from the poker game a few days prior. He lived on the hill with the finer homes with his brother Milton and his family. "Mr. Conley. It's good to see you again. I'm afraid we have no high-in game tonight."

"Didn't come for the poker. Came for the company." He shook her hand heartily. "Maybe I'll sneak into a nickel ante if I get bored."

"I'm certain that can be arranged. If you decide to join, let Edgar know. He's handling the floor tonight." Jane gestured to the door.

"You're not coming in?" Jeb quirked a brow. "I don't remember a night you weren't keeping an eye on the ruffians."

"It's a little ripe inside today thanks to this heat, even with the windows open." She kept her smile steady as she could. "Go on ahead and get your refreshment. I have a feeling a drink, and perhaps Glory's company, can distract you from the negative."

"Of that I have no doubt." He tipped his hat before disappearing into the saloon.

Jane sank onto the bench, her energy drained by the interaction. "I can't do this."

"You can. You're doing well enough, have been all day. No one is the wiser. As for those of us that are, you are doing as well as anyone can expect. Once you get your man home and see he's safe, it'll be better." Leanne patted her hand. "Why don't I go inside and get you some more tea?"

Jane kept her handkerchief at her lips, but shook her head. "There's no need. I just had some. It doesn't seem to be as effective today as usual, but I don't think the baby is to blame."

"I'm sure it isn't." Leanne leaned back against the window. "If you change your mind, it won't take any time."

"Thank you." Jane tried a genuine smile. "For coming here tonight. I really needed someone to be around before I went crazy. It's been a long day."

"I guessed as much. When I saw Kat at Turner's before I came here she said you'd been distracting yourself as best as you could. We both figured that didn't mean you'd succeeded."

"There was plenty to fill my day, and some worthy distraction—but you were both right, although I'm certain Kat knew as much after our tea."

"One shattered teacup is a small price to pay." Leanne sat straighter as a horse pulled up beside the porch. "Good evening, Dr. Young. To what do we owe the pleasure?"

Jane rose to greet her brother as he descended from his horse. "Charles Emerson Young, what do you think you're doing?"

"Millie is spending the evening with Lee and Cora working on some stitch work or tatting or, Lord I don't know what. They've taken over my home with all their bits and bobs and gossip." Charlie threw his reins over the hitching post. "I thought I'd come into town for some distraction."

"Which you never do." Jane breathed her fury out in gusts. "Why today?"

"Millie rarely comes to town in the evenings, nor does she usually keep such vibrant company what with the wedding coming and all, it's an unusual sort of night. I rarely have reason to come in town for distraction as I truly enjoy my lovely wife's company." Charlie set his hands on her shoulders. "That is why."

"Liar," Jane muttered. Despite her attempt at anger, she found herself only grateful. She wrapped her arms around him in a tight hug.

"How are you really?" Charlie kept his voice low as he returned the hug. "Did you sleep?"

"Fine. Coping." Jane sighed deeply. "Leanne will tell you herself I only managed a round two hours or so worth of sleep. I can't sleep not knowing."

"I'm sure he'll be back soon." Charlie released her from the hug before she felt ready. Still, she was glad he didn't overdo it. He turned his attention to the bench. "Leanne. Good to see you. I expected you to still be occupied."

"Turns out Mr. Underwood enjoys opium even more than absinthe. I found myself with a bit of free time, and I'm needed here more than there." Leanne didn't rise from the bench but smiled pleasantly at Charlie.

The two continued on in pleasant chatter, at one point disappearing inside to get drinks for them both. Jane remained where she was, her vigil on the street growing more intense as the night continued to deepen.

Horse after horse passed by over the course of an hour, in pairs and alone. Many going to the Inn itself, others heading to the saloon down the way. None of them bore the men she searched for in each rider.

About to give up and return to the bench, she noticed another pair of horses moving in the shadows near the library. Their pace remained lazy and slow. The bulkier man hunched over his horse, tilting on occasion in his seat. The taller, leaner man was unmistakable to her, but it wasn't until he passed under the lamp before the reality brought relief.

Jane's gasp choked in her throat.

Leanne was at her side in a moment. She gripped Jane's arm tight. "Oh heavens. Tom."

That was when Jane saw Cole reach over to right Tommy in his saddle again. She took one step toward them, then another. When Cole slipped from his saddle, she could no longer contain herself. At a dead run, she tore toward him. She hit him with such force that he actually took a step back.

Cole's arms wrapped tight around her. A soft kiss landed on top of her head. "Jane."

She sobbed into his chest. "Thank God you're home."

"Tommy!" Charlie's holler distracted Jane from her reunion with Cole to focus on the brother hunched in the saddle next to them. Charlie grabbed the reins from Tommy's hands. "I thought you were supposed to be hunting, not drinking yourself into a stupor."

Jane met Cole's gaze, fear shooting to her gut. Not once had she known Tommy to get drunk. Plus, it wasn't any sort of time for it. Was he injured? She whimpered, "No."

"Easy." Cole gripped her arms to keep her in place. "Let's get inside. Let Charlie handle the drunk fool."

Jane followed more out of the demand of his dragging arm than free will. Leanne remained on the porch, seemingly frozen where she stood. Her white-knuckled grip on the post belied the fear she'd somehow managed to cover with a grin. She finally let go of the post as Charlie brought Brag closer, Tommy still hunched in the saddle.

Tommy sagged over, a low groan blowing the strong scent of moonshine over them. Sure enough, a jug toppled from his grasp to the dirt.

Jane managed to contain her gasp at the smear of blood across the jug. While Leanne tucked under one of Tommy's arms and Charlie under the other, Jane stared at the bottle. Jane turned to Cole while they maneuvered Tommy onto the porch.

"Jane," Cole warned.

"Hush." She reached up to yank the bandana from his neck.

"What?"

"Hush." If they were trying to cover Tommy's injury with drunkenness, a bloody jug of moonshine wouldn't do any good to be seen by all. She picked it up with the bandana, wiping it best as she could. Satisfied the bottle could pass for filthy instead of bloody, she tucked the bandana in her skirt.

Leanne spoke loud and clear as they headed into the Inn, "I told you not to drink that rotgut Cole was taking with you. You're used to the watered down crap he serves."

Cole didn't release his tight hold on Jane, but a nasty smirk crossed his features. "I don't water down my whiskey, you hussy."

"Right. That's why the bottle I brought with me is so much richer in flavor."

"Keep it up, Leanne. You'll regret it."

"I'd like to see you try."

Cole sighed. "It's my fault. He bought some moonshine out at Petey's on our way outta town. I dared him, actually."

Jane didn't trust herself to speak the whole way to Tommy's room. She kept the bottle tight to her skirts to keep it covered as best she could. The grip she had on Cole's arm must have been tighter than she realized, because he pried her fingers off, squeezing and releasing his hand a few times as if to let blood back into the limb.

They got into the room where Leanne and Charlie deposited Tommy on the bed. Cole closed the door behind them. Jane found her voice. "What happened?"

"Bastard got off a couple of shots. He was aiming for me. Bullet overshot, hit Tom in the shoulder." Cole rubbed his hand over his face. "I'll tell ya what, he didn't falter for nothing. I didn't even know he was hit until we'd taken care of business."

"He's got plenty of padding to soften the blow." Leanne's laughter was weak, but she smiled at Tom. A single tear shimmered on her cheek, a fact they all chose to ignore. "Don't you, Tom?"

Tommy chuckled low. When he spoke his voice slurred and lingered in gruff tones. "Why do you think I eat so damn much?"

"Not funny," Jane whispered.

"Aww, come on Janey. You'd laugh too if you weren't so pissed and scared." Tommy's body jerked when Charlie peeled the shirt from his shoulder. His breath exhaled in a low hiss. "Damn. Bullet's still in there. I can barely move my arm."

"Get more whiskey," Charlie instructed. "He won't let me knock him out."

"Leanne can distract me." Tommy pat the bed next to him, opposite the wounded shoulder. The grin he wore when she climbed in beside him broadened. It gave Charlie enough room to work at least, and Tommy faced her instead of the approaching forceps. "Does sympathy soften your resolve, my reverse Madame Bovary?"

"Not in the slightest." Leanne kept a hand surreptitiously on Tom's face, holding his gaze her way. "However, whiskey has been known to soften many a men's resolve. I imagine moonshine makes matters much worse. Now let Charlie get the bullet out, you big galoot."

"What about the plan?" Tom winced, a deep grunt slipping free. "Damn it all to hell. Work faster you insipid know-it-all. Leanne, you should be…damn…elsewhere."

"Some things are more important than the plan." The look Leanne gave him was so caring and intimate, Jane turned her attention to Charlie's work. "Besides, do you think I am so ill-equipped to handle intrigue and deception because I'm no Pink?"

"Madam, you could be."

"Flattery will get you nowhere, sir." Leanne tried a stern expression, which missed its mark with the tremble of her lip. "Mr. Underwood believes he and I are rather enjoying ourselves. However, you may rest assured my record is still clean as a whistle."

Tom whistled in response.

Jane startled as the meaning sank in. While she knew Leanne and Tom had been enjoying each other's company, she didn't realize that the truth of Leanne's virginity had emerged. "Wait. Thomas knows?"

"Yup." Tommy grinned. "She even told me your nickname—*ah, gah, geeze!*"

"Sorry." Charlie held the bullet in the forceps. He offered a dry smile. "I figured the young lady had you distracted enough. You are so blinded by a pretty woman if they dare show you any attention."

"Not nearly enough," Tommy muttered. He groaned, his head dropping to the side, right at the top of Leanne's breasts.

Leanne patted Tommy's head. When his eyes flickered open, she turned her attention to Jane. "We'll discuss what Tom does and does not know another time. He's going to live.

The big dope is going to piss and moan to get me to snuggle with him. You go on."

"Go on Lou. You can yell at me later." Tom sat up over Charlie's objections. "I'm more drunk than hurt. Cole wasn't kidding about the moonshine."

"I noticed." Jane lofted the jug. "You dropped it."

"Keep it. I only got it to dull the pain. Stuff's horrendous."

"Where did you get the moonshine?" Leanne eyed him. "Or do I want to know?"

"Doubt it." Tommy jerked his head to the door. "I mean it, Lou. Get. You can yell at me later. Yell at him now."

When she opened her mouth to protest, Cole scooped her right off her feet. She yelped, the jug hitting the floor with a loud thump. He ignored the weak fight she offered as he carried her next door to their room. Once inside, she managed to scramble free of his arms to tear across the room. He stared at his empty arms before he turned a helpless gaze on her.

"I'm sorry. I…I don't know why I ran from you." A crazy wave of emotions rolled right over her, stampeding through her heart in a mad rush for her stomach. She turned to bend over the bucket, but only dry heaves escaped.

"You don't gotta be sorry."

"I waited all day for you to come home, but now I can't…" She took several long, deep breaths. Fear over what he thought of her now won over all else. A maddeningly weak whining whimper slipped free. "I…Logically I know I had no choice. He didn't give me one."

"What do I need to do?"

"I don't know. I only know that I'm disgusted with myself. I'm terrified you are as well, even though you wouldn't ever admit it. I know I want you to erase his touch, but I still feel too filthy to let you. I know I want you to take it all away. I know that I need you. I need you."

In two long strides he was at her side. Gently, he pulled her into his arms. "I can't take it away. I wish I could."

"I understand now why Clara wanted to forget, to run away. Part of me wants to just like she did. I don't want to be weak like her. I'm so afraid I will be."

"You ain't Clara, and I ain't Davie." He tucked a finger under her chin. With some effort because of her fear, he managed to bring her gaze to meet his. "You already proved it by telling me."

"What if I'm not strong enough? What if I finally break? You said they all do. We all do."

"You never did, and you won't."

"I feel like I could. I feel broken. Weak."

"You ain't. You're here, asking for help. You're not running."

"I don't feel strong enough…"

"You're stronger than this, and you're not alone."

"I can't lose you."

"We're stronger than this."

"I want to be." She buried her face in his chest. When his arms wrapped around her, she didn't pull away from his encompassing strength. She allowed his arms to return to the sanctuary she'd known them as for so long. When her tears began to slow, she sagged in his arms.

"What now?"

"I should get to work."

"No way in hell.

"You said I'm stronger than this."

"Have you slept?"

"No."

"Then that's what you're doing."

"I don't need to," she protested.

"Now."

She didn't shy away from his demanding tone, only nodding. "Stay. Please."

"Whatever you need." The sanctuary of his arms withdrew slowly. He didn't follow her when she went to the bed.

She sat to remove her boots, keenly aware of his gaze on her every movement. Once she'd set her boots aside, she returned to him. With her eyes level to his chest so she wouldn't falter if she met his intense, concerned gaze, she reached for his holster.

He didn't move a muscle while she removed his holster and set it aside. As she got to his vest his hands twitched, but no other movement slipped through.

With the vest removed she went for the buttons of his shirt, but her hands shook so bad she couldn't undo one of them. His hands closed over hers in a gentle grasp.

"You don't gotta," he said quietly.

"Just your shirt. I need to feel you. I need to feel safe."

"It ain't safe if you're shaking."

"You're safe. You're my sanctuary." She pulled her hands free with determination. This time her hands didn't shake. In short order she undid his buttons and pulled his shirt free from his trousers. She left him to remove his shirt and shoes while she removed her own clothes, save for her chemise. Perching herself on the edge of the bed, she patted the space beside her.

Cole took her cue, but only set his hand on hers.

She lifted her eyes to meet his finally. Concern creased his brow, with something far less familiar mixed in. Fear. That was it. "Lie down with me. Hold me. Stop looking so scared. If you're scared, I'm scared."

"I'm trying. I don't want to do something wrong and upset you."

"You said everything was handled."

"Definitely."

"There's no way for him to come back."

"Not a snowball's chance in hell it'll happen."

The ridiculous fear that Joe would return faded into the background. Not totally gone, but diminished significantly. After a shaky breath, she nodded. "Good. That makes it better."

"Does it?"

"Yes." She slid back, turning to her side and curling up on the bed. When he settled in beside her, relief washed over her nerves. "Forgive me."

"I told you. Nothing to forgive."

"Forgive me." She couldn't help herself, the words tumbled from her lips over and over.

He slid his arms under her shoulders and turned her toward him. A soft kiss landed on her temple, stilling her repeating pleas. "I forgive you. It ain't your fault, but I forgive you."

She shuddered against her own revulsion at herself. Needing to feel safe, she curled into him. "I love you. I didn't—didn't want…"

"I know."

The tears she'd forced back all day seemed to all spill from her at once. He did nothing more than hold her, and for the moment that's all she needed. Through it all, sleep continued to elude her.

After a while her tears slowed. His thumb brushed along her shoulder. "What do you need?"

"Just talk to me."

"About what?"

"Anything." In his silence, she took a deep breath. "I have news."

"What?"

"Graham came by today." She nestled in closer and told him the story of her day. While she spoke, she nestled as close as possible to enjoy the warmth and comfort of his embrace. For the first time in over a day her body began to relax.

When she finished, Cole's thumb had stopped its absent wandering. "Tuck agreed?"

"He signed the contract. I don't know how we'll come up with the money."

"How about a few more high-in poker games?" He smiled when she tilted her head to look up at him. "We made a killing that night."

"True."

"We should add gambling to the plans. Have more than poker. Ain't your brothers talked about some of the games they played during the war? Monte, roulette, and something French?"

Jane blinked a few times in surprise at the idea. "That isn't a bad thought."

"If we're losing the whores, we can do it up right. There were places in California that had exclusive rooms, cost plenty of money to gamble there."

Jane propped herself on her elbow to stare down at him. "Colton James Spencer, why could you not come up with this weeks ago? I'll have to get those plans adjusted immediately before Cutler leaves, and contact the other—"

His finger pressed against her lips, stopping her tirade. "Didn't mean to excite ya. You're supposed to be going to sleep, remember?"

"I do, but what took so long?"

"Didn't think about it until that poker game. Then things got…"

"Right." She sighed, sinking back into his arms easily. "First thing in the morning, we have to make plans. For now, back to the hot springs."

"Tuck ain't asking much for the claim, but who would we get to squat?"

"I don't know. They'd have to be wlling to have only a small cabin to live in."

"And we'd have to trust them." He kissed the top of her head. "And trust ain't easy to come by anymore."

"It never was for you."

"I always trusted you."

"And I always trusted you. I still do."

*Truth, when not sought after,
rarely comes to light.
-Oliver Wendell Holmes*

Cole nursed the coffee Jane set before him. She herself wandered through the saloon righting chairs so they could open in an hour. By all rights the woman should have been heading to the library, if it were a normal day.

Nothing seemed normal right then, though. Not even Jane setting up the saloon for business. The liveliness she wore so often had all but disappeared. Instead of the occasional bouts of melancholy she'd been prone to since her hanging, it was all melancholy with occasional bouts of hope. It was not a change he cared for.

The stairs creaked loudly, drawing both of their attention. Tommy leaned hard on the railing, a determined furrow to his brow.

Jane set her hands on her hips. "What in blazes do you think you're doing?"

"Getting whiskey to dull the pain."

"Bull. You've got booze in your room. Charlie would kill you if—"

"Say the woman that never listens to him." Tommy moved down another two steps. "So shut your cock hole and let me be."

Jane's features lit with the fire of indignation. "You rotten, no good, son of a bitch. I'll tell on you and get you a babysitter. I bet Mabel Greene wouldn't mind performing another act of attrition."

"Don't you dare."

Cole leaned on the bar, trying to hide his amusement at the argument. Jane rarely argued with Tom, if ever. Having both of them in a mood and in pain had brought out a spark of fire. He wondered if that wasn't Tom's intention, then again, the man might be in too much pain to carry out any sort of plan.

"Mudsill. Rake. Hugger mugger. Foul, loathsome—"

"Jane." Cole chuckled low. "Stop."

"He started it. Cock hole. You dumb bastard." Jane had moved to Tom's side by now. She slipped under his arm and led him toward the bar. "Cole, would you please keep this idiot occupied. He's off his chump if he thinks I'm going to put up with him today."

"I'm right here," Tommy grumbled.

"You're lucky you are, I've got my Remington always at the ready now." She cast a glare at her brother. After he'd tucked in with the glass of whiskey Cole slid his way, she turned her ire on Cole. "Tell him what I got us yesterday, and *your* brilliant idea, would you? I've got things to do that don't involve sitting around listening to foul language."

The second she'd wandered away, Tom muttered, "She was the one cursing."

"And the both of ya call me immature." Cole polished off his coffee, trying not to be amused at Jane's now angry attempts at setting the room up.

"But she doesn't look like a scared little bird anymore, does she?"

Cole shrugged. "No, but for how long?"

"Tell me what idea *you* could have had that Jane found brilliant." Tom poured himself another drink. His hand shook as the bottle hovered, but he used his bad arm anyway. "Or whatever damn thing she wanted you to tell me."

"Graham got us a trick for the new place."

"Graham?" The glass paused halfway to his lips. "You're shittin' me."

"He got Jane a lead on Tuck Crumbie's claim."

"That worthless pile of river rock and pine?"

"Not so worthless, apparently. He's got three hot springs out there. While we were feeding the pigs, she was getting a contract for the land. We just need to find someone to squat on it, and the funds to finish the purchase. I figure another high-in poker game'll do it."

"Hot springs, eh? That's more Mikey's health resort." Tom's fingers ran along his short beard thoughtfully. "Then again, that'd be a feather in our cap, pulling his clients for poker and hot springs? Good bonus income."

"That's what she thought. It'll take work to get a clear path and to fix them up right for use."

"Good news. We needed that." He polished off his whiskey. "What about your brilliant idea?"

"After that poker game, the money we made, I got to thinking. Maybe we should include gambling in the plans for the new place. Include Monte, Roulette, and the like."

"Poker, Faro, Vengt-et-un." Tommy tapped the bar with his finger. "There were some places during the war that made a killing. "

"I heard of places in Frisco had exclusive rooms cost thousands to get in."

"I'm liking the idea."

"We're likely losing the brothel, and we gotta recoup that money somehow."

"Only one problem I can see." Tommy leaned on the counter. "The poker and occasional Faro 'round here isn't so bad. You're looking at a full saloon of them like the Silver Saddle had."

"Right? They had one, so what's the problem?"

"No government then. Looser laws."

Jane perched on the stool beside Tommy. "You think they'll object, then? The Town Council? What for?"

"Some of the more uptight lot will worry that we're replacing a seedy element with another." Tom frowned. "I've heard a few of the laws they're bandying about. Including no brothels, and no gambling. No weapons too, but that'll never pass."

"No whores, no gambling. I smell a Daugherty." Cole's lip curled. "She wants us all respectable-like, and we ain't. Can Kathy talk to her?"

"I don't think that's the way to handle this" Jane glanced over at him. "Gun law will never pass, neither will the brothel law. Too many miners, and with the ranchers coming in, cowboys will be next."

Tommy frowned. "Which means they'll want to pass something Lillian proposed. Gambling is most likely."

Cole turned his attention to Jane. "You said it ain't the way to handle it. So what is?"

"Once we have the alternate plans for gambling set and extended to the potential investors, you have to get yourself ready." She leaned toward him, a hint of a real smile teasing her lips.

Her words sank in after a moment. "Wait. What? I have to get myself ready? For what?"

"Battle."

Tommy nudged her. "Battle's too harsh."

"Not if it's the law with the best chance." Jane met his gaze. "Your idea is brilliant. We could make good money, and you have to let the Council know how good that will be. Not just for us and The Hangman's Inn, but for the town."

"What do you mean?" Cole studied her features. The knowing smile she wore annoyed him now. "Jane, just tell me."

"Think it over. You're not as dumb as you act. Think about how we could use our good fortune to benefit the town." Her attention had wandered to the door. She slipped from her seat without another word.

Cole frowned her way when she went to meet Leanne at the doors. He didn't miss how Tommy's attention was immediately diverted to Leanne as well. The man tracked the path of the two women as they tucked themselves into a table in the corner, their conversation intense.

He poured another drink for Tom, and added a whiskey in for himself. "Well?"

"What?" Tom threw back his drink, slamming the glass on the counter. He rolled his shoulder, hissing as he did so. "Damn. This is gonna smart too long to make me happy."

"What of Leanne?"

Tom's brow furrowed in a frown, but a smirk twisted his lips. "She's going back to Denver in a few days right along with Alma. It doesn't much matter, does it?"

"It sure does." Cole leaned on the bar. "I don't know what she's told you."

"I only know about the Virgin Madam bit—at least from her lips." Tom met his gaze, not a lick of embarrassment there. "The rest is all because I'm good at what I do."

"Nosy bastard."

"Not nosy. Spent too long digging. It became a habit."

"Handy excuse. No reason to dig here, but ya did anyway."

"No reason?" Tommy chuckled heartily. "Really?"

Cole glanced Jane's way, then back to Tommy. "You got your secrets, too."

"I like to know who I work with, and who's screwing my sister. I dare say I knew about your extended family well before Jane did." Tom poured them both another glass. "Once I knew about Leanne, Alma, and what you did for them? I knew that Jane wasn't being like Clara—blinded by the notion of love."

Cole stared into his glass of whiskey in hopes of figuring out how to say what he wanted. The last thing he was used to doing was protecting Leanne through honesty. Still, he hadn't kept her pure from the riff-raff around these parts just to see her get hurt. "Look."

"I don't know," Tom interrupted. "She's a good woman, Cole. You did right by her. She's funny. Sarcastic. Strong. You did a good job protecting her, and it made her smarter. Look what she did with Underwood."

Cole downed his whiskey rather than answer yet.

"I wouldn't do anything to mess up all you did. I like you too much. Not to mention, you're family—so I wouldn't double cross you."

"I know that."

"She's going back to Denver. For now. You know that, so do I. She's still clean as you made sure she stayed all those years." Tom glanced over his shoulder. "Last I heard is she'll probably come back with Alma at Christmas."

"You gonna court her?"

"Still trying to figure out how, exactly, you would go about courting a renowned whore."

"I gotta say it, just like you said to me." Cole leaned on the counter close to Tom. "You hurt her, we're no longer family."

"I know. Don't intend to." Tom held up his glass. "To family. All of 'em. Whether they remember us or not. Whether we openly claim them or not."

Cole clinked his glass with Tom's tossing back the whiskey. Glad to have it over, he poured another drink. "Jane'll kill me for having whiskey this close to open."

"Have another. You can switch to coffee after."

"Don't have to tell me twice." Truth was, he would rather not stop, even for Cutler. With a gut full of whiskey, the past few days seemed fuzzy enough he could function. Jane may glare at him every time he pulled out a fresh bottle for himself, but it was better than the alternative—thinking about what he'd failed to protect her from.

"Plus, Cutler will be here in about an hour." Tom checked the clock, tossing back his whiskey. "We'll both switch to coffee next."

"Damn. Good point." Cole polished off his whiskey, clearing both glasses from the counter once he had. For the arrival of Cutler alone he'd stop. Jane'd kill him otherwise, and Cutler frowned on drinking at work. They needed the money too bad to muck it up. "You sure we should do this? We got no concrete proof beyond the tie between Warren and Underwood."

"That's all we need. A hint of doubt. Hopefully with that nugget, and the charms of those women, Cutler will at least take our advice and look into Underwood."

"Can't believe we got 'em to stay on extra because of the springs."

"Can't believe Leanne got Underwood handled so expertly all while handling Jane and you."

"She wasn't handling me. I'm fine."

"Right. And I'm an innocent farm boy from New York." Tom took the coffee Cole offered.

Cole narrowed his eyes, but changed the subject. "I can't believe Tuck managed to keep the springs a secret all these years."

"I can't believe Graham made him swear to tell only you first."

Jane smirked as she walked up behind Tom. "He's still feeling repentant for the bastard he's been to me these past few years, alternately between being decent, that is. Perhaps he might even be a little mad at himself for selling out now."

Cole leaned on the bar. "Telling us about the springs might have knocked off some of his debt, but he has a long ways to go."

"At the rate of interest you put on debts like that, he may never pay it back." Leanne hopped into the seat next to Tom. "Then again, you pay yours back in spades, so I suppose it shouln't be a surprise you expect the same."

"Sometimes the debts aren't even mine," Cole muttered.

Jane perched on a stool, her fingers twisting in front of her. Despite her claims of being fine, she was still pale and jumpy as hell. Cole didn't blame her one bit, but he hated not having any clue how to help, or which way was up for that matter. One minute she'd want his touch, his humor, or comfort; the next she peeled away and cowered.

Leanne piped up into the sudden uncomfortable silence. "Can I ask something?"

"You certainly can—and you may." Tom grunted when she punched his arm. "What?"

"Smart-mouth." Leanne stuck her tongue out at him. "As I was saying, why would Cutler believe a whore and two people that want money out of him over the partner he's had for years?"

"Funny. Cole here was dancing around the same question a few minutes ago." Tom tapped his finger on the bar top. "We've got little hard evidence. The rest he'll have to do some digging for himself to verify. All we can do is give him what we've got."

"Did Nick ever find anything?" Jane seemed to come to herself to reenter the conversation.

"He should be here soon. When I last talked to him, he was still searching." Tom rubbed his hand over his face. "He was in Denver for two days. I can only guess he found something."

"So now we wait." Leanne propped her cheek on her hand. Her lip puffed out in a childish pout. "That doesn't seem much fun."

"It's an hour," Cole pointed out. "You'll live."

"That's debatable."

Suppressed grief suffocates,
it rages within the breast,
and is forced to multiply its strength.
—Ovid

"Pssst."

Jane stopped her trek down the street at the hiss. Unsure it was meant for her, she glanced around.

"Psst. Janey."

"Graham?" Jane turned toward the undertaker's to find Graham's head poked out of the door.

"Janey, come here."

Jane drew closer. The nearer she got to his place, the more she heard the wails of a baby over the standard noise of the town. "Is there something wrong?"

"I need your help. I can't make him stop." His features twisted in distress. Impatiently, he waved her closer. "He woke up before Linh got back."

"He's probably hungry or wet. You can't help with the hunger, but you can change him." Jane remained outside the door, though he held it open for her. He had to learn, and honestly she had little desire to enter his place of business. To this day, the smell of death made her cold to her core.

"Change him? I don't know about that."

"You've seen Linh do it, have you not? I'm quite certain you can figure it out."

"Wait." Graham frantically grabbed her arm. "Won't you help?"

"I could, but this is more fun." She freed her arm, her grin spreading wider. When his shoulders drooped, she chuckled softly. She set a hand on his shoulder. "Graham. That is your son. You'll figure it out, I'm certain of it. Maybe he just wants to be held by his pa. Why don't you try that first?"

"Thanks, Janey." Graham patted her shoulder, disappearing back inside.

Jane lingered near the door for a few minutes. After a short while the crying slowed, and eventually all went quiet.

Satisfied Graham had a handle on the situation, she resumed her path back down the street. Though she returned greetings as she walked, her distraction remained too great to truly engage with anyone.

Since the attack she'd been trying to recover, and Cole had devoted all his attention to helping her. When he wasn't doing that, he was swimming in whiskey.

Somehow the man had to heal, too. Granted, it had only been days since the incident, but she couldn't live like it defined her, like it was all there was anymore. Life wouldn't stop simply because she was wounded. She'd learned that lesson years ago.

Maybe if they took the time to talk about it, and not in the sense of how it had affected her, but how it had wounded him—maybe then they could learn how to move on. Perhaps then her nerves would ease further.

Determined to confront him, Jane picked up her pace toward the Inn. Before she got to the entrance, Marshal Lewis and Mr. Cutler rounded the corner. They stepped onto the porch.

"Miss Spencer." Lewis tipped his hat. "I hope we aren't interrupting your day."

"No, not at all. I was just returning from a walk." Jane nodded to Cutler when he tipped his hat as well. "Was there something you needed?"

"We were hoping to speak with you and Mr. Mitchell." Lewis indicated to the Inn. "Is he available?"

"I would imagine he is," Jane acknowledged. "I'd offer to step inside and inquire, however lately I prefer the fresh air."

"I'll go in and get him," Lewis offered.

Cutler gestured to the bench when Lewis disappeared inside. "I have not had the opportunity to speak with you since our talk the other day. With the new opportunities you've presented, and even before, my associates were duly impressed with all of your plans. I'm seeing positive things for your future.

Jane smiled as bright as she could manage. The idea of a bright future battled with everything else. Damn, she hated feeling broken. "I do hope so, Mr. Cutler."

Cole and Lewis emerged from the Inn. Cole took a step toward her, hesitated a moment, then redirected to lean against the post on the corner of the porch. He nodded to Cutler. "What's going on?"

"I'll be leaving tomorrow." Lewis took a position near Cole. "I'll be taking Iris to the State Penitentiary. Along with her, I have another prisoner to guard until he's transferred to St. Louis."

Jane locked her gaze on Lewis for several quiet seconds. She turned toward Cutler. "St. Louis?"

"It wasn't easy to do, but after our meeting the other day, I contacted a friend in St. Louis." Cutler adjusted his glasses. "Using the information the Mr.'s Young provided, I arranged to have my accounts looked into by a neutral third party. They have only been working for a day, but have already found many discrepancies. My accountant has been taken into custody, and Marshal Lewis has arrested Daniel."

Cole's brow furrowed. "On what charge."

"Embezzlement," Lewis provided. "The funds he's been building, as Nick Young's research suggested, were not all his own profits. He's been skimming off Mr. Cutler's income in small amounts for a long time."

"Without finding his cousin, I'm afraid we may not be able to prove what he did to The Hangman's Inn." Cutler patted Jane's hand with a sad smile. "This we are able to prove. It will be enough to put him in prison for quite some time."

"What a relief." Jane sagged against the bench. As the callousness of her words hit her, she corrected them. "I mean, of course, that you were able to find out and have it taken care of so he won't be doing it any longer. It's not a relief he deceived you."

"I quite agree." Cutler held her gaze, a warm smile on his features. "I also wanted to let you know that while it will certainly not be enough for your grander plans, I intend to add more to my investment. Seeing as you are the reason my own funds are going to flourish again."

Jane's stomach flipped at the glimmer of hope. "You don't have to."

"I know I don't have to. I want to. I don't think I'll be alone, either—so I hope you're ready to begin at first word."

"We very much are." Jane turned toward Cole, excitement tingling through her.

Cole nodded. "We have construction schedules set up. Hammy checks with us daily to see where we are."

"The schedules are easily adjustable toward whatever plans we can fulfill." Jane hardly dared to hope Cutler was predicting enough for any of their plans. "As well as pre-sale contracts with the neighboring buildings. Should the best happen, we should be ready to reopen by next June."

"Then I'm certain I'll be seeing you then." Cutler offered his hand. "You are allowed to smile, Miss Spencer. This is all, in the end, good news."

"Of course it is." Jane shook her head to clear the cobwebs of shock. She took his proffered hand, forgoing a delicate shake in her enthusiasm. "I apologize. I have not been well the past few days, and I'm afraid I'm still a little out of sorts. Thank you very much, Mr. Cutler. Cole and I are more than grateful for your assistance."

Cole pushed off the post to move to Jane's side. He shook Cutler's hand when she finished. "She's right. You've been a real big help."

"Thank yourselves. You both could have let the situation get the best of you and let it fall to ruin. The fact that you didn't showed me far more than the plans for the business did." Cutler tipped his hat. "I'll let you return to your day. I have a few more telegrams to send, and then I must get packed for my return to St. Louis."

Jane kept her smile in place until Cutler walked away. She turned her attention to Lewis. "Alfred, I must apologize. We never had a chance to finish our conversation."

"Sure we did. Leastwise, I have heard and seen all I need to." Lewis held out his hand. "My business in Dominion Falls is done. Should I return it will hopefully be for matters that do not involve you or your place of business."

Jane shook his hand, a relieved smile taking place of her worry. "Thank you."

"Mr. Mitchell." Lewis held out his hand. "Good luck to both of you. You've had enough bad luck for a while."

Jane looked down at the spark of tears that arose from his mention of bad luck. "I quite agree."

"Thank you," Cole said. "For helping with this."

"No thanks needed. I was just doing my job." With a final tip of his hat, Lewis stepped off the porch in the direction of the jail.

Cole remained silent until they were alone. "You gonna come in?"

"I was taking a walk." Jane wanted to run into his arms and pour all her relief and remaining nerves out on him. Something held her back. She didn't understand why she couldn't breach the small distance between them. The mere realization that she couldn't seem to control this resistance made her angry. "I think I'd like to continue it."

"I can go with you."

"I don't need to be watched constantly," she snapped. Immediately she winced at her tone. She cursed under her breath for taking her anger at herself out on him. "I didn't mean—"

"Got it."

"Cole."

"I'll be inside."

Jane bit her trembling lip as he stormed into the saloon. Why on earth she kept taking out her frustration on him, she didn't know. Tears of frustration welled up so fast, she almost lost control of them.

She stormed off the porch in a fury. At herself, at him, at the world. No, at Joe. For what he'd done to them. She couldn't even enjoy the good news of Cutler investing more. Or the sanctuary of Cole's arms.

"Damn it." She swiped at tears, her feet leading her blindly through the street.

She stopped short when her feet hit boards, and she realized an old instinct had led her the last place she wanted to go.

The library.

Once a sanctuary for her as much as Cole, it now raised a cold stirring in her belly that wanted to rush out in a scream. Fear clamored up her spine until she shivered. This wouldn't do. After her death on the noose, she'd sworn she wouldn't let fear rule her again.

One man couldn't change that for her. Still, her heart would not beat in a normal rhythm, much less in her chest. The slow, cautious beat swam in her ears until she almost couldn't breathe from the fear.

A hand touched her arm, startling her back to the present. "Hi Jane!"

Jane jumped away from the touch, even though she recognized the voice as Isaac's. "My goodness. I'm sorry. You startled me."

"Sorry." Isaac offered a sheepish smile. "I came to get a book."

She realized she'd now have to open the door whether she wanted to go in or not. After a deep breath, she pulled her keys from her reticule to open the door. She fumbled with the keys trying to unlock the door. Once it was open, she stepped aside to allow Isaac in, but found herself unable to cross the threshold.

Isaac raced over to a shelf with one of his favorite books. He scanned the spines leisurely after that. Jane's gaze drifted through the library, the place she'd always loved so dearly. A scattered pile of books on the floor caught her attention.

Near the shelf in the same area were a series of dark spots. Her fingers drifted to the bun at the back of her head. The cut still smarted every time she did her hair, yet another daily reminder of the whole thing.

Her nose burned with the need for her to unleash the tears that wanted release. The library, her second home. It wasn't safe any longer. She stared at the keys in her hand, wondering who might want the post she wasn't certain she could hold any longer.

"Jane?" Isaac stood by the desk, a book in his hand. "Aren't you coming in?"

Joe was dead, he wouldn't be in there. Only his memory would be.

"Jane?"

"Of course." Jane gripped the keys so tight in her hand the ridges dug into her palms. The pain gave her the boost of courage she needed to cross the threshold. Panic whooshed through her ears before subsiding.

She paused when the door began to swing closed. Before it got far, she braced her hand against it, shoving it all the way open. With a chair normally tucked into the alcove, she propped it so the door couldn't shut. After that, she rushed to open the blinds, letting in as much light as possible.

As she approached the desk, Isaac's brow furrowed. "Miss Jane? Are you crying?"

"No." Jane wiped her cheek, surprised to find it damp. "Oh. Maybe a little. Don't worry. I cry a lot more with the baby on the way."

Isaac handed her the book when she circled the desk.

Jane set Isaac's book on top of *Dangerous Liaisons* so she wouldn't delay him any further. Her hands shook so hard she could barely write out his name or the book's title. "Enjoy your book. I'll see you in a few days."

"Ya sure you're okay?" Isaac clutched his book to his chest.

"I'm fine." Jane couldn't meet his gaze or drudge up a smile to reassure him in any way. "Really. Go on."

He trudged from the room, pausing at the door to look back at her.

She still couldn't manage to offer him any further reassurance. Her whole body shook against every warring emotion. Jane folded her arms tight across her chest to stop the shaking, sinking into her chair.

Dangerous Liaisons stared at her right where Joe had left it.

She flew to her feet so fast the chair clattered across the floor. With a lurch, she grabbed the book from the desk. She returned it where it belonged on the shelves, backing away from it as though it might bite.

The books on the floor tripped her backward progress. She caught herself on the shelves, and tried to regain a steady breath. The library should be open, but she needed to leave.

Eyes closed, she leaned against the shelves for several moments. When she opened her eyes, she found herself staring at the droplets of dried blood on the floor, the books scattered around them.

"I have to get through this. I have to. The library is mine. It's a place. He's not here. He's not here." She took several deep breaths, wishing the mere action of speaking the words would make them true.

Somehow she would get strong again. What had happened was in the past. The past couldn't hurt her anymore.

She knelt down to pick up the books. One by one she gathered them in her arms until the stack reached her chin. She'd put the books away, clean up the blood and then go on to the next thing.

Rising to her feet, she slipped the first book back in its place.

A shadow darkened the doorway. Panic hit her so hard she dropped all the books she'd picked up.

"What the hell are ya doing?" Cole hovered in the door, fists clenched at his sides. "Isaac told me you're over here. Why in blazes did ya come here?"

"I'm trying to work," she whispered. The tremor in her voice couldn't be helped. Determined as she was to keep going, she felt too broken. Worse, things with Cole had been completely off-kilter since her attack. "I have to work. I have to keep busy. This is just a place. I'm strong enough. I have to be strong enough."

"No. You don't."

"I do."

"Damn it, Jane!"

"Don't you yell at me!" She swiped at the tears that burst free. This wasn't the time or place for their conversation, but it was happening anyway. She stepped over the dropped books. Her finger jammed into his chest. "You won't come out from the bottom of a bottle for more than a few minutes at a time. You deal with it your way, and let me deal with it how I see fit."

"Thought your way was to run away."

She slapped him hard. "That was Clara, you ass."

He grabbed for her, but she was too fast. "You need to hit me, hit me. I deserve it."

She paused at the desk, her hand resting on the edge where she'd given up the fight. Her voice was raw when she managed to speak, "No. You don't."

"Sure I do. I let ya down."

"No. You didn't." She couldn't face him just yet. Her eyes closed as the memories rushed past at top speed. Her body jerked at the depth of her sob.

He caught her by the elbows, holding her upright when she was sure she'd fall. "I wasn't here."

"You couldn't know." Damn her voice for betraying her. "Stop."

"Stop what?"

"Let me go."

"I..."

"No, not me. Just my elbows." When he did, she managed to turn around. Torment lined his face in ways she'd not seen since her hanging. "Listen to me."

"Jane."

"I said listen to me!" Her hands trembled, but she set them on his still outstretched arms. "You're the one running away."

"I ain't."

"You're afraid."

"Am not."

"Yes." She gripped his wrists to keep her hands from shaking. "Afraid to touch me. Afraid you'll do something wrong. Afraid you'll move too fast and scare me off. You're only thinking about me."

"You're the one that was raped!"

"Physically, yes." She released her hold on his arms to back up one step. "I'm not the only one it affected, though. It affected you as well. You've done everything for me from the second you learned this happened. Including your hunting trip. It was for you, but for me as well. Everything you've done has been about me. You *are* allowed to grieve, too."

"Taking care of you is how I handle it."

"You're angry." Talking about him made her emotions more under control. This time she could control her own emotions when she focused on him. "Anger is easier, it always is. Focusing on me means you don't have to confront what you're feeling."

"Jane…"

She slid her arms around his waist, resting her forehead on his chest. "You're hurt. You feel helpless. You feel like you can't do what you usually do to deal with things. All of which makes you angrier. It does the same for me."

"What the hell do you want me to do?"

"I don't know." She stepped closer, flush against him. His arms slipped around her as they had so many times. "Love me. This wasn't your fault. Stop blaming yourself."

"I should've listened better."

"I should've listened to my own instincts. I was too busy not trusting myself because of what happened with Iris."

"You gotta stop blaming yourself too."

"I will if you will."

His chin rested on top of her head. A deep sigh issued from him before he spoke again. "I don't know how to help you—how to take it away like you want."

Her mind raced, unsure how to get close to healing. She stepped out of his embrace, leading him toward where the books were scattered. "I tried to run. He caught me here, slammed my head into the bookcase. He punched me the first time. I thought of our baby. I wanted to get to the gun in my desk."

His hand clenched in hers, a deep rumble in his chest.

She led him back to the desk where they'd stood moments before. "This is when I thought the baby was in danger, he shoved me into the desk so hard. This…is where I gave up."

"You didn't give up."

"Hold me. Make this place feel safe again."

He stepped back, his gaze drifting to the open door. When he moved the chair, she whimpered. His gaze shot back to her.

"Don't…"

His jaw worked with tension. The muscles in his arm tightened as he held the chair aloft, unsure. Despite her protest, he closed the door and clicked the lock.

The world dimmed, her breath labored under its own rapidity. "Cole."

His arms wrapped around her, pulling her tight against him. "It's me. It ain't him."

"Hold me tighter. I need…"

"Jane."

She shook her head, her own panic eased by his tight grip. "You. Tell me what you're feeling. Yell, scream, cry—whatever you need to do."

"What about you?"

"I've done it all. I've told you everything while you listened. I've cried, I've screamed, I've thrown up, I've had a hundred bouts of panic a day. Now all I need is you. I need to know that I'm not alone. I need to know what you're feeling. I need you. All of you."

"You always had me. Right from the start."

She smiled against his chest. "And you always had me."

"That bastard," his voice choked off.

She wrapped her arms around him in kind.

"He took ya. You weren't willing. He hurt you." His body leaned over hers, encompassing her totally.

"I wasn't willing," She whispered. "I was never his. I've always been yours."

"I wasn't here, and I shoulda been. I'm supposed to protect you. Protect our kid." He sank to the floor with her still in his arms. She sobbed into his chest, curling as tight against him as possible. With her secure in his lap, his own tears dripped into her hair.

She turned her face toward him until their foreheads pressed together. "It's not your fault."

"I wasn't there. Now there ain't nothing I can do to fix it."

"Love me."

"I do."

"Forgive me."

He clasped her hand in his, pulling it against his chest. "Forgiven."

"Forgive yourself."

"Ain't so easy."

"Love me."

"Forever."

Hope is brightest when it dawns from fears.
–Sir Walter Scott

Cole leaned on the hitching post next to Jane. "You know he had the gall to say they ain't courting?"

Jane followed his nod to find Tommy and Leanne walking along the street together. Her arm draped through his, their mutual laughter brightening both their faces. Jane laughed quietly. "He had a disastrous first marriage, she's a madam with a very unique quirk, and she's leaving in two days—I imagine calling it courting might be a stretch."

"I still gave him what-for."

"Men." She nudged his shoulder with her own. "Such brutes."

"You like that I'm a brute."

"Perhaps." After the day in the library the week before, things had begun to slowly return to normal. Some areas were still a struggle for them both, but as those moments happened they leaned into them, and each other, instead of ignoring it. "Unfortunately, Leanne's departure also means Alma's."

"I know."

"I'll miss her a great deal, but she'll be back soon. By the time she returns, we'll have to tell her about the baby, she won't be able to miss it." Already her stomach grew by the day, as if the moment she'd removed her corset it felt it had permission to expand beyond the bounds of decency.

"I got a feeling you'll figure a way to tell her before Thanksgiving."

"I might." She sighed deeply as she continued to watch the couple on their walk. One arm slipped through Cole's until their hands embraced. She rested her cheek on his shoulder. "I didn't think I ever wanted a family."

"I told you—stop taking in strays."

"I'll take it under advisement."

"Meaning you're going to ignore me."

"Probably."

He shrugged her off his shoulder. His low chuckle warmed her heart. "Wicked woman."

"You like that about me."

"Perhaps."

She dropped her chin to her hand, letting her gaze wander around town. At that moment she knew Alma and Sally had gone off to play with Jesse and Cora's boys again. Once Alma came to stay it might all seem normal. For her, that wasn't normal. She didn't quite know what to think of it.

Cole's finger swept a stray curl from her cheek. A soft kiss landed on her cheek.

She closed her eyes at the simple gesture, a happy sigh escaping. "Thank you."

"For what?"

She turned her gaze to his. At his continuing questioning look, she offered a half-shrug. "That is the first time in days you've kissed me without asking permission first."

His smile faded.

"Don't run away on me. Don't start to defend yourself, and don't you dare feel regret over it. I didn't mind, in fact I believe I did thank you."

He turned away and stepped off the porch anyway. His back to her, he leaned against the post. He stared off through the town at nothing in particular that she could see.

"Cole." She walked behind him, then leaned her shoulder into the same post. "I won't want you constantly worried you're going to scare me."

"We gonna always be like this?" He focused on his feet before squinting against the sun as he stared down the street. "Or we gonna have fun and cause scandal again?"

Jane glanced at him out of the corner of her eye. A smile teased along her lips. Hope that they'd move past what had happened burst forth in her heart. "You want to cause scandal again?"

"It's always been fun."

"Well, sir. I am already pregnant. By all accounts I'm a divorced woman, still unmarried despite my current state. I live in sin with an utterly delicious man. You are a man with a shady past. A penchant for prostitutes. You've been known to do a fair few of unseemly and ill-thought out deeds. What more can we do?"

Cole turned to face her, his eyes alight with laughter he'd managed to keep off his lips for the moment. He cupped her cheek. His thumb traced the outline of her lips while she continued to smile. "I missed that."

"What?"

"That smile. I ain't seen it since Denver."

"Not a soul could have found it but you." She stepped closer. His hand slid around her waist easily. With her on the porch, and him on the street, she was much closer to his wonderful lips. "I love you."

"Nah. You just like seeing me outta my shirt."

Her laughter burst forth to join his. To shut him up, she kissed him soundly. "Oh goodness, no. That's only the bonus. The very, very large bonus."

"That so?"

"Oh yes. I really hope the investors pull through. I'd like nothing more than to see you pitching in to help with the construction again." Her laughter faded when he leaned in toward her. All the joy and hope she'd felt moments ago were chased away by unwelcome panic when his lips hovered near hers. Her body tensed against her will, her lips sucked in between her teeth.

Frustration welled when he shifted to kiss her temple instead. The action did little to soothe her, instead it frustrated her with its abnormality. He ran his hand along her back. "It's all right, Jane."

"No. No it most certainly is not." She pushed out of his arm. Without another word, she tore through the saloon to their room. "Damn it, damn it, damn it."

Tears spilled down her cheeks. She dropped to the bed, punching her pillow in her frustration. All she wanted was normality, and she'd been so very close. Something had made her afraid…afraid of Cole? If Joe wasn't already dead, she'd kill him again for robbing her of the man she loved.

Sobbing again, she wept into her pillow until sleep won over tears.

There is peace and rest and comfort in sorrow.
–Soren Kierkegaard

Cole slipped into the room with Jane nearly an hour after she'd run off. He'd only meant to give her time to catch her breath, but distractions in the saloon had kept him away for much longer. He closed the door, only to find her asleep on the bed.

He kicked off his shoes to join her, but then noticed she'd fallen asleep with her own shoes on. With a few minutes frustration he managed to slip them off. He didn't bother with her dress. He doubted she slept well enough for the struggle it would be to completely strip her down, and he'd rather let her sleep.

The second he slid into bed behind her she turned toward him. Layers of petticoats rolled with her, right over his legs in a waterfall toward the floor. Her head tucked into his shoulder, her soft breath even against his hand where it lay over his heart.

His frustrations over their situation took a hard left when her hand slipped along his cock. Even through his trousers, the touch after well over a week of nothing sparked him to life in a way he knew he couldn't act on. Not with her asleep.

A few weeks ago he wouldn't have hesitated a second. He would have taken her the second she'd touched him. Now everything had changed. He wanted to soothe her, but he also wanted to love her like she'd asked.

Light touches danced along his length again. The whole time her breath remained steady, even as his own caught in his throat. He groaned low, trying to regain control of his faculties before his denied libido took right over.

Another touch right at the tip made him jump, and was immediately followed by what he could have sworn was an intentional squeeze.

He released his breath in a low chuckle. Talk about ridiculous. For as much pain and worry as they'd had, Jane didn't appear to have as many fears when she slept.

Jane stirred at his shoulder. Eyelids fluttered open, her deep blue gaze locked on his. Her brow puckered delicately at his continued laughter. "What?"

"Nothing." He tried to contain his grin, but it wouldn't be tamed.

"What is that smile for?"

"You talk in your sleep."

"Liar."

"All right. You grope in your sleep."

She released an indelicate snort. His stomach smarted when she smacked him.

He caught her hand. "What? I wasn't lying that time."

"I know you weren't." She dared to pout, and he had to resist the urge to bite the protruding lip. "I simply think you're enjoying it too much."

"Can't enjoy a good groping too much."

"Vile."

"I know."

She collected her hand from his gently. He would have sworn a wicked smirk lifted a corner of her lip in the moment before she turned her back to him. "What makes you think I was asleep?"

Cole's laughter cut off dead. His stomach twisted in nerves. God help him if she was serious. He didn't know how to keep it up without her scaring off. With one near-kiss outside she'd looked like a startled deer. When she didn't speak again, he pushed to sit. A touch to her shoulder got no reaction. "Jane?"

She rolled to her back, a sad smile on her features. "You look absolutely terrified. I'm glad to know the thought disgusts you so."

"That ain't it. You know it isn't."

Her hand clamped over his mouth. "Stop. I do know it."

He peeled her hand away. "I ain't gonna say I don't want to. There hasn't been a day I've known you that I didn't want to, but I'm not gonna push you. I wasn't trying to push you—it was a joke."

"Cole."

"I don't want you to feel obligated."

"Colton."

He frowned, determined to let her know he'd wait forever for her. It wouldn't be the first time he'd waited to be with her. "I mean it."

"Colton James Spencer, you shut your trap." She pushed to sitting, one leg sliding to circle his hip. Her fingers brushed along his forehead, easing the worry that pinched his brow. "You have never once pushed me. Not once since I first swished my petticoats at you—even though I could tell you wanted something."

Despite all his worries, he cracked a smile. "I wasn't the only one."

"You most certainly weren't. I did too—although I wasn't entirely certain what that was."

"You learned fast."

"I had an amazing teacher." She set her hand on his chest. Though a bit of fear lingered in her shaky hands, and a tick in her brow, she appeared to contain it all in a deep breath. "You wouldn't ever push me. And now, more than ever, you're going to hold back. I don't know that I want you to."

"You freeze up at a kiss."

"I know, but like the library last week, I must face my fears. The longer I hide, the worse I will feel."

He set his hand on hers where it rested on his chest.

"I told you I don't want to live my life in fear. To add to that—I don't want to let a horrible bastard of a man take this from me. I won't let him take *you* from me. My life, my happiness? He can't have any of it. I want to feel safe again. I have to feel safe again, and I sure as hell don't want his touch to be the last touch I've felt. You should be the one that lingers on my skin, not him."

Concern held him back, but he wiped a tear from her cheek. "All the words in the world ain't gonna make you ready."

"I need you."

His heart constricted at the break in her voice. "What if you aren't ready?"

"I need you."

"I won't hurt you."

She inched closer, her head tilted back to meet his gaze. Tears shimmered in her eyes, but they were dark with other emotions. "You never could."

His jaw clenched, worry and doubt holding him back. Still, he slid his arm around her. "There ain't been a day I didn't want you."

"There hasn't been a day I didn't want you." Her hands slid up his chest to circle his neck. Lips he ached to kiss hovered close to his. "You were all I ever wanted. You're all I ever needed. I need you now."

When her lips pressed to his, all arguments fell away. His hold on her tightened to bring their bodies flush. Relief rushed through him to have her close again. Every move he made was cautious, unwilling to scare her. He'd let her lead the way if it killed him.

With shaky hands, she unbuttoned his shirt. Her fingers slid along his bare chest toward his shoulders. At her gentle urging, he helped her get his shirt off.

In the breath of her hesitation, he cupped her cheek. He ran his thumb along the apple of her cheek before slowly trailing his hand down her neck to her shoulder. Never taking his gaze from hers, he waited for her nod before he released the hooks of her bodice.

Moments of uncertainty filtered into every motion as they slowly undressed each other. By the time they were skin to skin, her body trembled in his arms, but she sought out his lips, and he obliged her with a warm kiss.

Fear and self-doubt clouded every movement, the familiar traces of tender touches felt foreign, but began to ease the ache in his soul. At every resistance, whispers of love filtered in, soothing him back to a place of peace so long as she was in his arms.

One final moment before they reconnected completely, he found himself frozen. Ready to take the plunge, he held her close. The whisper of fear in her eyes locked him up until he couldn't move.

"I love you," she whispered.

"I love you too."

"I need you."

The plea soothed his last fear. He pressed his lips to hers again as they joined together completely. With every movement, every feather light touch she came alive again, responding to his loving touch and returning it in kind. They built on the burning fire inside until it burst into a joyous inferno.

He clung to her as they lingered in the moment, their tongues dancing together as the tremors of release subsided. Slowly he pulled back from the kiss to search her eyes. He trailed his fingers along her spine when she kept her eyes closed. "Are you all right?"

"Yes." She smiled, and her eyes fluttered open to reassure him. "You're still safe—even more so now. I might still be afraid, but not of you. Never of you. I love you."

"I love you too."

As he rolled onto his back, she rolled with him until her head rested on his chest, her body still lying on his. After a few minutes she lifted her head. "No more guilt. You didn't push this, I did."

"Just worried you weren't ready."

She planted her hands on either side of him. As she hovered over him, she smiled. "I might not have been, but I had to. You give me strength. Trust me."

"Of course I trust you." It was never a question.

"Then stop worrying. I'm where I want to be."

"I'm always gonna worry."

"That's how I know I'm where I want to be."

Peace comes from within.
Do not seek it without.
—Buddha

"Cole!"

Cole jumped awake. Disoriented, he fumbled until he felt Jane trembling by him. He pulled her close. "I'm right here."

She turned so fast she almost knocked him off the bed. Her breath came in ragged gasps. "Oh God. You, I—oh."

A familiar groan edged out of her. He released his hold as she flew off him toward the bucket. With a sigh, he rose to follow. On the way he grabbed her robe to drape over her shoulders. "Need tea?"

After a minute she managed a nod. "Teapot should be hot. I set it to boil before I—oh." She got sick again before she could say anything else. The moment the second wave eased, he offered a handkerchief. She snatched it from him quick.

Cole sat beside her, tea in his hand. Once she'd settled enough to take it, he rubbed her back. "Hope that ain't my fault."

"It sort of is."

"Damn."

Somehow she managed a smile, though her skin still lacked color. "I was far too comfortable. I didn't want to get up to get tea, nor did I wish for you to leave my side to do it for me."

"What was that scream?"

The smile faded away. Her gaze drifted to the window. "Bad dream."

"Was it…you know."

"I can't lose you."

The subject change startled a frown out of him. Confused, he moved closer. He wrapped his arm around her. "You aren't gonna."

"What if someone finds out what you did out there? I mean, I know it was necessary and I'd never begrudge what you had to do. What if they figure out he's missing?"

"They won't know he's missing for a good long time."

"How can you be so sure?"

"Tom said when the bastard would take off, he always did what he did here. He'd have his things sent home to Salt Lake, and head out on horseback for months. I heard him tell Tom myself that he told them he'd be gone 'til after Christmas."

"Then no one will think to look for him." She almost relaxed, only to tense again. "What if someone finds the body?"

"Ain't no body to find." He wasn't surprised by the sharp gaze she fixed on him. "You know Petey."

"Of course. Petey Burns. He only comes in now and then. Lives way out at the southern edge of the valley."

"Yup. He's got that pig farm and don't spend much time tending the pigs since most in town get them from China town."

"It's closer."

He nodded. "Exactly. Plus, he'd rather spend all his time making, and drinking, moonshine. Them pigs is half wild and plenty hungry. We made sure they had good full bellies before we got the rotgut for Tom."

"Oh." Her jaw went slack. "Oh! So you…fed the pigs…"

He nodded at her correct conclusion. "Pigs'll eat anything, even a pile of trash like Joe. He's long gone, for good."

She sagged against him. "Thank God."

"You got plenty to worry about, but that ain't a part of it." He ran his hand along her back in hopes of soothing her. "It ain't ever gonna be a part of it."

"I'll try to remember." She swiped away a few tears. "The nightmare may take some time to stop anyway."

"Guess I'll have to be there to wake you up."

"I guess so." She lifted her head to meet his gaze, a warm smile lit her features. Her soft hand cupped his cheek tenderly. Whatever she might have been about to say got cut off by the chime of the clock striking six, immediately followed by a knock on their door. She gasped. "Oh dear. It's six o'clock. That's what time we told Alma we'd take her to supper."

"Damn it. Get yourself dressed." Cole scrambled to get into his trousers quick. A change in schedule always upset Alma. It was something they'd been struggling with since Jane's attack.

"Hurry up." Jane clamored across the floor, grabbing clothes scattered through the room. "Much longer and she'll be upset. It's her last night, we can't have that."

Cole threw open the door the second Jane disappeared behind the curtain. "Alma."

"It's six o'clock." Alma rocked onto her toes and back to her heels. "Supper with Jane. It's time."

"That's right." Cole chuckled before he could help himself. Jane's struggle behind the curtain was well displayed thanks to a few muttered curses, along with the billowing of the curtain every time she hit it. "We're having supper with Jane. Anyone else joining us tonight?"

"Le-Leanne." Alma stopped her rocking as she thought. "Tom. Mike. Sally. Arthur."

"Practically the whole town." Jane emerged from the curtain, flushed with life again. Amusement tickled her lips into a wonderful smile. "They're all going to miss you, and want to see you before you leave."

Cole squeezed Janes hand when she walked up beside him. "Let me get my shirt and boots on, and we'll get going."

"It's six o'clock," Alma protested.

"Yes it is." Jane set a hand on Alma's, which had begun to twist together. "Why don't you and I begin our walk to Cora's. Cole can catch up. That way we can leave when we said we would."

At Alma's nod, Cole did the same. "Works for me. Don't walk too fast."

"Don't take too long," Jane countered.

Cole swatted her ass as she scooted out the door. Her yelp and glare bolstered his amusement rather than dampen it. Outside of a few bad moments, things were looking up. Cole raced to get dressed soon as they hit the stairs.

Jane's reassurances eased his worries, and being able to be with her again soothed the savage beasts of loss and anger.

Unfortunately they now had to face the loss of the company he was surprised to say he'd grown used to. Both Alma and Leanne had become a fixture in their few short weeks in town. For the first time in a long time he'd have to admit he would miss them.

At least Alma would return first for Thanksgiving, and then for Christmas. Eventually she'd move in to wherever they ended up living when the baby came.

Cole shook his head of its wandering musings. Any longer and he'd never catch up with them until they got to Cora's. With a hop start, he jogged all the way out of the Inn. Luckily, Jane seemed to have followed his request to walk slow, for they were only a short way down the street.

"When you come back in the spring, can you teach me?" Jane's question hit his ears as he caught up to them.

"Teach you what?" Cole set his hand at the small of her waist as he'd done for ages. He was glad to feel no hesitation to resume the habit.

"How to make a garden that will bring the butterflies Alma loves."

"You?" Cole chuckled. "You plan to handle a real garden? You killed the flowers at the library."

"That's why I need to learn." A sharp jolt from Jane's elbow hit his rib. "I was asking Alma if she wanted me to request the school let her learn from Miss Cunningham so that she can come home and teach me."

"I would like that," Alma said quietly.

Cole smirked. "Good luck, Alma. She ain't no good at keeping plants alive. They finally gave up at the library and tore down the flower boxes."

Jane smacked him in the arm. "You are not funny, sir."

"I think I am."

"You would."

Hope is like the sun, which, as we journey
toward it, casts the shadow of
our burden behind us.
-Samuel Smiles

"*Ma!*" Jesse's voice startled Jane from the book she read.

Jane rose as Jesse and Isaac tore around the corner. She rushed toward the street when the wagon tilted dangerously to the side. "Jesse! What do you think you're doing?"

Jesse laughed boisterously. His good hand gripped the side of the wagon as it drew to a stop. "We came to say goodbye to Alma and Leanne."

"Jesse Michael Schaffer, you still have a broken arm and foot! Are you trying to get hurt again?" She pursed her lips, hands on hips. Both boys ducked their heads at her glare. "Isaac, I cannot believe you gave into his begging after our last talk."

"Aw, I wouldn't let him fall." Isaac's attempt to appear reticent dissolved into a sheepish grin. "We were in a rush."

She turned back to her son. "You need to stop begging to go so fast. You're already banged up enough as it is, young man."

"Where's Alma, Ma?" Jesse grinned through his change of subject. "We wanted to see her before she left."

"She's spending a little time with Cole before she leaves. They should be back soon."

"Can we keep goin' round 'til she gets back?" Jesse hopped in his seat. "Please, Ma? It's lots of fun."

Jane sighed her acquiescence. Though she hated to see him hurt again, she knew he was having fun. "Fine. But go slower this time, all right Isaac?"

"I gotcha." Isaac picked up the rope. "We'll be real careful."

"Good. We don't need any more reasons for me to faint. I have more than enough already." She ruffled Jesse's hair and stepped back so they could take off down the street again.

Right as she turned to return to her book, approaching hoof beats drew her attention back to the street. Jane smiled as her horse, Tempest, arrived with a familiar rider on her back. "Leanne."

"I brought Tempest back for you." Leanne hopped down from the saddle. "Thank you for letting me borrow her while I was here."

"I'm glad she was able to get out and be useful. My doctor is limiting how much I can ride." Jane took the reins. She patted Tempest's neck, leaning into her when she nipped at her hair. Tommy rode up a minute later, bringing another smile to Jane's face as Leanne had clearly won the race. She could get used to this happy feeling. "Good morning, Tom."

"Janey." Tom frowned at her continued grin. "I'm injured. Be nice."

"Is that your excuse for losing yet another race to the lovely Leanne?" Jane giggled at Leanne's bright laughter. "Seems pretty weak to me."

"Har har." Tom dismounted with a modicum of difficulty. On the ground, he grabbed both sets of reins. "Let me put the beasts up, Leanne. Then we'll get to the depot. Mike said he'd be dropping your things off this morning."

"Thank you." Leanne's smile remained insatiably bright as Tom led the horses around the back of the Inn. She sank onto the bench next to Jane. "Such a shame to go home already. I was having a lovely time here in Dominion Falls. That's something I never thought I'd say."

"And how lovely of a time did you have?" Jane leaned closer. "You, my dear, cannot stop smiling."

"Not quite that good of a time, you devil woman." Leanne grasped Jane's hand. "Stop trying to corrupt an innocent such as myself."

"How could I possibly corrupt a whore?" Jane winked. "Does this mean you'll return with Alma when she visits in November? I certainly wouldn't mind. I'm certain Mike would let you use one of his rooms again, or perhaps Tom would offer his bed."

"With him in it." Leanne laughed, but the foreign sight of a blush lit her cheeks. "I've certainly considered a return trip. Tom and I were talking about it, and I might. After all, you won't be up for traveling by then, and I know Cole doesn't want to leave you alone ever again."

The simple reminder brought Jane's happy mood to a screeching halt, the nerves springing to life. Her smile faltered, but Tom's arrival saved her by diversion alone. "Well, Thomas. I don't know what you've done, but Leanne is fairly glowing."

"You really aren't funny. I'm a gentleman, damn it." Tommy offered his arm to Leanne. "Vile creature, you are."

"Takes one to know one, dearest brother." Jane smiled. "You two go on ahead. I'll see you at the depot shortly."

Leanne winked and fell into step with Tom. Even as they walked away, Jane could hear Leanne soothing Tom's grumpiness away. She knew those two would be officially courting by Christmas one way or another.

Jane sighed and dropped her head back against the window. While she was feeling better, she was far from back to her old self—and pretending was becoming more exhausting every day.

She forced herself back to her feet and paced the length of the porch. At the end of the porch she paused, forcing a deep breath to calm her riled nerves. Leanne's innocent mentioning had sent her into a tizzy again, and that simply wouldn't do.

Jane leaned against the post, watching the crowd of people milling through the street. Everything was so ordinary in its motion. As it always had, the simple daily action of the town began to sooth her more.

Hands slipped around her waist. Jane startled so fast a shriek escaped moments before she spun, swinging on the way around. Her fist made contact with Cole's eye dead on. "Oh! Oh my goodness! Cole! I'm so sorry."

He grunted as he tapped the eye with a finger. "Jesus, Jane."

"Sorry. I'm so sorry. I was—sorry."

When she touched his eye, he flinched. "Next time I'll remember to let ya know it's me first."

"Sorry," She repeated. Guilt nagged away her earlier worries as she pulled a fresh handkerchief from her pocket to dab at the drops of blood. "Oh dear. I cut you."

"Yeah. With the ring. I noticed." He chuckled low. "My fault."

"For startling me."

"No. For seeing you got that ring at all."

She pursed her lips in an attempt to cover her own amusement. With a little more force than necessary, she pressed the handkerchief to his eye socket again. "Not funny."

"Ow. Damn. Not even a little?"

"No."

"Aww, come on." He slipped his arms around her waist again and pulled her close. "I see a smile."

Shaking her head, she finished dabbing at the blood before she met his eyes. "Keep it up and you'll have the ring back."

"Nah." He brushed his lips across hers. "You'd never do that. You like me too much."

"Don't count on it," she murmured when he kissed her neck. "I don't care for inconsiderate fools."

"This feel inconsiderate?"

She sighed to cover the moan she was suppressing. "Yes."

"How's that?"

"Because, we have to get to the depot."

"Five minutes."

"I can't do five minutes right now."

"Sure sounds like you could." He winked at the tremor in her voice. His fingers trailed down her back and over her bustle to cup her bottom. "This is me. Just me, and a little scandal."

"Scandal?" She couldn't stop her smile as she leaned into him. "How so?"

"Clock's running down. It would take too much time to get to our room, so we'd have to improvise."

"It doesn't take any time to get to our room."

He captured her lips with his and pulled her tight against him. When she responded immediately, he chuckled into the kiss. "But, if you want to wait. I guess we can."

"You don't play fair."

"Never have, so I sure ain't gonna start now."

"Maybe I should—"

"Can't the two of you knock it off and be decent for one day?" Graham laughed and clapped Cole on the back hard enough to make both him and Jane stumble.

"Graham." Jane sighed in a mix of frustration and relief. "Can't you manage to not be an obnoxious beast for one day?"

Cole smirked. "No."

Graham snorted. "Who're you answering?"

"Both of you." Cole kept his arm around Jane's waist when she untangled herself and turned more toward Graham. "What d'you want?"

"Just passing by." Graham winked.

"Then keep passing." Jane laughed. "Unless you're looking for tips on how to be a real man, of course."

"From you? Nah." Graham shook his head. "You only got lessons in the opposite."

Cole tried to pull Jane back into an embrace when Graham walked off. "What is that you were saying?"

"That we need to get to the depot." She braced her hands on his chest. After she'd extracted herself from his embrace, she tugged on his hand. "Because I'm assuming you being here by yourself means my son and Isaac found Alma and took her to the depot themselves for you?"

"Yeah."

"All right. As for the rest of our conversation, we'll discuss it later."

"Damn."

"Patience," she chided.

"Never had much of that."

"I think you're wrong there. You have a great amount of it when it's important."

Laughing, he wrapped his arm around her waist and walked with her to the depot. Their cheer faded as they got closer, and he pulled her close again. "Wish we weren't saying goodbye."

"Soon enough we won't have to say it again," she said quietly. "Until then we should be happy with the progress we've made—and that we'll be seeing her more often."

"You don't sound like you believe it."

"I'm trying to convince myself as much as I am you."

He winked as they got to the platform. When Alma looked up from where she sat with Isaac and Jesse, he sighed. "I still ain't convinced."

"Me either." Jane took a shaky breath when the train whistle blew. Across the platform, she spotted Leanne and Tom. "I think we'll be seeing more of Leanne, too."

"Sure seems that way."

She glanced up at him. "Are you ever going to tell the truth about them?"

"Don't know. I used to say never, but you sure changed a lot of my nevers."

With a giggle, she elbowed him in the ribs before stepping forward when Alma rose. As Alma approached and opened her arms, Jane gladly accepted the hug. "I'm going to miss you, Alma. But we'll come see you next month, and then you'll come home again for Thanksgiving."

Alma hugged her back. "Bye."

Tears in her eyes, Jane pulled back. "Goodbye." She stepped aside to let Cole have his turn. After she'd wiped at her tears, she moved closer to Leanne and Tom.

Leanne and Tom had separated from their close conversation, so as soon as she was in range, Leanne wrapped Jane in a tight hug. "We'll see you in a month. Don't worry about a thing. I'll keep up my visits with Alma and send you so many letters you won't have time to miss me."

"Not true. I miss you already." Jane squeezed Leanne's hands when they parted. "You take care of yourself."

"You do the same." Leanne leaned closer. "And take care of these boys, too. They really are helpless."

Jane nodded and glanced Tommy's direction. "I'm sure we'll manage."

After another hug, they parted as Cole and Alma walked up. The rest of the departure was rushed as the conductor called final boarding. A last round of hugs went by fast until it was just Cole, Jane and Tom on the platform. Jane clasped both men's hands tightly as the train's brakes hissed in release and the train jerked into motion.

Once Leanne was out of sight, Tom excused himself. Jane sighed and wrapped her arm around Cole's waist. "I think he's going to be grumpy for a few days."

"At least."

"Hey, Jane!" Norman's gruff voice called from behind them.

"Let me see what Norman needs." Jane bumped her hip with Cole's. "Then perhaps we can get home and finish that conversation."

"Oh?" Cole's frown was wiped away with a bright grin.

With a wink, she darted away to the office. "What did you need, Norman?"

"Telegram came for you." Norman held out the paper, a big grin on his lined features. "Thought you'd wanna see it right away."

Jane took the paper and read it over. With every line from Cutler, he eyes grew wide and her pulse raced. "Oh! Oh, goodness. Norman, thank you."

"What?" Norman straightened. "I didn't do nothing but give you the telegram."

"It was enough!" Jane felt light as air when she ran from the office. Without ceremony, she raced up to Cole and threw her arms around him, kissing him deeply.

He chuckled when she finally released him. "Well. I thought you was waiting until we got back home for that."

"I couldn't resist."

He wrapped his arms tight around her when she pressed into him. His brow quirked. "What's that you got?"

"You."

"No. That, there in your hand."

With a wink, she grinned. "Oh, that's definitely still you."

He groaned at her teasing. "I can tell, but I meant your other hand. That paper."

"Oh, this? This is hope." At his furrowed brow, she pulled back and handed him the paper. "Go ahead. See for yourself."

He read the paper quietly. She didn't need to read it again, she already had it memorized. Cutler said all but three investors were on board. Based on the numbers, they'd have more than enough for even her grandest plans for the inn.

Cole shook his head. "You can't be serious."

"Looks pretty serious to me."

His head snapped up, and his grin grew. With a loud whoop, he wrapped his arms around her and spun her around.

Laughing, she wrapped her arms around his neck and met his kiss with equal enthusiasm. Quickly getting lost in the kiss, she clung to him until they finally parted breathless. "It's more than I'd hoped for."

"More than I expected."

"We can do everything we'd hoped to with our grandest plans, Cole. Three floors. A stage, more staff, all of it. We can do it all."

"Not gonna have to scrimp, neither. Only the best."

"We'll have to tell Mr. Hamm. He's got a lot of work ahead of him."

"Can we wait to tell him?" Cole grinned. "At least a few hours?"

"But why?" She widened her eyes in mock innocence. "Whatever would you want to wait for?"

"I'm feeling like celebrating."

"Right here?"

"Nah. I think this time we'd better be behind closed doors."

"Oh?"

"Yeah. If you think you can handle it."
"I think I'm handling it right now."
"You don't play fair."

Yesterday is but a dream,
tomorrow but a vision.
But today well lived makes every yesterday
a dream of happiness,
and every tomorrow a vision of hope.
—Sanksrit Proverb

Jane leaned over the plans. That afternoon they'd signed papers to purchase the tailor shop next to the Inn, as well as the two buildings behind.

She had another idea she'd been stewing on for some time but wasn't sure she could make happen. Soon she'd know, for she'd invited the subject of her query over for tea.

"Jane?" Cora stepped into the saloon, glancing around the building uneasily. To be honest, she couldn't remember a time when Cora had been inside, with the exception of the times they'd used it as a hospital.

"Cora, thank you so much for coming." Jane hugged her friend, gesturing to the table next to the one with the plans laid out. "Can I get you a drink? Tea? Perhaps coffee?"

"Tea would be lovely, thank you."

"I'll be right back." She hustled to the storeroom to get a tray together with tea and a few cookies.

Cole stepped into the room. "See you got Cora to come in. Think she'll go for it?"

"I haven't the slightest idea. It'll take some convincing, though not as much as you're going to have to use." Jane accepted his kiss easily before turning back to her tray. "Are you ready for the town council meeting?"

"It's in three weeks, Jane." Cole almost groaned.

"It's best to be prepared, especially since neither Tom nor I are going to put words in your mouth. You want a casino; you tell them why it's good for the town."

"Nag."

"Ass." She bumped his hip on her way out to the bar. At the table, she got everything set. Rather than comment on Cora's nervous fidgets, she set out the small spread.

"I have to say, I can't imagine what you wanted to discuss, that had to be discussed here." Cora took her teacup as though desperate for something to keep her hands busy.

"Well, you are already doing a wonderful thing by offering us a discount for our visitors to eat at your place." Jane remained calm. She took a small sip of tea. "With the new hotel, we were hoping for more."

"Don't know I can give you a bigger discount."

"No, I don't expect that." Jane set down her cup to face Cora proper. "We want to have a restaurant inside the new hotel. It would be easier to offer things like meals in rooms, tea service, and the like with a restaurant on property."

"Oh." Cora's features fell. "So, you wouldn't be using my services any longer?"

"On the contrary. I was hoping you would run the restaurant. Your meals are well loved by all, and I'd hate to have to search for a woman as good at cooking and business such as yourself."

Cora sat in silence for several long minutes. "I couldn't run both a proper restaurant, and the mercantile and my restaurant there."

"No, I don't expect you could." Jane set her hand on Cora's gently.

"What are you saying?"

"You've talked of selling the mercantile. I thought this would be an opportunity for you."

"The store was Kelly's. I've kept it running for—"

"I know, it's a difficult decision, and I don't expect an answer today. I wanted to offer you the chance. A good reason to perhaps take that step. You and your boys could have your own place, and you could decide what you got in your kitchen. Rather than a single stove, stuck in the back of the store like you have now."

Cora still sat wide-eyed, her teacup half to her mouth.

"Let me show you what I'm thinking." Jane pulled Cora's cup free of her weak clasp to set on the table. She helped her friend to her feet, guiding her to the next table. "Here is the lobby of the Inn. You'll see we have tables here for seating. Here is the counter for check-in. Then behind that wall…"

Cora followed Jane's gesture toward the bar. "Where the tailor shop is?"

"Yes. That will be the kitchen." Jane pointed at the spot on the plans. "We're using the entire footprint of the tailor's main floor for the kitchen."

"That's—that's a lot of space."

"Quite a bit more than you're working with at the mercantile. You could have one or two stoves, or ovens, whatever you need. Mr. Hamm said there's already a cellar, but it isn't very large so we could make it bigger for your dairy and whatever else you need kept cool."

"Oh, Jane." Cora sank back into her chair.

Jane took the seat beside her. "I told you; I don't expect an answer today. We would work out the details for what your profits would be with Nicholas. I'll be fair as I can while still getting a little profit from the venture."

"It's all very generous anyhow, I just…"

"It would be leaving another piece of Kelly behind." Jane scooted closer to wrap an arm around her friend. She understood what a difficult decision Cora faced. She'd loved Kelly a great deal by all accounts. Before Jane and Cole, Cora and Kelly had been the most scandalous couple in town once upon a time.

"We've been in the mercantile for so long. I don't know that I'd know how to sell it."

"I know. It's an immensely difficult decision. I only knew Kelly a few months, but it was clear how much you both loved each other, and he loved his boys."

Cora sniffled. "I've talked about it, but it hasn't been a real possibility before. I mean, not really. I would have had to start all over."

"I'm hoping this way you won't. You'll have time to find a buyer for the store, and we'll furnish the kitchen with no expense at your hands, which would leave you free to find a small home for you and your boys with your profits."

"I don't know what to do."

Jane patted Cora's hand. "Again, I don't expect an answer today. I have months before this hotel is anywhere near completion. I only wanted to make the offer, so you knew it was there."

"I appreciate that. I have to talk it over with the boys. I know Arthur didn't plan on running the place, but Isaac might have designs on it. Plus, they grew up there."

Jane handed her a napkin to dab her tears. "This was a very sudden offer. Take your time and think on it. I won't look elsewhere for some time, likely after the first of the year. You've got a few months to think it over."

"Thank you." Cora hugged her fiercely.

"No thanks needed. The good Lord knows I couldn't be the cook."

Cora laughed heartily at that. "No, certainly not."

"Not unless I found many visitors willing to eat burnt eggs and uncooked biscuits."

"Don't forget the fire you set attempting soup."

"I never knew you could set fire to water." Jane laughed along with Cora. "Good thing I can handle a tea kettle. I would quite upset if I couldn't make my own tea."

"That's still boiling water, so I'm surprised."

"Ah, but it's not boiling water with the intent of cooking anything. I believe that's the difference."

"Fair enough." More relaxed now, Cora took a cookie from the plate.

With the difficult part of the discussion passed, the rest of their shared tea passed in pleasant conversation. By the time Cora left, some of the regular crowd filtered into the saloon for their drinks.

Jane cleaned up her mess. With the plans returned to their place in the storeroom and nothing else to do, she slipped from the saloon into the cool afternoon air.

Tom waved from a few buildings down. He jogged up, a smile bright across his features. "You look in a good mood."

"I am. I asked Cora if she'd like to run our restaurant."

"And?"

"I think she might. The biggest hurdle to overcome is the need to sell the mercantile that is a link to Kelly, and where her children were raised."

"Tough sell." He laced her hand through his arm. "Are you certain she'll agree?"

"Not completely. However, I think she's intrigued by the idea of being able to build the kitchen how she would like it." Jane's free hand settled on her stomach as it fluttered with excitement.

Tommy, not one to miss a trick, took notice. "Are you feeling well?"

"I just finished some tea. This was nothing more than excitement. Our grandest plans realized."

"It'll be good for the town. Even more than Mike's. If Cole manages to convince the town to allow for gambling, it'll be even better."

"The draw of our hot spring will get us patrons from Michael's health resort. If only we had a small claim that yielded smidgens of gold, we could advertise a real chance to mine without encroaching on a claim."

"Look at you." Tom chuckled. "Want me to keep an ear out for any claims light on gold that the Daugherty's wouldn't be interested in?"

"Let's wait until the investments prove true and we've spent all we plan to. If there's money in the coffers, we can look."

"Good plan. How's Cole coming with his proposal for the Council?"

"He's procrastinating. Even though I've told him Edward Young's statement that 'procrastination is the thief of time'. He feels as though he has all the time in the world."

"He has three weeks."

"Precisely what I reminded him of a few hours ago. Has he shown you anything he's come up with?"

"No. You?"

"No." She smirked. "He'll figure something out last minute. It'll be brilliant, and I'll hate him for it."

"At least you're prepared for the inevitable."

"Doesn't mean I'll like it any better when it happens."

He slowed their pace when they crossed the railroad tracks. "How are you holding up?"

She frowned at his new tone. Concern had made his voice heavy. "Must we?"

"I'm your brother. I'm allowed to worry."

She exhaled her frustration. He didn't deserve it. She knew he was worried still. "Some nights are worse than others. I still have some difficulty being at work by myself. The library is…used to be my sanctuary."

"I thought Cole was."

"He is. Which has been a big help. We both still struggle. It hasn't been that long, after all. I do best when I have plenty to keep me busy. I've asked Katherine to handle the library more often while I deal with it. She understands."

"In other words, you're coping."

"A little more every day. It's better knowing—knowing Petey's pigs were well fed."

"Better for all of us." He cleared his throat. "I'll pester you no longer on the subject for today."

"Thank you." She cast a sideways glance his way. "Have you heard from Leanne?"

In a rare occurrence, Tom's cheeks grew ruddy. He adjusted his hat, staring off toward town. "Haven't you?"

"Of course I have, but I'm not the one sweet on her."

"I'm a little too old to be getting sweet on anyone."

"Pshaw. You are."

"Knock it off, Lou."

"Oh no. This is too much fun." She laughed when he took off toward town. "You wait, Thomas Eugene. I'm not letting you off that easy."

He took off running.

The chase was on.

She pursued him all the way back to town, teasing him the whole way.

*A wave of panic passed over the vessel,
and these rough and hardy men,
who feared no mortal foe,
shook with terror
at the shadows of their own minds.
-Sir Arthur Conan Doyle*

Silence fell over the saloon for the first time in two days. Cole straightened in the sudden quiet, not surprised when Jane emerged from the storeroom.

Tea in hand, she approached the bar. "Does that mean it's time for lunch, or he's done?"

"Maybe both." Cole winked at her. "I'm sure we'll know soon. Hammy won't keep his Lady Jane waiting."

"Oh, stop that." Despite her protest, Jane flushed at the comment. "He's a good, kind soul. He doesn't need your teasing. He has everyone else's."

"Not teasing. The old coot adores you. Can't blame him for it, neither."

"Flattery will get you nowhere, Mr. Mitchell."

"Oh, I think it might." He leaned over the counter, encouraged by her smile. "You've been in too good a mood lately to deny me."

"Your ego is getting far too big. Perhaps you need to be put in check." In the days since their good news, her mood had improved enough he didn't worry about her as much.

Nights were still rough, but they were working through it all. It was good to have things looking up as much as they were. It was helping them get past the rough year they'd gone through.

Moments before he managed to capture her lips, a throat cleared near them.

Jane turned on her brightest smile, turning toward the man that had interrupted. "Mr. Hamm. Please, have a seat. Would you like a beer?"

"Wouldn't ever say no to a beer, Lady Jane." Hammy hopped onto a stool. "Finished knocking down the tailors."

"We were hoping that was what the end of the clatter was." Jane set his beer before him. She didn't move away, taking up position comfortably close to Cole.

Not quite satisfied, he moved behind her so he had her in his arms. He nodded to the man. "You work fast when you put your mind to something. Makes me wonder at how long that blasted theater is taking."

"That ain't me. Mrs. Daugherty is fussing over the plans. Keeps changing how big she wants it. Can't rightly work if I don't know what I'm making." Hammy slurped his beer. "Thinking we can start on the two other buildings next week."

Cole's brow furrowed. There were two days left in the week. Both buildings could be down if they put their minds to it. "Next week?"

"Reverend has some repairs he needs done on the church. Would like 'em done by Sunday. Hope ya don't mind since we got some time on your stuff." Hammy wiped the foam from his lip with the sleeve of his shirt.

"Of course not. We certainly aren't your only clients." Jane patted his hand. "You should think about hiring some help, Mr. Hamm. With the town growing like it is, you've got quite a bit on your plate."

"Don't mind the work, none."

"Perhaps, but you're one man, Gilbert." Jane hardly used the man's Christian name, but it had the effect of getting his full attention. "Any man can overwork himself, and I don't want to see you overextending yourself. I wouldn't want you to get sick."

Hammy flushed again under her kindness. "I'll think about it."

"Good." Jane tilted her head to look up at Cole. "We're in no rush on the buildings. We're waiting on the remaining funds to come in so we can truly start construction."

Cole tilted his head in agreement. "She's right. We got time. It's good to see some progress, even if it is only destroying a building."

"And that's the easy part. The rebuilding like ya want is gonna take some doing." Hammy finished off his beer. "Gonna head to the church and see what the Rev wants done."

"Would you tell Mark I've received the books he was wanting? I won't be seeing him until Sunday, we are far too busy for visiting right now." Jane ducked out from under Cole's arms to give the man a hug. "We'll see you this evening."

"Will do." Hammy fumbled his hat back on his head.

Cole shook his head, chuckling as the man left. "You're going to flatter that man into an early grave. He don't need to worry about overworking they way you work him over."

"The man needs flattery. He hasn't gotten nearly enough in his life. You, on the other hand, receive far too much."

"I do, do I?"

At his stalking approach, her eyes widened. She took a step back, then another. "You'd better behave, Mr. Mitchell."

"Or what?"

"Or I'll—"

"Jane!" Kat's voice raced into the saloon, a panicked squeak to it. She flew in moments later, her red hair in a tizzy to match hers.

Jane froze at her friend's approach. "Katherine?"

Cole's nerves tautened at the clear worry on the red heads features. "Kathy? What is it?"

"This just came for you. I thought you'd want to see it right away." Kat held out a telegram.

Jane took the telegram, reading quick. "Oh no. Oh, dear."

"What?" Cole snatched the telegram from her outstretched hand. It was from Cutler.

Just got word. Jay Cooke is folding. I fear more to follow. My funds are secure, but you'd best check other investors. Best, T.R. Cutler

Cole stared at the telegram, unable to fully take it in. Jay Cooke Bank, going under? He feared more to follow. What did this mean for them? How much would they lose?

He registered Jane pacing near him, words seemed to have failed her as well. Kathy stared at them both, wringing her hands.

Kathy broke the silence first. "What's this mean?"

"It means we were likely premature in moving forward." Jane paused her pacing, wringing her hands. "If it's true, a hotel might not even be needed, the whole country could suffer, including this town."

Cole set down the telegram, unwilling to stare at the words any longer. "We need to talk to Nick, find out if we've got binding contracts with them investors."

"Binding contracts won't mean anything if the banks fold. They won't be able to get their money, much less use it—not that they would use it." Jane had a point. "As for the buildings we just bought, one of which we've leveled…"

"We made them binding ourselves," Cole finished.

Kathy sank into a chair. "I should tell mother. If she doesn't already know, that is."

"If you have anything in the bank here, I'd pull it all before Jacobs gets word and shuts his doors." Jane rubbed a hand across her forehead. "Fortunately, I haven't used the bank since the previous owner turned out to be a snake that easily caved to Jackson Krenshaw."

Cole grasped her shoulders to stop her pacing. His nerves were bad enough without Jane panicking too. He tried to put some conviction in his words. "We'll get it figured. No matter what we get."

"Maybe it won't be so bad." Jane's hands wrung. There was little surety in her tone. "Maybe it'll stop there. It won't happen as I've feared for a while. Oh, I shouldn't have stopped worrying when it took this long to happen."

Cole let out a laugh at those words. "It's not anything you could have stopped, you know."

"Maybe I could have." A smile twitched her lips. "I'm a powerful woman, after all."

"You sure are, but not that powerful."

Kathy rose. "I'll be at the office. I imagine you'll have some telegrams to send soon."

"Us or Nick, or both." Jane squeezed her friend's hand. "Be careful what you say and who you tell. We don't need the town in a panic yet. Not until it's well-earned."

"Which I'm afraid will be sooner rather than later." Kat hugged Jane quick, then surprised Cole with one as well. "You two will come out all right. I know it. You've suffered too much this year. Something's going to go right."

"Your lips to God's ears." Jane leaned against Cole. A deep sigh sprouted from her lips. "We should get to work. Go see Nicholas and try to get ahead of this."

"Yeah."

Neither of them moved. They both stood staring at the door Kat had just left by. One by one, Jane's plans flashed through Cole's mind.

Many grandiose ideas that could be pulled back, and other necessities. He supposed they didn't need the plumbing since perhaps the town wouldn't be getting it after this news. That would save a lot of money.

"I can practically hear you running numbers in that head of yours." She squeezed him around the waist. "You're already tossing out the plumbing aren't you?"

"First to go."

"I was looking forward to that." Jane rubbed her nose and made a surreptitious dab at her eye. "Stop calculating. We don't know how bad it is. We can't know. We have to wait for the fallout."

"I hate waiting."

"Me, too."

Silence fell between them again. They both continued their silent vigil of the town outside the door as if evidence of the steam engine that had bowled them over would show in the people milling around outside.

After a time, a familiar figure jogged toward them. Larger and larger until Tom burst through the doors, breathless. "Jane. I just got word from a contact—"

"Jay Cooke is folding," Jane and Cole said at the same time.

"Oh." Tom straightened. "You heard."

"Cutler sent us a message." Cole kissed the top of Jane's head. "We're trying not to panic."

"Want me to talk to Nick?" Tom moved closer.

"No, that'll be our job." Jane sighed again. "Now that you're here to watch the place, we'll go meet with him. We need to get on top of this before everything falls apart. There's still some hope. I hope."

"There's always hope." Tom set his hand on her shoulder. "Don't you worry. One way or another, it'll work out. We gotta believe. You've got a good plan."

"Good plans won't save the investor's funds."

"But it will save the investor's ideas of you. Your plan and acumen got them on board." Tom nodded to her, then Cole. "Go talk to your lawyer. I'll watch the place."

"Thank you." Jane gave her brother a half-hug. Not once did her arm leave Cole's waist.

He walked with her out of the Inn, still thinking hard on their predicament. "Casino's our best bet. Even broke men'll gamble in hopes of riches."

"Then you'd best get to work on your speech."

Obstacles cannot crush me;
every obstacle yields to stern resolve.
—Leonardo da Vinci

The worst came to pass.

As Jane had feared for months, the economy collapsed.

Eight days before, the stock market completely closed. Shut down. Nothing moving, done. The latest news didn't contain any firm predictions on when business would resume.

Jane wondered how long it would be before the investors themselves backed off. They'd been stupid to start before all the money had come in. As it stood, they'd received funds from Cutler and one other investor, enough to buy the surrounding buildings and begin work.

Of course, all that work involved was tearing down two of the four buildings they'd bought. The old tailor shop next to the Inn was already gone. When Hammy was put to a job, he worked fast.

Jane picked at a splinter in the railing. Nerves left every muscle taut. Cole wasn't much better. The man was good enough with numbers to understand what the closing of the market meant. Everyone in town was on pins and needles, the bank had closed its doors with the stock market, which was fortuitous for the owner in the ensuing panic. Everyone with money in the bank now sat broke, all of their savings gone with little more than a whimper.

The townspeople had tried to break into the bank only to find it empty. Jacobs had cleaned out and skipped town before anyone had a chance to try to get their funds.

The mines themselves sat silent. A breathless anticipation of when life would return to normal. Jane could only hope it would be soon. If it didn't, their plans would mean little to a future where nothing was moving.

Down the street two of Jane's brothers walked toward the Inn, their heads together in conversation. Tommy had a handful of papers in hand, and Nick carried his attaché. Neither of them looked particularly happy, not that Nick's expression was every truly readable.

Jane backed away from the hitching post at their approach. She slipped inside the Inn where she figured they were heading anyway. After she caught Cole's eye, she moved to a back table. The current standstill in town meant even the saloon was quiet, so there wasn't much effort in finding privacy.

"What is it?" Cole took the seat beside her.

"Thomas and Nicholas are about to walk in here with what could very well be bad news. Neither of them appears all too happy." She set her hand on his. "We have to hope it isn't all bad."

"It won't be." Cole laced his fingers through hers. "They're smart men. Maybe they did like you did."

"Even if they didn't invest in the market, there could still be problems. Look what Jacobs did at the bank in town. Took off with whatever was still inside." She pursed her lips. "Not certain if they would still want to invest in a hotel with the economy like this, either."

"Here they come. It won't be all bad." Cole sounded surer than Jane felt.

"Jane. Cole." Nick sat without waiting for acknowledgement. He set his attaché on the table. "Thomas and I just got back from the depot. We have all the responses to your queries to the investors back already."

"How bad is it?" Jane clenched Cole's hand, willing all her nerves into the tight grasp instead of the waver of her voice. "Are we done for?"

"Not entirely, but we aren't as well off as we were." Tommy set down the telegrams in the middle of the table. "Obviously we know Cutler is still in. Between his gratitude, and the fact he already sent us money, he's still in."

"Thankfully. We wouldn't be able to return money we've already spent." Jane sighed. There wasn't but a hundred dollars left after their purchase of the surrounding buildings, but Hammy hadn't been concerned about getting paid up front, so they still owed him.

"Half of the investors lost big and can't put up the funds they'd promised." Nick's goatee twitched. "Honestly, I expected more of them to say the same."

"Another four men aren't ready to invest in anything right now." Tommy leaned on the table. "That leaves Cutler, with his sizable investment, of which we've only received half of. He's assured us the rest will be here next month."

"And?" Cole practically vibrated next to her. He hated delays as much as she did.

"And three other investors are still in. Unfortunately, two out of the three were on the smaller end of the investment scale." Tommy furrowed his brows.

"Here's how much you have to work with now." Nick pulled a paper out of his case and pushed it across the table to them.

Jane's heart sank at the number as all her plans flew away with the lessened investment numbers. The plumbing was certainly out, as was the restaurant. It no longer mattered if Cora was willing to sell. They'd be lucky to be able to afford to upgrade the building they currently occupied.

She ran her finger over the number. "We need to tell Mr. Hamm to not tear down the remaining two buildings. We'll have to sell them. Maybe we should consider selling the hot springs to Michael, too. It's more in keeping with his Health Resort concept."

"We can't sell the hot springs. It'll be good income," Cole protested.

"We don't have the funds for what we want to do. Not even close. At best, we'll be able to fix this building up nicer. We'll have to keep the whores, too."

Cole shook his head. "I think we can do more."

"Really?" Jane pulled the paper closer. "How?"

"We can add the kitchen since we already tore down the tailors. We can fancy up the rooms, add gambling tables, and close in upstairs to add more rooms. If we add the gambling, we wouldn't need to keep the whores more than a year or two. Think we can keep the old cooper shop behind us for us to live in, too."

Jane smiled as Cole managed to find more in the numbers before them than she had. "Do you really think we can accomplish all of that on this?"

"Sure. If we ain't tearing down the structure, Hammy won't charge us near as much to fix it up right." Cole tapped the paper. "The old cooper shop would be big enough for us, Sally, Alma, the baby, and even for Jesse to stay now and then. Should just need a couple walls and a good cleaning."

Across the table, Tom's brow remained furrowed. He sat unusually silent, an intensity to his dark look at the numbers. Abruptly, he pushed to his feet and strode to the bar.

Jane rose to follow. She set her hand on his arm. He didn't react, so she squeezed his arm. "Thomas?"

"Just thinking." His answer was abrupt, even harsh.

"And what, pray tell, were you thinking?" She leaned back on the bar, her gaze on the table where Cole and Nick resumed their discussion. "We'll be fine, Thomas. It isn't my grandest dreams for the hotel, but it will suffice for now. The economy likely won't be as such that it'll allow for a need for a hotel."

"This town needs more than a gussied up saloon."

"It will be more. We'll have our restaurant, more rooms, and the casino. It's better than we've got. The Hangman's Inn will be better in the end for it. Maybe in a few years when the economy improves we can expand again as we wanted."

"You're awful calm for a woman that just lost thousands of dollars."

"You can't lose money you never had. Would I have preferred this never happened and we had every penny we'd been promised? Without a doubt. Would I have preferred we hadn't been set for those grand plans so it would be easier to accept a lesser plan?" She sighed deeply. "Definitely."

"Those grand plans are perfect for this town. The crisis will pass, and the town will keep growing. Colorado is heading for statehood. I'll bet anything the Daugherty's aren't giving up their plans for the theater and dress shop. We'll need another hotel to accommodate for their plans."

"We'll have one. Just fewer rooms than we'd hoped." Jane wrapped her arm through his, leaning her cheek on his shoulder. "Cole is calm about this, so I have to imagine he's already got the numbers set in his head. It's going to be fine."

"I should probably let Hammy know he won't be tearing down any more buildings." Tom brushed her off, storming outside in a huff.

Jane frowned at his departing back.

"What was that?" Cole walked up beside her.

"I think he's more upset than we are."

"You're plenty upset." Cole kissed her temple. "But we'll figure it. We always do. We managed after the fire, we'll manage on these funds."

"I'm much calmer than I would be because you're calm." She hugged him tight, her cheek on his chest. "Plus, there's also that other thing."

"What other thing?"

"The worst has already happened. Anything now is just a stumbling block." She withdrew from the hug to meet his gaze. "After the hell we've been through the past few months, what is this? Funds that weren't ours anyway. A change in a dream."

"We're getting used to those." He tapped her nose. "Between the strays you keep taking in and that baby."

"We have had quite the summer." She laughed, nipping at his finger when he tried to tap her nose again. "Do you think you can talk Thomas down? He didn't appear to care for my reassurances."

"I'll try. Ain't making no promises." Cole stole a kiss before he slepped away.

Jane frowned when she realized Nick still sat at the table. "Nicholas?"

"I had something else to say. I wasn't so sure Cole would appreciate it." Nick rose from the table. By the time Jane had slipped behind the bar and poured him a bourbon, he'd taken a seat on a stool.

"Out with it." Jane leaned on the bar. "Or I will make it far worse in my head."

"It's nothing bad, just not a gesture I was sure Cole would appreciate considering the source. Mrs. Daugherty sent a telegram a couple of days ago."

Jane straightened. "Lillian Daugherty? What on earth would Kat's mother want with you, Mr. Young?"

He chuckled. "It's not me she wanted something with. She just let me know that with their vested interest in the town, she'd been keeping a close eye since the stock market closed. She continues to have high hopes for this town, and grand plans."

"She always has grand plans. Did she mention the library?"

"Not in this missive." Nick pursed his lips. "I guess Kat has been keeping her informed on your status as well as others in the town. She offered, should the worst happen, to add to your coffers."

"Cole would not like to be beholden to Lillian."

"I figured."

"Besides, Lillian is like family to me. I wouldn't ever take money from family, not even her. We'll make do with what we have. Any improvement to our current state is better than nothing. Although I do hate that we need to keep the brothel running, even if only for a couple of years."

Nick's brow arched. "Are you really going to keep it? I thought that was off the table, period."

"It was. However, I had contingency plans in place for it to remain at every level of investment. We must be flexible in times like this." Jane shook her head. "No. Tell Lillian I appreciate the offer, but we have enough to make do. I'd rather a new library for the town than for her to invest in us. I don't want such a thing between us."

"Good. That means I can share some information with you off the legal record."

Jane eyed him in suspicion. If she wasn't mistaken, there was a wicked smirk hidden under that blasted goatee. "Nicholas? What are you up to?"

"I'm hoping word will get around, and perhaps the general morose state of the town will subside a bit. As I am not the Daugherty's lawyer, I'm not harming any attorney client privilege."

"If you want word to get around, Mr. Hamm is the one to tell, not I." She leaned closer, unable to stop her grin. "I'd still like to hear it myself, though."

"I heard Norman in the office going over the maps with a surveyor. Turns out the Daugherty's had more claims than they were mining."

"Really? Why?"

Nick paused, his glass half to his lips. His sharp gaze met hers. "Why do you think a person wouldn't mine all of them at once?"

Jane pondered for a minute. "If it were me, I'd not want more than I needed. It's their town so they would want to keep their miners employed to have the settlement grow. You mean Lillian and Henry Daugherty were being frugal?"

"They live rather well, so frugal might be pushing the boundaries of what they are." Nick rubbed his fingers along his goatee to smooth it out. "For their status and the amount of land they have available to mine? Yes. They were being frugal."

"Mines are only good as long as the gold or silver is there." Jane pursed her lips. "I've heard some of the miners that came from other places rave about how fair the work practice is here. They only work eight hours a day, they're paid fair wages. No one is pushing them to pull in ever more gold, only what's done on a good day."

"Not to mention the health care. Daugherty's have always taken care of those injured in the mines."

"I know. After the cave-in last year they were here in town seeing to the injured and their families."

"The Daugherty's have always been smart. With money and business. From what Katherine has said, Lillian got swept up in society for a time, but it happens to the best of us." Nick took a sip from the fresh glass she'd poured.

"Wonderful. Wait. You said there was a surveyor?"

"They're possibly going to expand into the next region to get more work for the miners. Seeing as gold is still worth something, they can sit on the silver until its value increases."

Jane smiled brightly. "More work for the miners is wonderful."

"And this is free knowledge. Two more ranchers have bought land. We'll start getting cattle in here next year."

"I've met Mrs. Edwards. She and her ward were her to buy a horse. Who's the other?"

"A pair of brothers, Mort and Marvin Keenan. Bought land right next to the Edwards. Good place for ranching, the grass is better near the join of the valley."

"Then we'll hope some ranchers are enticed by the land south of here as well."

"I think David is speaking with a friend of his. Could get us a third ranch."

"Excellent. That'll mean cowboys to use the gambling tables and whores." Jane couldn't deny the news stirred excitement despite the earlier blow of losing so many investors.

"I thought you might appreciate that." Nick adjusted his hat. "Now I should send a telegram to Mrs. Daugherty. If there's any news of any kind, I'll let you know."

"Thank you. I appreciate all you're doing for us. I hope it's not too big a conflict of interest for you, with the Sage Brush Hotel and all."

"Not at all. I'm silent partner there, and really, your success is our success. It's not going to be great news all around when word of the loss of investors gets around. That means outsiders are losing faith in the town."

"Which is why you want to get the word about the mine expansion out." Jane smiled.

"I'm sure word will get around one way or another." Nick winked.

"Of that, I have no doubt. Give my regards to Mr. Hamm."

"Will do."

I am only one, but I am one.
I can't do everything, but I can
do something.
—Edward Everett Hale

Jane followed Cole into the old cooper shop. The scent of fresh cut wood lingered in the building. Otherwise, the place sat clean and empty. At some point in the past few days Cole had come in to clean. Even the floor was free of sawdust.

She turned a full circle to take in the large front room. Free of the counters and shelves, the room was open and airy. The walls facing the cross streets were full of windows. "Lovely. The windows will make this a nice gathering space for us. A fitting living room, even if it is a bit public on Third Street such as it is."

"I thought so. When we save up for a piano, it can fit over here. The stove'll go in that corner to help keep it warm in winter. I had Hammy take out the counters and such. Sally did a good job cleaning it up for you." Cole waved her to the door between the front and back of the building. "Come on. I'll show you where we'll put our room."

She took the hand he offered, following him through the door into the narrow hall. When he paused halfway down, she cast a curious glance his way.

He tapped the door beside him. "Used to be a storage closet. Gonna make it into our bathroom."

"We had to lessen all of our plans, and yet you still included a place for us to share private baths? You are a true boor."

"You bet I am." He winked and pulled her close. "Got a problem with that?"

"Not a one." She yelped when he tugged her suddenly to head further down the hall. When he stopped in a room, she glanced around. "Yes?"

"This'll be our room. It's big enough, already got a stove."

"Yes, a stove for cooking, not heating. This was the Donner's kitchen!"

"Figured you had no use for a kitchen anyhow. It's a big enough space for us. Can use the pantry as a closet."

"Well, you're correct in that I don't need a kitchen. The only thing worse than my singing is my cooking." She opened her mouth to say more, but the front door banged open before she could.

"Jane! Cole!" Nick's voice was unusually animated.

"What the devil?" Cole's brows pinched together. "Is your brother excited?"

"I wouldn't know. I can't say I've ever heard him excited before." She raced down the hall to find both Nick and Tom in the front room. The pair each wore shit-eating grins. "What in heavens name? Nick? You really do know how to smile!"

Nick chuckled. "Keep that up and you won't get your news."

"Aw, hell. Just tell them. If you don't, I will." Tom crossed the room to stand in front of Jane. His hands dropped on her shoulders with such enthusiasm her knees buckled. "I've told Hammy we're going to tear this down after all."

"What? We can't!" Jane set her hands on his wrists. "We don't have the funds."

"We do now." Tom grinned. "Got a new investor, or rather, an investment group."

"What?" Cole's jaw went slack. "When? How? Who? And most importantly—how much are we talking?"

"The 'who' is somewhat easily answered." Nick held up his attaché. "Is there somewhere we can sit?"

"I'll sit on the floor if you're serious." A small fear it was too good to be true kept her excitement in check. Hope still revved an excited flutter in her belly. "Are you?"

"You bet we are." Tommy stepped back only to plop on the floor. His legs crossed in front of him, he gestured to the floor. "Join me."

Jane dropped to the floor fast. Unable to fully curb her excitement, she wiggled on the spot. "Well? Tell us everything."

"A telegram arrived from the Armermann Investment Group." Nick joined them on the floor. He popped open his case. "They are also located in St. Louis."

"Really? Did Cutler speak to them? Have you looked into them, Thomas? Are they truly legit?" Jane twisted her hands together. "Why would they invest?"

"Would you stop, breathe, and listen?" Tom chuckled. "We're not sure if it was Cutler or maybe the Daugherty's. The Investment Group is very tight lipped about the whole situation."

"Wait." Jane's mind raced, a familiar tug from the black hole of memory drew her attention. "Armermann. Why does that sound familiar?"

Nick and Tom exchanged glances so fast, Jane thought she might have imagined it.

Tom shrugged. "Could be anything."

"What was that?" She pointed between them. "Do you know something about why I should know it? Why did you look at each other."

"I told you to stop, breathe, and listen. I mean it." Tom pointed a finger at her. "Armermann is a German name. Maybe Clara recognizes it as such. It doesn't matter anyhow, I did the research."

"Clara recognizes it?" Jane frowned. When Cole's hand settled on hers, she squeezed it. "Is this a relative? You know how I feel about that."

"We have no relatives named Armermann." Nick fixed a serious gaze on her. "As Thomas was saying, even though we've only had a day since the initial telegram arrived, we were able to get fast responses on the validity of the company. Everything is all clear financially and legally."

Jane relaxed at the reassurance.

Cole cleared his throat. "Still ain't said how much."

"Makes up the difference of what you lost, plus some extra." Nick withdrew papers from the attaché.

"What? That's so much," Jane protested. "From one source? Why would they—"

"Lou, stop." Tom glared her way. "Let Nick finish a sentence, would you?"

Nick held out the papers. "This is the benefit of getting funds from a group instead of an individual. I have everything here for you to go over."

Cole took the papers when Jane remained still. "You're sure they're legit?"

"Absolutely," Tom assured him.

Jane couldn't put aside the nagging feeling there was more to the group.

Nick spoke before she could question again, "Jane. Don't look a gift horse in the mouth."

"It's enough for all you wanted, Jane. Plumbing and all." Cole tapped her arm with the paperwork. "Nick's probably right. We should go about resuming our plans without second guessing this."

"Take it, Lou." Tom's words rang familiar, he'd said it to her on several occasions when he was the gifter. She could not imagine he had this sort of money, though. Thus such an idea didn't make sense.

She studied him a long minute, trying to find a crack in his story or demeanor. None came, so she nodded. "We'll go over the paperwork this afternoon, will that work? Or would you rather I sign blindly?"

"Never." Nick smiled brightly at her. "Go over it all. We'll meet for supper, and I'll answer any questions you have."

Jane allowed Cole to help her to her feet. "Sounds good."

"Oh." Tom snapped. "One more thing."

Jane stopped smoothing her skirts to meet Tom's gaze. "What?"

"The Daugherty's are here." Tom grinned. "Got off the train when I was at the depot checking the alcohol shipment.

Lil's all fired up about her own plans. Seems she wants to make our town better than, say, Colorado Springs."

"I know. A theater, a fancy dress shop, I've even heard rumors of her wooing a confectionary to come all the way here from Boston." Jane wrapped her arms around Cole's waist. "The rumors are flying far and fast these days in the wake of rumors of an expansion of their mines."

"Which have turned out to be true, shockingly enough." Nick winked her way. His joviality crinkled the corners of his eyes. "Norman already had a posting for mining positions up on the board outside the depot."

"Finally. Some hope for the whole town."

"Never thought it'd come from the Daugherty's," Cole muttered.

There is no law of progress.
Our future is in our own hands,
to make or to mar.
-William Ralph Inge

Cole stood in the empty saloon, the plans for the new Inn laid out before him. They had too many gaps to fill in. Jane refused to sit still for any of it.

Perhaps it was nerves. Fear that it would all fall apart again. Heaven knew he had the same worries. However, they'd received the bulk of funds from Armermann, and Hammy had already started on the new barn.

In next to no time he'd be ready to start on the structure itself. First in line was their apartment, seeing as it was on the back of the building.

The flurry of excitement had Jane running hither and tither, to where he didn't know. In the past weeks as she'd grown stronger, she still avoided the library frequently. Kat worked there more often than not. Jane only seemed to go when she'd have company. The colder the weather grew, the more she seemed to avoid it.

Tom emerged from his room upstairs. He was still strapping on his weapons as he walked along the balcony above.

"Tom. You seen Jane?"

"No. Figured she was with you. Then again, I just woke up." Tom quick-stepped down the stairs. "There a problem? Figured you'd both be taking advantage of the couple of hours before opening."

"She was down here. Disappeared when I went to get the plans so's we could figure out the apartment."

"You still don't have that figured out? All that space and you're leaving it blank?"

"Can't get her to sit still long enough to decide between ideas. Think she's nervous the investors will change their mind with all the railroads crumbling."

"Wouldn't worry about that. You've got most of your money. You're good to go." Tom paused next to the table. He pointed to a spot on the second level. "I don't need anything that big. I told you as much. What I've got now is more than enough. A place to hang my weapons and a wardrobe is all I've needed for a long time."

"Jane insisted you have a proper room. It'll be attached to our apartment with a locked door for your privacy, but so you're welcome to join us whenever you wish." Cole sighed. "About the only thing she's been clear on. No idea how many rooms she wants. I know this half is our room."

Tom quirked a brow. "Half the width of the hotel. Even much as you two like the bedroom, isn't that extreme?"

"Won't be the whole thing. Stairs will cut out part of it. It's not as deep as all that." Cole drew a few lines along the upper floor. "Alma there, and Sally there. Leftover space could be as much as two rooms if we wanted for company."

"Or any other kids that come along."

"Shut your trap. We got plenty."

"Tell that to your—" Tom looked around to be sure they were completely alone. Even with the place empty, he dropped his tone to finish, "Wife."

"She knows. I'm done. No more strays, and this baby is enough." His hand clenched convulsively. The pencil snapped in his hand. His track record with babies wasn't good. Anytime thought too hard, the fear struck.

Tom clamped a hand on Cole's shoulder. Blessedly, the man said nothing. Even if Cole suspected Tom knew about his deceased wife and child, the man never said a word. "You might change your mind."

"Alma, Sally, the baby, Jesse, and…"

"Cindy," Tom finished for him. "One of these days you and Kat will get that squared away. Don't think there's a person in town that doesn't suspect. That girl looks too much like you to deny."

"Until she knows, no one else will." Cole blew out a breath. "And Jane is like a second ma to Lizzie, so they visit often enough. That's a few too many kids for my liking."

"Pretty sure you like it more than you admit."

"Clamp it."

Tom laughed outright. "Fair enough. Question is—are you ready for tomorrow night? You've got to tell the town why we need a casino."

"Think so. Jane took a look at my notes. Said my points were strong." Cole didn't bother to cover his grin. "She seemed almost impressed, actually."

"I was." Jane's voice drifted over him moments before her hand slipped along his back. "What are you two troublemakers up to?"

"Cole's worrying over your apartment." Tom pointed to his room again. "It's too big."

"It is not. It's the same size as the room Cole and I currently occupy. To adjust the size would throw off the rest of the floor. We'd have to put rooms in odd configurations to fit around yours. Stop complaining and say 'thank you'."

"Thank you," Tom muttered.

Jane leaned over to see the lines Cole had drawn. "Do you think that's big enough for Alma?"

"It's bigger than she has at the school. Besides, the piano will be in the living quarters. She won't be up there a lot. Don't think Sally will, neither." He pointed to the space next to Sally's. "One room, or two?"

"Two. We'll also have the spare room downstairs next to the baby's for when Jesse comes. We should have two upstairs should ma and pa visit, along with James and Ida."

"You know we can put them in rooms in the hotel."

Jane's eyes flicked to the side to stare him down. "Do you really think once we have a true apartment and the baby here that Ma would allow us to keep her in the hotel?"

"She's got a point." Tom chuckled. "Guess the extra rooms are a good idea. Besides, you never now."

"Get the hell out of here, Tom." Cole sneered at his brother-in-law. "Don't need any more of your lip?"

"What is going on?" Jane straightened, pursing her lips.

"Been teasing him about you having more kids after the baby comes."

"Oh, heavens. I think our lot is enough. With the way this pregnancy has gone? I'd rather not do this again. I don't care to ever drink that tea again once this is passed." Jane stared her brother down. "Maybe you should talk to Leanne if you want more babies around here."

In a surprising turn, Tom darkened several shades of red before he turned on his heel to leave the Inn.

Jane didn't bother to keep her triumphant smirk hidden. "I knew that would get rid of him."

"Wicked woman." Cole tugged her close. "Glad you're finally talking about the plans."

"I don't want too much set in stone before the meeting tomorrow night. The entire plan depends a great deal on what the saloon area turns out like." Jane draped her arms over his shoulders. "However, I suppose planning our apartment won't do much harm."

"Thought you were afraid of it all falling apart again."

"I won't deny that fear is there. I'm more concerned about the hotel itself. Much depends on your eloquence and fortitude at tomorrow night's session."

"I'm gonna do my best."

"Of that I have no doubt." She looked back down at the plans. "Now. Are you sure these measurements are calculated properly? Our room looks awful large, and we have to plan for seating, a table for learning, Alma's piano, and a desk all in our living space."

"Hammy did the measurements. This gives us all this room for a private bathroom, with a stove inside it, plus a stove in our room."

"I was looking at furniture. Katherine got a new catalog in, and I was able to look through it before Cora arrived. The piano is more difficult to suggest, but I think I found a nice sofa and desk for the living space."

"You were at the depot? Looking at stuff for the apartment?"

"Yes." Jane shifted to study the first level of the apartment closer. "With the corral and barn, have we planned for a place to have a garden for Alma?"

"Behind the barn there's going to be a big space, even with the larger barn."

"You'll be able to do more with the horses. Will you breed now that we have the room?"

"One business venture at a time, woman."

She winked his way. "I thought you wanted me excited."

"Sure I did." He drew her close again. "Maybe not here, though. We still got whores to contend with, and the doors aren't closed."

"I do like the way you think. You're right, though. I'm expecting company."

"You are?"

"I am." She brushed her lips across hers. "Cora arrived while I was there. When I gave her the catalog, she said she'd come by to see me. Apparently, she's made a decision."

He eyed her quietly, trying to read her take on the news. "What do you think she means?"

"I'm hoping it means yes. I don't want to predict, though. I'm no spiritualist."

"You're not?" He grinned, pulling her close. "But you were a ghost once."

"Out of desperation, necessity." She flicked his forehead. "And not funny. I am the one that almost died."

"You did die." Cole's stomach turned at the memory. "Wait. I don't like talking about that."

"Neither do I." She claimed his lips in a kiss filled with so much heat, it purged the depressing thoughts straight away. When they broke apart, she sighed. "I shouldn't have done that."

"Not unless you planned on finishing," he agreed.

"I will—later." Her body pressed into his. "Before you ask, yes. That's a promise."

He groaned, which turned into a second when a knock came on the door. "You don't play fair."

"Trust me, it's not fair to me either." Jane turned toward the door. "Cora! Glad you could stop by. Can I get you anything to drink?"

"No, thank you." Cora's cheeks were flushed, likely from the compromising position she'd caught them in. "I can't stay long, gotta get the store open."

"Of course." Jane left his side to approach the woman. "I could walk with you, if you're in a rush."

"Oh, I don't know. I just…"

Jane took Cora's hands in hers. "If you aren't ready to give us a decision, I told you there's time."

"No. No. It's not easy, but the boys and I talked about it a lot the past few weeks. We all think it's time."

Cole was surprised to find he was holding his breath. What did she mean by that?

"Is that a yes?" Jane glanced back at Cole, a hopeful smile crossing her lips.

"Yes," Cora spit out the word fast. "I think it is. Now, I don't know how long it'll take me to sell the place."

"No worries about that. I'm sure my brothers could help you find a buyer. Oh, how exciting." Jane threaded Cora's arm through hers. "Come. We'll walk together, and you can start telling me all you'd like to have in your kitchen. We have plans to make, after all. Grand plans."

Cole chuckled as the pair left the Inn. No matter that he and Jane had plans of their own make, he was just glad to have one more obstacle out of the way. They wouldn't have to find a cook for the restaurant.

He glanced back at the plans. The saloon area drew his eye in particular. He definitely had to work on his argument for the council. The casino would bring it all together nicely. He couldn't have the Council banning what could be their biggest money-maker whether they had guests or not.

Nature cares nothing for logic, our human logic; she has her own, which we do not recognize and do not acknowledge until we are crushed under its wheel.
—Ivan Turgenev

"Very good, Sally." Jane couldn't help but be pleased with the progress Sally had made in such a short time.

"Really?" Sally set down her book. Wide eyes on Jane, she wiggled in her seat. "Did I really get it right?"

"You most certainly did. In the past few months you've shown great improvement. I'm proud of you."

A deep red flush filled Sally's cheeks. "I don't know about all that."

After three months living as their ward rather than a contracted prostitute, Sally's growth continually surprised Jane. While there were still flashes of impertinence, Sally had put forth great effort in growing. Still, bits of pains she'd gone through lingered in her self-doubt. Jane squeezed the girls' hand. "Take a compliment when it comes, Sally."

"That's what you keep telling me." Sally cleared her throat. "I should get to the Inn. You need anything before I go?"

"No. I'm all set, thank you. Oh, wait." Jane smiled knowing Sally would appreciate the task Jane was about to ask of her. "Would you run to the depot and see if there was any mail for me on today's train?"

Sally gathered her book to her chest. Pink lingered on her cheeks through her affirmative nod. "I sure wouldn't mind."

"I didn't think you would. Give my regards to Arthur while you're there." Jane chuckled softly as Sally darted from the building. In the past month the friendship between Sally and Arthur had turned into a sweet courtship involving sleigh rides and candy treats.

The door slapped close behind Sally, startling Jane out of her amusement. Familiar tingles of cold fear raced up her spine. She flew to her feet when her stomach twisted in panic. Quick as she could, she crossed the library and yanked open the door.

Despite the cold wind that blasted into the building now that the door sat open, Jane lodged the nearby chair firmly under the knob. If the nerves didn't have her jumpy as a jackrabbit she might have been embarrassed. As it stood, she still couldn't breathe if she got shut in the library alone.

She rubbed her arms against the cold air. In a rush, she threw on her shawl and drew close to the stove. She stoked the fire until it blazed warm again. If she remained on this side of the library she would be warm enough.

The sound of hammering filtered in over a whistle of wind. Jane peeked out the door in the direction of the Inn. The past three months had been a whirlwind. The offer from Armermann Investment Group had proved solid, and they'd signed the contract the very next day. Right after the signing they'd resumed with their initial plans.

Hammy began working immediately. First step had been to move the horse barn and paddock to where the cooper and ironsmith's shops had been. Soon as that was done, he'd begun on the new hotel. The work began from the back toward the front in hopes of keeping the saloon open to earn money as long as possible.

Among the amenities of the new hotel they'd planned for, Hammy had brought in a plumber to install pipes that would connect to the sewage system the town would build in the spring. The Hangman's Inn would have indoor plumbing before Mike's Sage Brush Health Resort and Spa. However, Jane and Cole had no designs to make the Inn a grand affair. Though it would be larger than it had been, and even larger than Mike's, she wanted The Hangman's Inn to be comfortable.

They'd continue to have a saloon, a larger one with a stage for entertainment and burlesque. The saloon would boast a casino with two private rooms for higher paying clientele.

Their private quarters would be much larger. Two levels with a large living space where they could gather with the children. Jane and Cole would have a large bedroom with a private bathroom. The baby would have its own room, as would Sally, Alma, and even a smaller room Jesse for when he stayed over. Cole had even suggested another room just in case she took in any more strays.

Tom would have his own quarters within the layout of their apartment, and have his own door into their place should he care to join them. There'd be a series of smaller rooms for the staff as well. The hotel would then have fifteen full rooms including smaller spaces as well as full suites.

Outside of the hotel, life had been just as crazy. The pregnancy continued to give her issues, and she'd grown rather large much faster than she'd expected. Just that morning Cole had needed to reassure her again that her size didn't bother him.

Jane settled back in her chair, letting her hands rest on her belly. A smile tugged her lips as she remembered every detail of Cole's rather enthusiastic reassurances. The assurances had continued on so long they'd both almost been late to begin their day.

Jane shook her head to clear the thoughts enough to focus on the now. The memories helped keep her warm enough that she hardly noticed the breeze from the door. She grabbed the books she'd set aside at Sally's arrival.

She rose to put them away, and as she slid one into place a fresh gust of cold air flew through the room. The book to the right of the one she'd just put away caught her eye. *Dangerous Liaisons* remained in its place on the shelf. Though tempted many times, she'd refused to get rid of a book because of her own seemingly unconquerable issues.

Taking a bracing breath, she clutched the remainder of the books to her chest. She circled back to the stove to warm up again. Before she moved on, she poured herself another cup of tea. The warmth coursed through her and restored her strength. She returned to shelving the books in hand.

Cole's voice rang through the empty building. "What the hell are you doing?"

Jane pushed the book she held into place on the shelf. "Well, I don't know, Cole. What does it look like I'm doing? I'm working. This is part of my job, putting books away."

"That ain't what I mean. Are you trying to get yourself sick? It ain't good for the baby." Cole grabbed the chair and yanked it out from under the door handle.

"Don't!" The squeak in her voice caught her off-guard. Panic snaked along her spine so fast, her hand shook when she lifted it to try to cover the tremor in her voice. "I'm fine. I have the fire going strong and my tea. I-I don't like the door closed."

"It's closed when I come by every day."

She set the final book on the shelf, then realized it left her with nothing else to do but face him. Embarrassment and fear collided in an ugly tangle in her gut. "Sally is always here when you come by."

"You saying the rest of the day you sit around with this open?"

"I prefer it open."

"It's the middle of winter!"

"I prefer it open," she repeated quietly. She didn't dare admit how utterly suffocated she felt every time the door clicked shut. Outside of the library she'd done so well, managed to work through her fears and pain with Cole by her side. She hated how it still frightened her in this place that had once been a sanctuary.

"Thought you didn't want to be scared no more."

"Some things aren't so easy to shake."

The door clicked shut. Cole took it a step further by turning the key.

Jane's throat closed shut, air left her lungs.

"You come here every day and let it scare you."

"Cole…" The word barely made it past her lips. Her hands shook so violently she grabbed her skirts to try to still them.

He walked to the window, drawing closed the shutters. The light drained from the room as they shut.

"Stop."

"Not yet." He crossed the room toward her.

She flinched when he brushed aside a lock of hair with his fingers. Her eyes fell shut, air stubbornly refusing to return to her lungs. The betraying lump in her throat refused to budge an inch.

"You told me this place was safe. You wanted me to help make it safe."

"I—we—" She backed away from him until she hit the shelves. The impact startled a shriek out of her. At least the lump was gone from her throat. "I thought it was. Logic says it should be."

"Logic?" Cole moved back in front of her. With his finger he nudged under her chin until she met his eyes. "What's logic got to do with it?"

She wrenched her chin free to stare at the floor. Tears burned her eyes as she fought the emotions again. "Logic has everything to do with it. It must. Logic is how I handle everything, and logic says it should be safe. The man is dead. He can't hurt me. It was months ago."

"Logic don't always win. Even Charlie'd tell you that."

"He'd likely use the words of Oliver Wendell Holmes, 'Insanity is often the logic of an accurate mind overtaxed'."

"And yours is."

"I know. You think I don't know? I know none of it makes sense and logic isn't working, I know. I know. I know." She steeled herself, hands tightening into fists. "I can't make it make sense."

"Some things don't make sense."

"I hate this. I shouldn't still be afraid."

"You need a new memory."

"I don't think—"

He cut her off with a kiss, his body leaning into hers until she was flush between him and the shelves. Gentle, but insistent, he kept her pinned.

Her hands, which had braced on his chest to keep him at bay, splayed to grip his coat. She held him close against her, letting his warmth overtake every trembling fear.

He pulled back and held her gaze.

She pushed the coat from his shoulders. "Help me make a new memory."

Apprehension, uncertainty, waiting, expecation, fear of surprise, do a patient more harm than any exertion.
—Florence Nightingale

Jane curled on the floor of the library, Cole flush against her back, her body lax, lungs breathless. She trailed her fingers along the back of his hand where it lay against her rounded belly. "Now that is one hell of a memory. I may need to still keep the door open."

He chuckled low. A soft kiss landed on the nape of her neck. He skimmed his hand along her hip, then back to the swell of her stomach. "That so?"

"Oh yes. If I'm left alone with thoughts of this, I'll need a good blast of cold air once in a while."

He reached up to turn her face his way. His lips captured hers in a gentle kiss. When he withdrew, a wicked smirk crossed his features. "Then you use a fan. You ain't allowed to get sick, not for nothing."

"Perhaps I should pretend to be. If I were, I'd be cooped up in our room all the time and you'd be forced to take care of me all day long."

"Nah. You'd have Daisy and Katherine and Sally all butting in to check on you. Then Leanne'll be here in a few days and she'd join in the distractions."

"Such a shame." She sighed, lacing her fingers with his. "We could have convalesced together."

"Sure wouldn't mind that."

"Maybe I need to get a little cold. Alma and Leanne won't be here for Christmas for another three days. I feel a sniffle coming on."

"You do, do ya?"

Jane jumped, a shriek startling out of her at the knock on the door.

"Jane!" Charlie's voice boomed through the wood and glass.

"Charlie?" Jane frowned, not moving an inch away from Cole. "What the hell do you want?"

"Open the damn door." Charlie's voice was gruff with annoyance. "I just got to the clinic. Daisy said you missed your appointment, and she came by to check on you to find the door locked. Tommy said you weren't at the saloon. Cole, I can't believe you'd let her miss an appointment."

Jane laughed outright by the time his tirade was over. She spun and curled into Cole's chest as she tried to regain control of herself. It figured they'd been found out.

"Sorry Charlie," Cole called out. "We got to talking."

"Bull." Charlie hit the door again. "The last thing the two of you do is talk. Now get some clothes on and get to the clinic."

Right when Jane thought she might gain control of her laughter, Cole started to tickle her. She shrieked and twisted to get out of his hold. "Stop. All right, all right. I'm sorry!"

"You're too distracting. I forgot why I came by." Cole chuckled and rose to his feet. He pulled her into another kiss, and lingered there until she leaned into him again. When he withdrew again, he growled. "We'd better go or he's gonna be busting down the door next time, or shooting out the lock."

"They're always telling me to relax." Jane sighed. She slipped into her dress as quick as she could. "Then interrupting me when I actually am relaxed. That seems so counter-productive."

"It'll be a quick appointment. They've all been lately. Daisy even let ya go down to two weeks for a while." He hopped into his trousers and then into his shirt. When she'd finished dressing and ran her hands along her stomach, he set his hands over hers. "I told you—if it ain't clear enough already, I still want you, just as much as I always did."

A ripple of pleasure tickled her belly and she nodded. "I suppose you'll have to keep proving it to me. On a very regular basis."

"Jane!" Another slamming hit to the door from Charlie interrupted them.

"I'm coming," she hollered. With a giggle, she pushed Cole away. "We'd better go before Charlie manages to break down the door. Will you grab my coat?" At his nod, she didn't take her eyes from him. When he bent over to pick up her coat, she sighed and bit her lip as she enjoyed the view.

He smirked over his shoulder. "Enjoying yourself?"

"I always do when I'm looking at you." She winked as he approached, but turned to slip her arms into her coat rather than meet his oncoming kiss. As she walked to the door with Cole, she couldn't contain her grin. However, when Charlie glared at her the second she opened the door, she managed a semblance of a pout. "I thought my relaxation was of the utmost importance."

"Don't be smart." Charlie didn't waver in his glare.

"Well, being dumb's my job," Cole started. He grunted when she elbowed him straight in the ribs. "Hey!"

"You are far from dumb, so shut it." She turned back to Charlie and smiled. "It wasn't on purpose. I had every intention of going to my appointment. Then Cole arrived."

"You don't need to continue." Charlie held up his hand. "I am quite clear on what happened after."

"I was still having trouble with the library." She huffed and took his proffered arm. When Cole fell into step beside them, she grinned. "Cole was helping me get over them."

"Nice excuse," Charlie muttered.

"Thank you. I like it rather well." She smiled when Cole started laughing.

Charlie shook his head. "You're both helpless."

"Think you knew that all along, Charlie." Cole held open the clinic door for them both. "So tell us something we don't know."

"Jane." Daisy rose from the reception desk. "Are you all right?"

"I'm wonderful, Daisy. I'm terribly sorry to be late, I got a little distracted at the library." Jane nudged Charlie away. "Now excuse me Charlie. You're not my doctor."

"That's getting annoying." Charlie kissed her temple. "You know I'll get filled in when I go over your files."

"I suppose you will." Jane walked with Daisy to the room. As Cole closed the door, she climbed onto the table.

"So how have you been feeling the past couple of weeks?" Daisy pulled over her instrument tray. "Any improvement?"

"I'm still terribly moody, and big as a barn." Jane sighed. "I thought I'd have a little more time before I got quite this large."

"And you aren't finished." Daisy laughed and draped a sheet across Jane's legs. "You're only halfway there—there's still plenty more room to grow."

Jane groaned and clutched Cole's hand as the exam started.

Cole smirked. "Like you're gonna let it stop you. You're still getting sick all the time and you don't stop for nothing."

"It's hardly all the time." Jane frowned. "And it's not nearly as bad."

Daisy patted Jane's knees. When Jane straightened her legs, Daisy pulled down the sheet to display her belly. She pulled a stethoscope from the table. "I take it the nausea is improving, then?"

"I'm still almost constantly nauseous, but it's not as severe as it was. Only in the mornings and sometimes in the afternoon do I feel like it's out of control." Jane pursed her lips. "Then I drink tea until it goes away."

"Good." Daisy set the stethoscope on Jane's stomach. A smile lit her features. "The heartbeat is strong."

Jane grinned, but her smile faded when Daisy's faltered. Cole's grip on her hand tightened when Daisy moved the stethoscope around. Jane took a deep breath to brace against the sudden rush of fear. "Daisy what is it? What's wrong?"

Daisy's brow furrowed and she shook her head. "It's nothing major, but I'd like to have your brother come in here for a moment."

"No. You can't do that. Tell me what it is first!" Jane struggled to sit, grateful that Cole helped her do so. "What's wrong?"

Cole frowned. "Just tell us. We saw that look."

"I'd rather get confirmation first," Daisy started.

"Then check again yourself, but tell us what's going on please." Jane gripped Daisy's hand. "You're worrying me."

"All right. I don't want you to worry," Daisy said quietly. "Lie back down and let me have another listen. I'll let you hear as well this time, how about that?"

Jane nodded, shaking as Cole helped her lie back down. She kept a tight hold of Cole's hand as Daisy listened again. "Well?"

"Here," Daisy handed her the ends of the stethoscope, "Listen there. Do you hear that sound?"

A rushed whooshing hit Jane's ears, like listening to Cole's heartbeat, but not quite the same. "It's so fast."

"Yes it is." Daisy laughed. "That's normal. Now, keep listening."

Jane nodded, waiting as Daisy moved the end of the stethoscope across her belly. The heartbeat faded, but almost diagonal across her abdomen, a new rapid beat hit her ears.

Cole's gaze flickered between the women. "Jane?"

"I'm sorry. I should have seen it sooner." Daisy squeezed Jane's hand and smiled. "It sounds a little different, right?"

Jane blinked rapidly as the meaning hit her hard. She grabbed Daisy's hand and moved the stethoscope back to the other side of her stomach. "Is this what I think it is?"

"Yes. This is your baby, and this," Daisy moved it back to the second heartbeat, "is your other baby."

Cole's head popped up. "What?"

Daisy laughed. "Twins."

Jane stared up at Cole with wide eyes. "Twins?"

"*Twins*?" Cole shook his head.

"I think I'm going to be sick." True to her word, Jane rolled to the side, and proceeded to throw up all over the floor. The action was enough to stir Cole and Daisy back to life.

Once Jane had relieved the sickening void of her stomach, she managed to get herself back together. She knew Cole hovered nearby, but she didn't know what to say at this point. Facing the idea of one child had been tough enough, but two?

"Why don't you take a few minutes to get used to the idea and let me get Charlie?" Daisy took Jane's hands in hers. "Jane."

"Hm?" Jane stared at Daisy as the words sank in. "What?"

"I'm going to get Charlie. We'll need his participation now that there will be two babies at the birth." Daisy smiled. "And it will give the two of you a few minutes to come to terms with this."

"We'll need more time than that." Jane tried to force a smile. "Go on. Just—no one but Charlie. Not yet."

"No one else will hear, I promise." Daisy chuckled. "But I'll make sure Charlie knows what he's walking into."

With a shaky breath, Jane managed to nod again. After the door had closed, she turned to face Cole, finding him staring at her with his jaw dropped.

No sound passed between them for several minutes. Finally, the humor of the moment caught up to Jane and her lips quivered. She couldn't fight the smile, and the oncoming onslaught of giggles any longer. "You are one virile son of a bitch, did you know that?"

Her laughter must have caught up to him, because he started to chuckle. "Yup. I'm *all man.*"

"Don't I know it?" She held out her hand, her laughter fading with every step he took closer. When he got close enough, she wrapped her arms around his neck and pulled him close. Pressing her forehead to his, she sighed. "Did she really say twins? Two babies? I—I'm not sure I can handle one."

"Sure you can. There ain't nothing you can't handle."

"Says the man that does not have to give birth to two children at once."

His brow furrowed. "We should check with Daisy. I ain't so sure it happens like that." He chuckled when she smacked him.

"Don't be smart."

"Just trying to help you stop being so scared."

"You're here. I don't feel scared. ..."

When her silence lingered, he filled in the blank. "Shocked as hell."

"Damn straight."

He cupped her cheek and met her gaze. "I ain't gonna say I got any clue what we're gonna do, but we'll figure it out."

"I know."

*Do not anticipate trouble,
or worry about what may never happen.
Keep in the sunlight.
—Benjamin Franklin*

Throughout the ensuing exam with Charlie, Jane was stunned by her brother's quiet nature. Certainly, Charlie wasn't the loudest of her brothers, that award would always go to Tom.

It still seemed well out of character. He didn't react to Cole's, or her own, sarcastic comments. All he did was listen to the heartbeats and make notes on the chart. Daisy had full control of the meeting.

Jane listened to her instructions best she could with the distraction of her brother's silence. Cole's hand held hers with surprising ferocity. He, unlike her, listened to every word Daisy said.

Daisy glanced at Jane. "Do you think you can handle your instructions?"

Having only heard half of what was said, Jane hesitated. After a moment she nodded. Cole had hung on every word, and she didn't doubt he'd make sure she abided every rule. "Yes, of course. Whatever it takes to make sure the babies…"

Babies. Plural. Would she ever get used to that idea?

"Jane." Cole's brow creased. "What's wrong?"

"Nothing, I'm not used to saying that. Babies." She turned her attention to Charlie. "We're not telling anyone, not yet anyway. We need time to figure this out."

Charlie nodded once.

"I mean it. Not Ma, not any of our brothers, Charles."

When Charlie lifted his gaze, his face was stoic. The light fell in such a way she couldn't read see his eyes to gauge any emotion. What was wrong with the man? He cleared his throat. "I understand. We couldn't tell, anyway."

"All right." Jane frowned when his gaze dropped to the floor again. She released a breath to ward off her anxiety, and mild frustration. "As I was saying. I'll do whatever it takes, as I have been trying to do, to keep the babies safe."

"That's all we needed to hear." Daisy reached out to squeeze Jane's free hand. "Congratulations."

"Thank you." A giggle rose, unbidden. "My goodness. This has been all too much."

Cole chuckled along with her. When Daisy rose, he nodded to her. "Thanks, Daisy."

"Of course. We'll let you folks get accustomed to your news. Charlie?" Daisy paused at the door when she realized Charlie hadn't followed her.

"I'll be along in a few minutes. I want to—" Charlie hesitated a brief moment. "Share my congratulations."

Jane waited until Daisy had shut the door to speak. "Liar. What is going on, Charles? You've been morose since you walked in here."

Charlie released a long, shuddering breath. "I should have expected this. Prepared you long ago. I allowed myself to believe otherwise, and let your illness distract me."

Janes excitement deflated into concern. She returned Cole's tight grip until she felt they might break the bones in each other's hands. "Prepared me? For what? I thought this was supposed to be good news?"

"It is, of a sort. Of course." Charlie rubbed his hands together. Still, he said no more than that.

"Charlie," Cole rumbled. "Out with it."

Charlie took the stool Daisy had abandoned. He met Jane's gaze. "Twins run in our family."

She pondered that a long minute. "How can it? There are seven of us. None of us were twins."

"That's not, precisely, true."

"But, it is. None of you are the same age. Even Nicholas and I, though we are only nine months apart."

Charlie cleared his throat. "Let me go back first. Ma is a twin. There are several sets of twins that her parents brought into the world. Ma, on the other hand, and her twin, had far less success. No twin was born alive."

Jane's heart skipped a beat. Immediately, she set a hand over her belly. "What?"

"James was a twin, as was Nick. Neither of their twins survived. Ma lost full pregnancies a couple times, as well." Charlie set his hand over hers. "I heard both of those babies and they are strong and healthy. There's no reason to think that will change."

"Then why tell her? Why scare her like that?" Cole pulled Jane close. "That isn't helping."

"I wanted you aware. Odds are, you've surpassed the curse that Ma and her siblings have faced bringing twins into the world. Aunt Effie gave up after two tries, started adopting. Ma wanted a big family, though." Charlie rose, his hands on both sides of her stomach as if holding the two babies inside. "You're already doing everything right, but I thought it only fair you knew, just in case."

"In case…one of them is born dead." Jane's voice caught in her throat. "You should have kept your mouth shut."

"Probably." Charlie grimaced. "I'm sorry. If it helps, I'm optimistic. Despite your troubles with your illness, their heartbeats are strong. It's a good sign."

Jane's hands shook as set them on top of her brothers. "Do me a favor?"

"What's that?"

"Next time wait until you've had time to think before revealing devastating information to a pregnant woman."

Charlie smiled at her, tears in his eyes. "Promise."

Cole rubbed Jane's back, surprisingly quiet. "Should she remain in bed? Would that be safer?"

Jane gasped. "No!"

"No." Charlie spoke at the same time as her. "Perhaps later if she starts acting like she'll go too early. For now, it would make her insane and give her far too much time to think over what could go wrong."

"We'll prepare for things to go right." Jane stuck her chin out stubbornly. "This is our gift for the loss of our first child. God wouldn't be so cruel again."

"I think you've had enough cruel for a lifetime." The tension in Charlie's brow eased. "For a woman that's only been alive for a few years, it's rather impressive the amount of trouble you've gotten yourself into."

"I've gotten myself into?" Jane grabbed at the playful mood like a lifeline. She couldn't handle any further moroseness. "I'll have you know Clara got me into most of it. I'm a delight and cause no trouble."

Even Cole's mood broke at that. "Sure. Them girls back at the Inn arc virgins, too."

The laughter took over, shaking the last of the dark mood from the room. Jane smacked Cole's arm. "You're terrible. How dare you insult the woman carrying your children!"

"You like a little insulting. Lets you know I care." Cole winked. He stood, pulling her to her feet. "If you don't mind, Charlie. I'm gonna see my woman gets real comfort instead of more scaring."

Jane squeezed Cole's hand at his dark tone. She hugged her brother. "I know you meant no harm."

"I didn't." Charlie returned her hug fiercely. "Just wanted you aware. I truly have all confidence that you're going to make it through."

"Thank you." She turned to take Cole's arm. "Let's go home. I'd like to rest."

Cole led her to the door where he swung her woolen cape over her shoulders. Even with it in place, a brisk wind wiped all the warmth from her bones. She shivered against it, leaning into Cole.

Rather than take her inside the Inn, he guided her around back to the newly completed barn. Inside was surprisingly warm, what with the body heat of horses and the large stove near the door.

"What are we doing? I can't ride." She turned toward him.

"We're not riding, just figured you didn't want to be around too many people after all that nonsense. Here, sit." He guided her to a haybale. Once seated, he draped a blanket over her legs. "Give me ten minutes."

"Ten? I'd rather you stay here."

"Trust me." He kissed her forehead and slipped from the barn.

Left to her own devices, Jane's mind spun around all Charlie had told her about their ma and her family. So many children lost. She'd already lost one infant before it had been born. Now that she'd heard the heartbeats of the two inside, how could she bear such a fate again?

She wasn't sure she could. Would she finally break? Would she become the sort of woman Cole pitied?

Her hands coursed over the smooth curve of her stomach. "Well, little ones. I think we need to have a serious talk. Your ma has been so ill, and Charlie has me so worried. I'll take every bit of illness you throw my way if you stay right where you are until it's time."

A soft thump hit her hand. She gasped, staring at the spot where it had happened. "Now, what was that?"

"What was what?" Cole carried a large basket into the barn. "You look—well, not sure how ya look."

"Come here." She waved him over, afraid to move the hand where the bump had hit.

He dropped the basked, rushing to her side. "Is something wrong?"

"Give me your hand." She only prayed it would happen again so he would feel it. Carefully she set his hand in the exact same spot hers had been.

He met her gaze, a curious lift to his brow. "What am I doing here?"

"Wait. Be patient."

"I'm not real patient."

"I'm aware." Sh set her hand on his gently. "Oh, I do hope it happens again."

"What happens?"

Right then it did. A small bump hit her belly she could feel. Cole's eyes widened. "Was that?"

"One of your children? Yes." Jane laughed, the earlier panic flying away. "My goodness. They're really there. I haven't just become far too plump for my liking."

He laughed with her. "Not for mine."

She accepted his kiss eagerly, pulling him closer until they both lay on the blanket he'd spread onto the hay. "In a few months they'll be here."

He kissed her again. "You're gonna be the best ma. I've got a few things to learn, though."

"No. You're a good pa. All you've done for Alma since you adopted her. How you handle Jesse, and Cindy, even Lizzie? You're better at this than you think."

"I don't know about all that."

"I do." She cupped his cheek. "I don't want to dwell on what Charles told us. I want to stay here, in this moment. Imagining all the possibilities."

"I'll do my best. Won't say I'm not worried."

"Me too. Scares the hell out of me, but I can't live scared anymore. I said I wouldn't."

"Bravest woman I know, right here." He tugged her close against him. "We'll manage it. We always do somehow. Even when it seems like we can't."

"We're lucky that way, I guess."

"Be luckier if the tragedy didn't come before the good, least to my way of thinking."

"That would truly be a nice change of pace."

He nuzzled under her ear. "I brung food for you."

"Food? Oh, you do know the way to my heart."

"Sure do."

Every gift which is given, even though
it be small, is in reality great
if it is given with affection.
-Pindar

Tickling light touches danced across Jane's flesh, pulling her from the depths of a very intriguing dream. Slowly his skillful fingers made reality a far more pleasing draw, pulling her wide awake with a small gasp before his lips closed over hers.

She buried her fingers in his hair and arched toward him. With fervent abandon they meshed together, exploring and searching, reclaiming each other as if it was the first time again.

By the time they both reached the peak, they were balmy with heat despite the cold temperatures of the day and the fading fire in the stove. Flushed, Jane sighed and laughed softly, curling against him.

"Merry Christmas."

She giggled. "I hope that wasn't my present."

"Well, it wasn't the whole thing."

"Not that I'm complaining because, believe me, I'm not—but how did we manage that? Usually first thing in the morning, that's the last thing I can do."

"You don't remember?"

She stretched luxuriously and shook her head. "No. What am I supposed to remember?"

"I woke you up and gave you some tea about half an hour before I started."

"You sneaky devil."

"Complaining?"

"Oh, hell no."

"Good." He laughed and tugged her closer. "'Cause I ain't done with you yet. I ain't ever done with you."

"I've noticed, but unfortunately," she laughed when he pouted. "The tea helped, but not permanently or completely. You'll need to give me a little time to get more."

"But if you get up now, you won't come back."

"Why in heaven's name wouldn't I?"

"I know you. It's Christmas. You can't keep to the bed when you got things for Alma and Sally, and designs on going to church."

She tilted her head to check the clock. "You've got me for another hour before I start insisting on all of that."

"Only an hour?"

"I promise to make it a fulfilling one if you let me take care of business."

He released his hold on her and lay back, grumbling under his breath. While she moved around the room making her tea and taking care of her morning illness, as well as her usual morning routine, the man didn't move a muscle.

She wondered how long his patience would last, and after fifteen minutes, he sighed in frustration. At that moment, she sat next to him and set her hand on his thigh.

He grinned wickedly. "Now what was that you said?"

"Trust me. It will be well worth the wait." Before he could even reply she slid her hand up his thigh and began to prove her point. Any smart remark he might have planned was lost in a deep moan.

She made good on her word and then some, using the entire rest of the hour and most of their remaining energy. Spent, she curled against him with a contented sigh. "Merry Christmas to you too."

"It ain't over yet."

"Hm?"

"I still gotta give you your real present."

"It can wait."

"No it can't. Get your robe on." He grinned when she lingered on the bed. "Your turn to trust me."

She stuck her lip out. "But it's warm and comfy here."

"Too bad. Now get your robe on or I'm carrying you like you are."

"Mean."

He laughed as she dragged herself to her feet and slipped on her robe. With his trousers on, he slipped his arm around her waist. "Let's go."

"Go? Where are we going?"

"Jane."

"Mean."

"It ain't as much fun if you know what's going on."

"You're still mean." She pouted and leaned against him as he led her downstairs and to the back door. Behind the door was the new unfinished portion of the hotel, so she paused there. "Cole?"

"Trust me." He laughed when she huffed, but opened the door anyway. Despite her continued attempts to pout at him, he kept a blind eye to her and led her down the hall next to the sunken area that would soon contain the new saloon and stage. Around the back of the large center room, he stopped at the back door.

She glanced at him out of the corner of her eye when he opened the door and led her down the hall toward their future home. "What do you have up your sleeve?"

"You don't got no patience, do you?"

"Not a lick."

"I'll give you a lick."

Giggling, she shook her head, pausing only when he opened the door. She smiled as she took in the wide room that would be their living space. "Mr. Hamm is doing a wonderful job. This is farther along than I'd expected."

"Hush."

"Cole!"

"Now close your eyes."

"You know I despise that."

He stopped where he was and folded his arms across his chest. "Do it."

"No."

"Jane."

"Nuh-uh."

"Mrs. Mitchell."

"No fair, pulling out the marriage card."

"Shoulda made you say obey." He smirked.

"But then you couldn't love me, because I wouldn't be me."

"Would you please close your damn eyes or we're going back upstairs and Christmas is over."

With a heavy sigh she closed her eyes, only to let one pop back open. "There."

"Close it, you loon." He laughed at her full-on pout, but when she closed her eyes he took her hand.

She had no idea where he was leading her, but she followed without further argument. Once he had her still again, she tapped her foot. "Now?"

"All right, all right. Open 'em."

The minute her eyes opened, she gasped. Before her stood a large tub, easily big enough for them both. "Cole! My goodness, it's exquisite."

"It's big."

Jane laughed and nodded. "Definitely. This isn't the tub I ordered. How did you get this one here?"

"The tub you ordered weren't no bigger than what we been using, and since this is our own private tub—I wanted you to have the best."

"Me?" She definitely detected an ulterior motive.

"Yup."

"Just for me? Or is this for you?"

He wrapped his arms around her from behind and kissed her neck. "For you."

"Are you certain?"

He kissed along her neck. "Maybe a little bit for me too."

"Selfish."

"Nope. You'll see."

"Show me."

"Gladly."

Age does not make us childish, as some say;
it finds us true children.
-James Anthony Froude

Alma peeked into the room, her eyes wide. Her hand skimmed along the smooth wood of the wall. "This is…mine?"

Jane followed her into the empty room. Alma's awe lightened her heart. "Yes, Alma. This room will be all yours. When you come home next, you'll be here to stay."

Alma turned in a circle, then crossed to the outer wall Jane had made sure to have lined with windows. A smile lit Alma's features. The young woman pressed first her hands to the panes, then her forehead.

"We put in lots of windows because we know how much you like the solarium at school." Jane walked up beside her. "I know you're on the second floor, but I thought you would like being able to look over the town and see more without having to be in it."

Alma pointed down toward the ground. "Garden?"

"There isn't anything there yet because it is winter, and I'm waiting for you to help me choose the plants, but yes. The square you see marked out will be the garden." Jane leaned on the windows to look down as well. "I cleared away the snow so you could see it."

Alma turned to take in the room again. "Mine."

"Yours. Your furniture will arrive in a few weeks, in time for your next visit. When you return you can tell us exactly where you want everything to go." Jane remained leaning on the window while Alma wandered the room. "Cole and I also ordered a piano for the living space downstairs. I thought the crowd in the saloon might bother you, and I wanted you to be able to play the music you like in quiet."

"I will live here."

"In a few months, yes. Are you excited for that?"

"With Cole?" Alma nodded.

"Where you belong." Jane moved to Alma's side. "Are you ready to go see Cole now? I think he's ready for church."

Alma's smile brightened. The entire way back to the saloon, she practically skipped along the hall.

Jane tried to hide her laughter when they found Cole glaring at Sally. Sally, for her part, was adjusting his tie, a wicked grin on her face. Jane's chuckle escaped despite her best efforts. "You aren't picking on Cole, are you Sally?"

"No ma'am." Sally's smile sobered, not enough to hide it entirely, but enough to appear somewhat contrite.

"Liar," Cole grumbled. "Ain't she teaching you not to lie?"

"Stop looking so miserable," Jane chastised. "It's one service, and it isn't a regular service because it's Christmas. Don't glare at me. I'm not the one that asked you to go."

Cole actually pouted. "I still say you encouraged it."

"I did no such thing, it was all Alma's idea." Jane turned her attention to Sally. "You look lovely this morning. Is anyone else joining us?"

"Me, of course." Tom hopped off the last step. His fingers skimmed the lapel of his suit coat. With a bright grin, he kissed her on the cheek.

"My goodness," Jane said with a nod of approval. "You clean up halfway decent, Thomas. Perhaps I should try harder to convince Leanne to stay if she brings out this side of you over the helpless sod you normally are."

Sally laughed outright. "He's not so bad. Alma? Do you want to walk with me? We can leave the adults to their strangeness."

Jane couldn't help but smile when Alma moved closer to Sally. The pair got along swimmingly, which helped ease her nerves over Alma's imminent residence. She squeezed Cole's arm as the pair headed outside. "She likes her room. I told her when she comes next time, we'll have the furniture and she can tell us where she wants it placed."

Cole set his hand on hers. "What about your stray?"

"Stop calling her that, or I will hurt you." Jane nudged him. Tommy laughed beside her. When he extended his arm as well, she hooked her free arm through his. She encouraged the men forward, and the three of them followed behind Alma and Sally at a slower pace.

"That girl's got expensive taste," Tom piped up. "I hope you two know what you're getting yourselves into taking her in as a ward."

Jane stuck out her tongue. "She actually used a bit of decorum picking out the things for her room. Unlike some big galoots I know."

Tom picked imaginary lint from his coat. "I don't know what you're talking about."

Cole laughed. "I think she's talking about the extras you got for your room."

"What?" Tom pulled aside his coat to reveal his holster. "I got a lot of guns. I needed a place for them."

Jane rolled her eyes. "It's obnoxious. No wonder you sleep alone. Three gun racks, plus a full cabinet?"

Tom managed to appear penitent. "Well…"

"Ma!" Jesse attacked suddenly from behind.

Jane nearly stumbled under the impact. To keep from falling, she gripped tight onto Cole's arm. "My goodness, Jesse!"

David's voice sounded from some distance off, "Jesse!"

"Merry Christmas, Ma!" Jesse squeezed her tight around the waist. "Thank you for my books. And my sled. Pa said it was from you too."

"Jesse." David finally caught up with the boy, Lee trailing behind moments later. David gasped for air. "Sorry, Jane. He saw you and took off."

"Seems to be his habit," Cole pointed out.

David nodded. "Noticed, did you? Anyway, he's had a real exciting morning. Can't keep him still for nothing."

Lee laughed. "I'll say. If I'd known Santa was going to bring so many gifts I wouldn't have bothered making him that quilt."

"Of course you would have." Jane hugged Jesse against her. "I bet Jesse loved it, too. It was beautiful."

"It's *warm*." Jesse hopped in place. "Can I go say Merry Christmas to Alma and Sally? Can I? Can I?"

"Of course—but not with quite so much excitement, all right? I don't want you upsetting Alma." Jane sighed when he darted off with a yell despite her warning. "I don't know if Alma will ever adjust to the amount of enthusiasm Jesse has."

"No one can." David laughed. "Merry Christmas Cole. Surprised to see you're coming to church today."

Tommy snorted, protesting when Cole smacked him, "Hey!"

Jane yelped when the pair began sparring back and forth. She moved closer to David and Lee, leaving the men behind. "Those two scare me sometimes. I didn't think you were supposed to get along with your in-laws."

David scoffed. "Well, technically they aren't in-laws."

Jane couldn't believe her slip-up, but directed a modicum of her anger at herself onto David. "Hush."

Lee chuckled. "Um, Jane? I think there could be a problem."

Jane turned to see what Lee pointed at. The two men were covered in mud practically from head to toe. "Cole! Thomas! What are you two, children? Look at yourselves."

"He did it," they said simultaneously.

Jane pinched the bridge of her nose. "Heaven help me. It's like I have two extra children."

David shook his head. "Jane is going to kill you."

"No." Jane set her hands on her hips. "I'm making them go to the service as they are. No changing or cleaning up. We're already running behind. Let's go."

"Aww, Jane."

"Come on, Lou. We don't take an hour like you do."

"In a pinch it only takes me two minutes, and that is not the point." Jane shook her finger at them. "Go on. You saw fit to fight in the muddy street, now you can go to service like that."

"Fine." Cole stalked toward her. Before she had the thought to run away, he'd pulled her into his arms. "But you do too."

"Cole!" Jane smacked at him. "This is a new dress!"

"Sorry, Lou…"

Jane let out a shriek when both men took her down in the mud. She managed to fight them off far too late, and flew to her feet, her whole dress ruined. Her breath came in rapid bursts as she tried to contain her anger.

She wiped the mud from her face, glaring at the pair lying in the mud laughing their immature asses off. "Colton James. Thomas Eugene."

Both men stopped at the use of their full names.

She straightened her back. "Now it's up to you to explain to Alma how her Christmas plans are ruined, and you've gone and upset her entire day. I'm returning home to clean myself up. I don't wish to see either of you the rest of the day."

"Jane."

"Lou."

"Shame on you both."

*I am a great friend to public amusements;
for they keep people from vice.
—Samuel Johnson*

"So how long do you think she can hold out?"

"She won't be able to keep away that long. She's never been able to."

"She's gone for weeks before—he's always the one that broke down first."

"I bet it's an act. She ain't really keepin' him at bay."

"Sally told me that she had the workers move that big oak bed into their new room along with her books."

"What's he doin'?"

"Sleeping on a straw tick in their old room."

"No."

"Yes."

"I bet she cracks first. Ain't you the one that told me pregnant women—"

"Do you really want go there, Norman?"

"Well what about Alma? Wouldn't she pick up on their fight?"

"She's astoundingly civil and even friendly when Alma is around—and then turns on the ice the minute she's out of the picture."

"So he's keepin' Alma around all the time."

"As much as possible."

"She's coming this way."

In a rush, the group fled from the window of Cora's and gathered around a table that already held a few cups of coffee. Graham picked up his cup and leaned toward Norman. "My money is on one more day tops."

Norman laughed. "I'll take that. I been around Kat enough to know that Janey's too stubborn. I'll put my money on Saturday."

Leanne giggled. "I'll take next Tuesday."

"A week from Saturday," Mike piped up before he took a sip of coffee.

"Today," Kat said with a smirk.

They all turned to her in surprise, and Mike raised an eyebrow. "You really think she'll crack today?"

Before she could answer the door opened and everyone tried to look busy.

As Jane pulled the door closed firmly behind her, she didn't miss the bevy of curious glances tossed her way. She chuckled under her breath and turned her back on them, heading into the store portion of the building.

Leanne dared to follow behind her, but didn't approach the subject Jane had no doubt they were curious about. "So you're going sledding today with the Schaffer's?"

"Yes." Jane stepped back out from one of the aisles, only to find everyone watching her again. "Jesse has been waiting all week for the snow to return so he could test out his new sled. Lizzie and Cindy are coming too, right?"

"Are ya kidding? They wouldn't miss it." Norman smiled brightly.

"Good." Jane smiled at Kat. "And I expect you'll be joining as well."

"Of course. A little cold doesn't hurt me." Kat grinned.

"So are you going to let Tommy off the hook?" Mike chuckled when mutters started around the room. "He's starting to pout."

Jane pursed her lips and shook her head. "I don't predict a rapid end, Mike. You all might want to reconsider your wagers."

"How does she do that?" Norman snarled, then straightened and cleared his throat. "I mean, what wagers?"

"Smooth, Norman." Graham snorted. "Been a long time since you kept Cole at bay, Janey."

"It's been five days." Leanne leaned on the counter next to her. "It hasn't voluntarily been that long in quite some time, from all I've heard."

"You are all sad people with far too much time on your hands." Jane paid Cora, who'd remained suspiciously silent during the conversation. "Gossiping around here like old women, and no, Graham. I'm not giving you any inside information on when this is going to end. I'll stay mad as long as I care to. Thank you."

Graham smirked when she left in a huff. "All right. I'm still on tomorrow. I'm in for one dollar. What do the rest of you want?"

Even the gods love jokes.
—Plato

If Jane weren't still so very annoyed, she might have felt bad about leaving her friends in the lurch like she had. However, considering when she'd looked back inside they were already all huddled up and money was changing hands, her guilt was quickly relieved.

In the days since Cole and Tom had seen fit to dump her in the mud on Christmas morning, she'd had to struggle against their first pitiful, and then increasingly heartfelt, attempts at an apology.

Being dumped in the mud and subsequently missing the Christmas service was cause enough to hold onto her anger. However, the disruption to Alma's day when the excitement of the day already had her on edge, had brought on some rough hours trying to help calm Alma down.

After hours of alternately playing the piano and reading, Alma had calmed enough that Jane's own nerves eased. She'd spent another hour with Alma, and when she'd left is when Cole had learned what she'd done with their sleeping situation.

In the end she'd had to lock their new bedroom door with him on the other side for him to realize she was serious. She was pretty sure by now Cole and Tom were conspiring against her, which made her question how long her resolve would last.

Jane shrugged off the doubt and steeled her resolve as she entered the inn.

Tom hopped out from behind the bar. "Jane!"

She ignored him and kept walking through the saloon.

"Aw, come on Lou." Tom touched her arm. "You've got to stop being so stubborn. Cole's getting cranky."

She stopped short and cut him a dark glare. "Oh, I'm sorry. *He* is getting cranky? Go jump of a cliff, Tom." She whopped him in the back of the head before storming through the back door into the new construction.

The new saloon was almost complete, the dropped floors had been covered with the smoothest boards available, and the walls were gorgeous panels. The railings surrounding the area were still minimal, but it was one thing at a time at this point.

"Lady Jane." Hammy leaped up the steps, a large grin on his wrinkled features. "I've got somethin' to show ya."

"I always like hearing that, Mr. Hamm. Please, lead the way." Jane took his arm, but was surprised when he didn't take her into the pit, or toward the steps for the upper levels. Instead he took her back toward her own apartment. She pushed aside her confusion to point out, "You were supposed to be taking this week off."

"No stoppin' me. Not once I get started."

"So I've noticed. At the rate you're going, we may finish ahead of schedule."

"That's the plan."

"Wonderful!" Jane hesitated when they got to her and Cole's new living quarters. "I've seen where I'm going to live Mr. Hamm, in fact I've been staying here all week."

"I know. Made it near impossible to finish. Lucky ya don't hang around here most of the day." Hammy dragged her through the living room toward the bedroom.

"Finish what?" She stopped short inside the room, surprised to see a new door on the wall to the right of the bed. "What is that door? It wasn't here this morning."

"That's what I wanted to show ya." He pushed open the door. "Hope I got it right."

She hesitated a moment, but curiosity won out and she rushed forward. Beyond the door was a small room lined with pegs and drawers built into the outer wall under a small window. "Oh, my! A closet? This wasn't in the original plans."

"You know," Cole's voice soothed through her rather than Hammy's expected reply. "When you pull a stunt like this, you make it damn near impossible to surprise you."

Jane frowned at Cole's voice, despite the warm fire it lit inside.

"Stop being stubborn." Cole chuckled. "Thank you, Hammy. I got her from here."

"Mr. Hamm." Jane turned and stepped around Cole to clasp the old man's hands. "Thank you so much. This is beautiful, and so much more elaborate than I would have asked for. I'd like to hear the details later when Mr. Mitchell isn't being such a bull."

Hammy shrugged and ducked his head. "Thanks, Janey. I best get back to work."

Jane turned her attention back to the closet. Along one wall sat the vanity from upstairs, and her trunks lined either side. Cole's solitary trunk and a row of five pegs sat beyond the door.

She couldn't deny the closet was a great touch and most definitely softened her resolve. While she'd had wild dreams of adding a closet, she'd never included them in the plans, so Cole thinking to add them himself warmed her heart.

Still, she thought back to Christmas and Alma's struggles and she pursed her lips. With a nod, she turned and tried to leave the closet.

Cole grabbed her arm. "Jane."

She peeled his hand from her arm. "It's wonderful. Thank you."

"That's it?"

She shrugged and walked over to the bed where she'd laid out a muffler and coat to replace her cape for sledding. When she heard him walk closer, she kept her focus on getting ready.

He leaned in until his lips hovered a short distance from her neck. His breath teased her flesh until she shivered. "Come on, Jane. It's been five days. You gotta forgive me sometime. I know you miss me."

Instead of a verbal reply, she grabbed her muffler and wrapped it around her neck.

"Damn it, Jane."

"Jesse is expecting me."

The minute her coat was on, he wrapped his arms around her and pulled her close. He turned her toward him. "Jane."

When his finger hooked under her chin, she met his gaze quietly. Without argument, she let him close the distance and left her lips soft and yielding to his kiss. She pressed her body close and her tongue battled his until a deep moan rumbled through him. Slowly she pulled back and smirked. "Suffer."

His jaw dropped and before he could react, she pushed him away and stormed from the room. She slammed the door behind her, and grinned. Not sure how long it would take him to get his wits about him again, she darted through the new construction into the old saloon.

As she reached the door outside, Cole's shout hit her. "Jane!"

She rushed out of the inn and was relieved to hear Jesse's excited shout from across the street. Meeting his rush toward her with open arms, she pulled him close and hugged him tight. When Lizzie and Cindy followed right behind, she hugged them as well before she rose. "Are we all ready?"

Once everyone had nodded and started to walk, Kat laced her arm through Jane's as they lagged behind the others. She sighed. "I think you're enjoying this too much. He looks utterly miserable."

"I'm not enjoying it at all." Jane frowned. "And he should look miserable. They were rotten, immature little children. They ruined what was a wonderful day not just for me, but for Alma. That's that."

"Apparently immaturity is contagious."

"Like the plague."

Kat laughed. "At least you know it."

"Of course I do. Just because I'm immature too doesn't mean I'm too idiotic to know it. I do have a modicum of intelligence."

"So when are you going to let him off the hook?"

"Well, he did gift me with a closet. I suppose I should try to be nice."

"A closet? Well, well." Kat nudged her. "Did he plan that before, or do it as a way of apology?"

"I'm not quite sure. I wasn't really speaking to him enough to find out." Jane winked. "So let me guess—you've put money on me giving in today."

"I've got two dollars riding on it, and I said you'd cave first."

"Just for that I should wait another few days."

"Graham has tomorrow—and he thinks Cole will cave. Leanne went all the way out to Tuesday and your brother thinks a whole week from now."

"I see." Jane snorted. "You're as childish as we are by betting on it. You're right. Immaturity is contagious."

"Like the plague."

They fell into laughter and rushed to catch up to the others.

The rest of the afternoon passed cheerfully, and Jane even took a spin on the sled with David and Jesse both pulling. She fell into the snow in her laughter as Kat took a turn and ended up flipped over into a large snow drift.

By the time they got back to town they were all cold and wet, but parted in good cheer. The second she stepped into the inn a blanket was thrown over her shoulders. She gasped and shrugged it off.

"Trying to catch your death?" Cole threw it back over her shoulders.

"No. I was having fun," she countered. Once again she peeled off the blanket. With him right on her heels, she walked all the way back to their new living quarters without saying another word. Once there she began to peel off the wet layers of clothes.

"I said I was sorry."

"You know they're betting on when we'll cave and who will cave first."

"Really?"

"Yes." She fought with the buttons on her dress. When he moved to help her, she didn't fight his assistance. "Kat put two dollars on today—with me caving."

"Are ya?"

"Not that I've noticed." She let him help her get the dress over her head before she sat on the bed. As he knelt in front of her and began to remove her boots, she smirked. "Besides, I think you caved a couple of days ago when you got Hammy to make that closet for me."

"I caved the second you stopped talking to me."

"No. Not the second I did—you thought it wouldn't last long."

"Good point." He tossed aside the first shoe and moved to the next. "So we gotta wait until tomorrow?"

"No. Longer. Graham has money on tomorrow and I'm certainly not going to let him win if I can help it."

He dropped the second shoe on the floor and rose to his knees. With his arms around her waist, he tugged her closer to the edge of the bed. "Nothing I can do that'll change your mind?"

"I don't know."

"You always do like my apologies."

"Oh, how very true."

"You're shivering." He frowned and brushed a damp curl from her cheek.

"I'm freezing. I think the fire went out."

"I know the right way to warm you up."

"Oh?"

"Wait here." He leaned up and kissed her hard before he stood and disappeared into the next room.

With a smile, she peeled off her stockings and hung them next to the cold stove. She put more coal in the stove and relit it. Once the fire began to grow warm, she settled back onto the bed and let her eyes drift closed.

"Jane."

She could feel the warmth of Cole's body covering hers completely. Nothing could have stopped her smile then, not even all her anger combined. "Hm?"

"I got your bath ready."

"My bath?"

"You gonna share?"

"I might."

"I'm sorry."

She sighed and tilted her head back as his lips brushed along her neck.

"Sorry…"

Biting her lip to keep back the moan, she arched toward him.

"Sor—"

Before she could stop it, she sneezed. A groan rose up but was interrupted by yet another sneeze. "Damn it."

Abstinence engenders maladies.
-William Shakespeare

"Jane?" Kat patted her leg.

Jane groaned and snuggled deeper under the covers. Every inch of her hurt and ached, she didn't feel like company. "Go away, Kat."

"Still not feeling better?"

"No." In the five days since the sledding outing, Jane had been in bed with a horrendous cold. As if the boulder that had taken up residence in her head wasn't bad enough, she'd missed Alma and Leanne's departure the day before. To put it mildly, she felt like death. "Go away."

"So tell me the truth. Before you got sick, were you going to give in?"

In frustration, Jane threw back the covers and sat. She sneezed into her handkerchief and glared at Kat. "You're still worried about the damn bet?"

"Not so much, but it did get you moving."

Jane sagged and groaned. She flopped back onto the bed and curled up, drawing the blankets back around herself.

Kat laughed and pulled back the covers. "Let's go. I have a nice warm bath drawn for you. Cole will be home in a few hours. We'll see if we can't improve your disposition before then?"

"Not going to happen." Jane couldn't have fought Kat if she'd tried, so she let Kat help her sit. Once she was upright, her lungs tightened, and she had to struggle for a breath. The minute she was able to, she asked, "How's Jesse?"

"Are you kidding? It barely slowed him down for more than two days. He bounced back in no time. So did Lizzie and Cindy. However, you and Lee weren't so lucky."

"She's still sick?"

"She pulled herself out of bed yesterday. You're running behind, Jane."

Jane's protest was cut off by a coughing fit, and Jane gripped the footboard until it passed. "Believe me. I'd rather not be feeling like this."

Kat led her into the bathroom. The steaming tub looked so inviting to Jane's aching muscles, she didn't need any help removing her chemise. Still, Kat was right beside her and helped Jane into the tub. "There you go. Now sit and relax. We'll get you out of this room yet."

With a groan, Jane rested her head back against the tub and let the warmth of the water soak through to her bones. Her closed eyelids did nothing to block the stream of chatter from Kat from the next room.

She chuckled at Kat talking without a response until the laughter spawned another coughing fit. Once she'd settled down, Jane leaned back again. That's when it started to sink in what Kat was doing in the next room. "Katherine. What on earth do you think you're doing?"

"Don't you worry yourself about it. Keep relaxing and let me worry about what I'm doing."

"Don't change my sheets." Jane sighed, it was already too late. "You didn't have to do that."

"Please. You've been sick in bed for a week, they needed changed. You'll feel so much better with fresh muslin under you."

Jane frowned, but didn't argue any further. Instead, she let the warm water relax her. Kat's stream of chatter kept going, but Jane gave into the relaxation and let Kat worry about being busy.

"All right. Let me help you wash up and then we'll get you something to eat." Kat bustled behind Jane to grab the sponge and some soap.

After days of being sick, Jane's stomach wasn't sure what to make of the suggestion. On the one hand, she was starving—on the other, she never wanted to eat again. "I'm not all that hungry."

"Jane. The baby."

"Right." Jane sighed and turned when Kat started to wash her back. "You don't even know the half of it."

"What is that supposed to mean?" Kat slowed and touched Jane's shoulder. "I don't know the half of what."

"Well. You know I asked you to be there when the baby is born."

"Of course. Cole would drive you crazy—besides, I don't think that's something he needs to see. It could scar him for life."

Jane laughed, glad that this time she didn't cough. The warm bath had helped more than she was willing to admit. She pushed to her feet and took the towel Kat offered.

"Well?"

"Oh, right." Jane took her help to get out of the tub and begun to dry off. "Well, I'm really going to need you there now. Now that it's going to be a twin birth."

"Of course, if it's..." Kat's efforts to unplug the tub ceased and she straightened to full height. Her already pale features were almost white. "I'm sorry. Could you repeat that?"

"We found out before Christmas. With the holidays, Alma, and me getting sick, I haven't had the chance to tell you. I'm having twins."

Kat squealed and hugged her tight. "That's amazing."

"It's frightening," Jane corrected with a laugh. "And amazing."

"How did Cole handle it? I mean—wow."

"We both handled it the same—we were incredibly shocked. We're still adjusting and—we aren't telling anyone, Kat. Cole hasn't even told Tom yet, and I don't know if he's going to."

"Why on earth not?"

"Because we're still trying to figure this all out—and we'd also like it to be a surprise." Jane squeezed her hands. "I'm only telling you because you're going to be there, and I know Daisy will be here soon for a checkup."

"Oh, how exciting. Twins. What are you going to do? Have you come up with more names? Did you tell Alma or Sally?"

"Slow down." Jane groaned and went back into the bedroom. She pulled on the new nightgown Kat had laid out. "The bath helped a lot, but my brain still isn't quite at full capacity yet."

Kat grinned and plopped onto the bed beside her. "It's exciting."

"It's frightening. It makes things more complicated, and more risky for the babies and myself. The fears I already had are so much worse."

"You're doing so well this time, outside of the sickness. You've got Daisy taking care of you."

"And Charlie now," Jane grumbled.

"And Charlie. Two very fine doctors. I'm sure everything will be fine and those little ones will be making your life chaotic in no time."

"My life is already chaotic enough!" Jane rested back against her pillows, a soft laugh tempting fate.

"I tend to agree," Daisy said from the door. "Sorry, but you didn't answer my knock on the door to the apartment and this door was open."

"Don't apologize, Daisy. I'm going to have to have Hammy install a bell so I know when someone is at the door. The walls of this room are extra thick." Jane smacked Katherine's arm at the loud guffaw from her friend. "I wouldn't ever hear a knock on the front door."

"That's not the only reason." Kat giggled. "Of course, that's why the walls are so thick in the first place."

"Katherine," Jane warned.

Kat ignored her and glanced at Daisy. "They had Hammy put double tar paper and triple the boards. I believe you could stand outside this room with the whole town and scream and they wouldn't hear a thing."

"Katherine," Jane scolded. "Would you stop? You are in a rare mood today."

"I'm making up for your miserable mood." Kat winked.

"All of that aside." Daisy set down her bag, but couldn't hide her own laughter. "How are you feeling, Jane?"

"Miserable, but I suppose it's tolerable now. Kat was kind enough to draw me a warm bath which helped most of the aching." Jane smiled. "Otherwise I'm feeling the same. I've told Kat about the twins so you don't need to be cryptic."

"Good. I'm glad you're feeling better." Daisy opened her bag and rifled through it. "When I came by two days ago you were thoroughly miserable."

"My throat is still raw, my head still feels like someone dropped a boulder in it, and I want to cough, but overall I think I'm feeling better." Jane remained still while Daisy did her examination. After her eyes and throat were checked, Jane smirked. "So I guess I'm going to live?"

"Yes." Daisy took her stethoscope out of the bag. "Your throat is still red, so try mixing some honey into your tea, that should help. Are we ready to see how the babies are faring with their mother so sick?"

Jane nodded. "Please. I've been trying to eat even when I felt miserable, but Cole had trouble waking me up enough to eat some days. At least he had trouble waking me up without getting yelled at."

"Oh!" Kat flew to her feet. "The twin talk distracted me, I forgot about your food. I'll go get that for you."

Jane laughed when she darted out of the room. "It could have waited."

Daisy listened to Jane's belly, first one side and then the other. When she pulled away, she smiled. "They both still sound strong, that's very good. You seem healthy, other than your cold. I'm glad you've been making yourself eat."

"Following doctor's orders. It's not my strong suit, but I am capable of being compliant when necessary."

"Not always when it's necessary."

"But this is everything to me."

Daisy squeezed Jane's hand and nodded. "I know. I'll want to check you again next week. We'll continue on as we have been. If you start to feel worse or feel like there's anything wrong, you come and see me or Charlie."

"Yes ma'am." Jane nodded.

Kat returned with some soup, and so Daisy excused herself. After she'd eaten and managed some more conversation with Kat, Jane drifted off to sleep again, tucked deep into the warm bed.

The next stirring she felt was Cole's familiar touch as he climbed into bed with her and set his hand on her belly. She turned toward him and curled close. "Hey."

"You still sound terrible."

"It was one bath. Did you expect a miracle?"

"I can hope, can't I?"

Jane hummed, soaking up his warmth as eagerly as she had the bath's heat.

"Am I forgiven yet?"

"Not entirely, but you feel too good to push away."

He chuckled and pulled her closer. "That's all I'm worth to you, ain't it?"

"You bet."

"Rotten."

"Scoundrel."

"That's why you love me."

She sighed and relaxed. "Damn straight."

"So I guess you're up to talking at least."

"A little, maybe."

"Leanne's selling the business."

"What?"

"Asked me to sign off on it if she found a buyer."

She untangled herself from his arms to sit up. After she'd wiped the sleep from her eyes, she stared at him. "Are you serious?"

"Yeah."

"What is she going to do? Why didn't she tell me?"

"Because you were lying at death's door and didn't even know who was in the room half the time."

"Damn." She turned and leaned against the headboard next to him. When he draped his arm across her shoulder, she pillowed her head against his shoulder. "I know she'd thought about it in the past, but I didn't know she was seriously considering it again."

"Guess she decided Dominion Falls ain't so bad after all." Cole grinned and winked. "I offered her a job here."

"Oh you did? And what did she say to that?"

"I don't think your delicate ears could handle it."

"I can only guess what sort of job you offered her."

"What? She'd be a big draw."

"Brute."

"Nah. I told her she had a job here if she wanted. Figured you'd know what she was good at. She ain't gonna be hurting for money if she finds a buyer, though, so she may not bother." His fingers danced along her spine and he kissed the top of her head. "She wanted to tell you herself, but didn't want to make you wait until we went to Denver for it, so she said I could tell you."

"It will be nice having her here, for me. Not sure how you feel about it."

"I imagine it won't be long until all my secrets are out."

"It's not so bad. Much more fun than looking over your shoulder all the time."

"I guess."

She sighed and ran her hand across his chest. "Cole."

"Yeah?"

"Your clothes are in the way. I want to feel you."

"But I ain't forgiven. Are you sure?"

"I'm not going to screw you, I'm going to lie with you."

"I dunno."

She frowned and pulled out of his arms. "Fine. Be that way. Go back to your straw tick and I'll stay here and use the blankets for warmth."

When she turned away and curled under the blanket, he didn't move at first. Then the bed shifted and he got out, and Jane had to fight the urge to reach for him. Instead of leaving she felt him climb back in a few minutes later.

She turned and curled against him, glad to find his chest bare. "You'll need to go back upstairs once I'm asleep."

"Not on your life."

"But you're not forgiven."

"Like hell I'm not."

Her giggles gave way to a coughing fit. When she settled back down against him, she sighed. "You did have Hammy build me a closet."

"Yeah."

"I still expect a proper apology."

"The minute you stop coughing, you can bet I'm gonna do just that."

"Then you're forgiven."

"Damn straight."

The happiest moments my heart knows are
those in which it is pouring forth its
affections to a few esteemed characters.
-Thomas Jefferson

Jane rifled under the bar, frustration welling. Getting down onto the floor was a huge challenge anymore, and the fact that she was down there was bad enough. Being unable to find what she was looking for threatened to ruin her mood for the whole day.

She was now eight months along. Miraculously, despite her early troubles and the actuality of having twins, she was still pregnant. Daisy and Charlie weren't sure how much longer she'd manage to stay that way.

For weeks they'd threatened to make her stay in bed if she didn't take it easy, and she'd tried. Unfortunately, her life was too full. Construction, while slowed during winter, had reached a point where they would have to finally shut down the saloon portion of the inn and let Hammy take the place over.

In the end, the changes would be worth it, but it meant being closed for two full months. Two months without income or profits of any kind. Their regular customers would be faced with having to find other places to find their booze and gambling. Would they come back when the saloon was a vastly different place?

"Jane?" Tom's voice rang through the saloon. "Where'd you go?"

"Tom!" Jane sat back and gripped the edge of the bar. Now her challenge lay in trying to stand up. Damn. She couldn't, and that annoyed her more. "Where are the damn receipts from last night?"

"Right here. I told you I was getting them for you."

"No, you didn't."

He stepped around the side of the bar, his lips pursed in a failed attempt to cover his laughter. "I did. Where did you think I went?"

She'd remember if he'd said that. With a curse, she tried to haul herself to her feet. To his credit, Tom helped her stand without a smart remark. "Just give them to me."

"When are you going to have that kid already? You're sending me to the looney bin with all of this."

"So sorry I annoy you."

"Liar."

"Just help me sort the receipts. We're shutting these doors soon and we have to make sure everything is straight."

"You've been set for weeks." Tommy walked her to a table and held out a chair. When she sat, he rubbed her neck. "Just relax."

"Don't tell me to relax. I'm going to go into labor any minute, right at the same time as this business is going through a *huge* transformation. There's a dance in a few days that I *so* don't feel like trying to put on a pregnant version of a fancy dress on for. And the furniture for the baby's room has been delayed for weeks, if it doesn't get here soon I might have the baby without it. I don't have any room to relax."

"Lou." He hugged her and took the seat next to her. "Why don't you let me do the receipts? You can go stretch your legs, have some tea with Kat. Try to take your mind off of things."

"There's no taking my minds off things now, Tom."

"Try. You've got us all helping you out here. Your doctor says you need to relax, and stressing about the Hangman's Inn is not doing that."

She buried her face in her hands and growled. While she appreciated his offer of help, it only frustrated her more that she wasn't trusted to do things any longer. "I'm not helpless! And I *will* relax if I get everything done."

"Fine!" Tom held up his hands. "Do whatever you want."

"I will."

Before Tom could snap again, Cole shouted from outside. "*Jane*!"

All of Jane's frustration flew away when she saw the wagon outside the doors. Cole leaned against it with a grin. She pushed herself to her feet with the help of Tom and ran outside. "Did everything finally arrive?"

"Not sure it's everything, but it's a lot." Cole laughed. When she began to climb on the wheel, he sprang forward. "What do you think you're doing?"

She gripped the side of the wagon, her feet secure on a spoke of the wheel. The cart was full of crates, almost over-full. "Thank goodness! We might be a few items short, but it looks like most everything."

"Would you get down?"

"I'm perfectly fine." She grinned down at him, but released her hold on the wagon so he could help her off the wheel. Once down, she kept her arms around his neck to pull him into a deep kiss.

Cole chuckled and pulled her tight against him. He pressed her against the wagon as their tongue danced together.

"Would the two of you knock it off?" Tommy jumped hard enough in the wagon to shake the whole thing. "I'm not unloading this all on my own."

Jane frowned Tommy's direction. "Weren't you the one that was just telling me to relax? So leave me alone and let me relax."

"When we get this stuff unloaded you two can relax for the rest of the night." Tom smirked. "Didn't you have numbers you wanted to run?"

Jane pouted. "I don't like you."

Cole nibbled her neck. "Soon as this is all in the kids' room we'll see about finishing what you started."

Hammy's voice interrupted her reply, "Mrs. Mitchell!"

"Hammy," Jane and Cole snapped simultaneously, even though they grinned.

"Pitiful," Tommy muttered.

"Sorry." Hammy's features scrunched in an uneasy look when he realized Cole was outside too. "Habit."

"Don't worry about it," Jane said with a genuine smile. "What is it you needed?"

"Got another question about the setup on the second floor." Hammy adjusted his hat. "Last time we changed the size of Tommy's room, we forgot something."

Jane sighed, teasing her fingers along Cole's thigh. "I guess that'll give you boys time to get all of these things into the baby's room. Don't unpack a thing and come meet me in our bedroom as soon as you can."

Cole groaned and dropped his head against the side of the wagon when she slipped away. "I bet I'll be faster than you."

"Don't count on it," she called back. "All right, Mr. Hamm. Let's go."

Jane took the old man's arm and followed him inside. Surprisingly, the meeting and discussion took almost an hour. By the time she got back downstairs she was exhausted.

With a sigh, she stepped into the apartment and closed the door. A loud thump startled her, but the stream of curses that followed made her need to cover a giggle. She crept across the living room and paused outside the door to the twin's room.

Muffled conversation seeped through the partially cracked door.

"You know she's just going to move everything around," Tommy complained. "Or more precisely, make us move it all around again. Probably again after that."

Cole snorted. "I know. Woman can't ever make up her mind, but it ain't like it's trying to move that damn bed. This stuff isn't heavy."

"Plus, you don't know what crib she's settled on."

"Both of 'em."

"And you talk about me being extravagant."

"No. It ain't extravagant. We're gonna need them."

"Why would you need—"

Jane had her hands firmly clamped over her mouth, tears in her eyes as she tried to hold back her laughter. Cole didn't offer a reprieve to Tommy's silence. By the sounds of things he was still moving furniture around.

"Cole?"

"Yeah. Put that one over there."

"Why are you going to need both?"

Cole chuckled. "I know you ain't that stupid. Now put that one over there."

"*Cole!*"

"Just put the damn bed there."

"Is she carrying twins?"

"Maybe you are that stupid. Why else would we need two cribs and cradles?"

There was a thump as the crib was set down. A soft thud preceded Tommy dropping into view on the floor against the wall. Jane stepped to the side so he wouldn't be able to see her through the crack in the door.

Tommy sighed. "Does she know about our Ma?"

All motion stopped, and Cole's voice grew quieter, "Yeah." Muffled rustling filled the empty vacuum of silence after another minute. "She's trying to be positive about it. So are Charlie and Daisy."

"Ma and her sister both had several sets of twins." Tommy's voice grew heavy. "Didn't ever work for either of them. Of course, Aunt Effie actually lost both before they had a chance."

"Don't tell her. She's scared enough."

"Well, Ma and Effie were twins, too—and they both came out all right in the long run. Aunt Effie just had some troubles when she was little."

"Don't tell her," Cole repeated.

"Sorry. I'm just surprised."

"We ain't telling no one. Kathy knows, and now you do. That's it, at least until it happens." A crack of wood echoed out signaling the opening of another crate. "She didn't want to be fussed over because of it, so stop looking like that or she'll kill me for telling."

Jane leaned against the wall and ran her hand along her stomach. Under her hand her stomach moved as one of the babies stretched. She closed her eyes and said another prayer as she had several times a day for months.

With a shaky breath, she wiped her hands over her face as if that would erase the dark thoughts from her mind. Exhaustion crept in over the fear, so she pushed off the wall and went to her bedroom. She set her hands on the two crates stacked outside of their room, which she assumed held the cradles.

Yet another prayer welled up, and soon as she'd whispered it, she went into her bedroom and closed the door part way. After she'd slipped off her shoes, she grabbed her book and sank into the bed.

It took her several minutes to find a comfortable position, but once she did she flipped open the book to try to read. With every line the words grew fuzzier and her eyelids grew heavier until she gave in and let herself sleep.

"Jane?"

She startled awake and rubbed her eyes to try to wipe away the sleep. Without a clue what time it was, she had no idea how long she'd dozed off for.

"Jane? Are you here?" Cole's voice drew closer. The bedroom door slid open, and he leaned on the frame with a smile.

"Hi." She smiled back and patted the bed. "Sorry. I heard you and Tom in the twins room and came in here to let you talk. I must have dozed off."

"You heard us?" A frown darkened his features when he sat next to her. "What did you hear?"

"Enough." She reached for his hand. When he'd kicked off his boots, she pulled him closer. "Sorry I took so long with Hammy."

"Don't worry about that. Since it was taking so long Tom and I figured we'd unpack the stuff you ordered. It's all set up, but we can move it."

"So I heard. I can't make up my mind, hm?"

He chuckled and nibbled her neck. "So you did hear."

"Yes."

"You all right?"

"As much as I am any other day. You know it's always on my mind."

"Everything is always on your mind." He smirked when she smacked his hand. "Am I wrong?"

"No, that still doesn't make you funny."

"You said yourself. There ain't no way they're not gonna make it." He set his hand on her stomach and one of the babies rewarded him with a solid thump. "So we aren't gonna be scared."

"Scared is all right. There are times when fear is good. We just have to keep it in perspective. Focus on the positive, just like Daisy said."

"She says that you made it this far is real good."

"Exactly. With twins she was worried I'd go into labor much sooner—far too early for the little ones to make it."

He kissed her temple. "And you don't get sick no more."

"That finally passed last month to be replaced with heartburn."

"You can still get me going with just a look."

She pinched his side and laughed. "And you aren't in the least bit dissuaded by the fact I'm as big as our bed."

"Nah. You aren't quite that big. Maybe the headboard." He ducked when she smacked him. His laughter escaped when she moved faster than normal to launch an attack.

She squealed when he gained the upper hand in no time and tickled her. Her fight was playful, but then she froze when her stomach tightened.

"Jane?"

After a shaky breath, the tightening eased. She managed to nod. "I'm all right."

"You sure?" He hovered close by, his hand encompassing hers where it sat on her belly. "Do we need to get to the clinic?"

"No. I'm really all right. I think it was another of those false ones. Daisy warned us they'd start happening more often."

"Sure that's what it was?"

"Yes. It's been happening for a couple of weeks, this one just caught me off guard." She met his gaze and offered a smile. "Really. Don't panic yet. I think these two are going to hold on a while longer."

"Oh, you do, do you?"

"Most definitely."

"How's that?"

"I had a little chat with them." Jane ran her hands along his arm. "Because they gave me so much grief early on—they need to stay right where they are until I say so."

"Think they'll listen?"

"For at least another hour, yes."

"Just one?"

"Or two."

"Or five?"

"Oh—bully for me."

The whole difference between construction and creation is exactly this: that a thing constructed can only be loved after it is constructed; but a thing created is loved before it exists.
—Charles Dickens

Jane rested on the bench outside the inn, enjoying the rare spring-like February day. Every one of Hammy's employees, along with Cole, Tom, and whomever else they could wrangle was hard at work to take advantage of the nice weather to further construction quick as possible.

That meant their projected closing date of a week out had already been pushed back to just three days. Several customers had already complained, but with the promise of a closing night party with free rein to destroy the furniture and just about everything but the bar itself, they'd cheered up somewhat.

"Clara." Mike winked as he stepped onto the porch. "How are you feeling?"

"For the moment I'm in a good mood." Jane grinned, though she couldn't seem to stop running her hands over her belly. "You wouldn't be out to ruin that, would you?"

"Wouldn't dream of it. I was only hoping you'd show me the progress on the Hangman's Inn. All I've seen is your apartment and the outside—which is impressive in and of itself."

"Are you trying to gauge your competition?"

"Perhaps."

She laughed and held out her hand. "Of course you can see, if you'll help me stand. Our hotel won't be much like yours anyway, and we'll have more rooms than you."

"In my defense, mine is a health resort. It's meant to be enjoyed by a privileged few." He chuckled at her snort. As they stepped into the saloon, he glanced around at the room that was now half the size it had been, and ceiling that now sat above them in place of the old open view of the second floor. "So where's Cole?"

"He's upstairs helping with the construction. Trying to keep himself busy." Jane stopped him in the middle of the room. "We both are."

"I thought you weren't due for another few weeks— although you sure look like you could go any time."

"I'm not, technically. Daisy says it could be sooner or after a time, and now that the saloon is shutting down in a couple of days, we really want to keep busy."

"Are you sure it's a good idea to shut this place down?" The saloon buzzed with activity around them, even as they stood still in the middle of the room. "You seem to have quite a bit of business going on these days."

"Well, it's either that or sell the liquor out of a wagon in the street. Try hard as he will, I don't think Cole would be able to convince the Town Council to allow that, no matter how skilled he's becoming at orating."

"Guess he's learned a few things from you."

Jane shrugged and gestured around the room. "This entire room needs to be redone. This is going to be our lobby and seating for Cora's restaurant. We're changing to a corner entrance there, so it'll be even more easily seen to those coming in from the train."

Mike nodded. "Good idea. I always wondered why Cole had a straight store front."

"It was the way the town was set up, he bought an existing establishment, but it was a good size, bigger than most everything but the mercantile so he didn't fight it." She turned to lead him toward the bar, and stopped by the front window. "So this area will still be tables, but we promised Cora something a little less—roughshod."

"I'm still mad you managed to get her to open her restaurant here."

"I admit, I had inside knowledge. She told me back after the fire she was thinking about selling the mercantile. I took full advantage to convince her to do just that. Once we had the investors in, and I told her what I'd hoped for, she was easy to convince."

"Still. Cora working alongside Cole? That's an impressive thing to manage."

"You're telling me." She laughed. "However, she didn't want to maintain the mercantile, and with Arthur nearly of age, she felt it was time. She and Isaac are going to live in the old newspaper office right across the street. It's a smaller building and required little work to make it a good living space."

"So where will her kitchen be?"

"Back here, I'll show you it along with the rest of our lobby." They walked past the bar to a door that had been installed on what had once been the outside wall. On the other side had once been an alley and then the tailor shop, but now was the rest of their lobby.

Just past the door to the left was an elaborately hand-built desk that sat right against the wall back into the saloon, with a set of stairs right behind. While the stairs led up to the second floor, a door was visible underneath them, with a barred window into an office. Directly in front of them beyond the stairs was another door.

Jane pushed it open and stepped aside to let Mike peer in. "That will be Cora's kitchen. I let her tell them what to do with it. At the general store, her restaurant was an afterthought, added afterward and as the business grew she still only had that small kitchen with the tiny stove."

"You gave her a lot of space to work with." He whistled. "And that stove."

"Don't even mention it. It cost almost as much as Alma's piano. That's what I get for promising Cora the best. I don't mind, if she's happy our customers will be happy for her food, so it's a win-win. Just because I'm clueless when it comes to how to use a stove, doesn't mean Cora can't have what she needs."

Jane set her hand on the railing to the stairs and leaned against them for a minute while Mike finished perusing the kitchen. Once he'd finished, she tapped the railing, "This is one of three staircases upstairs. Obviously this one will be used right at check-in and by the staff to take luggage to rooms if someone wishes to gamble first."

"We going up?"

"Not on these. First, the casino." She led him back through the door into the saloon. As they passed through the saloon, she returned greetings, but didn't stop to chat. Already she was feeling tired and wanted to get the tour over fast as she could.

When they got to the door into the back, Mike opened it for her. On the other side of the wall was another staircase hanging in mid-air. "Those stairs don't go all the way to the floor."

"That's because once this place is shut down, the stairs will split here." Jane set her hand on the bottom step where it hung in mid-air. "There will be a small landing and steps down into the restaurant and lobby or into the casino area. This section of the wall will be open to allow everyone to go from the restaurant into the show without having to go through an actual door."

Mike walked into the large room and leaned on the railing above the pit. The sunken casino was a large rectangle, with the game tables on the end where they stood. There was an empty area on the right wall where the bar would be placed.

At the far end of the pit sat the stage with rows of chairs in front. They'd put viewing areas on the main level so they could have those that didn't wish to mix in with the gamblers still able to enjoy the show.

They'd upgraded from just poker and faro to roulette and craps, among others. In fact, they were keeping secret their deal to bring boxing matches in once a month, and regular horse races to add to their coffers.

"The doors back there," she pointed to a door to the right of the casino, "will lead to the elite gambling rooms."

"You expecting much business with those?"

"We already have regulars for the high-in game and we host that weekly so I think we'll manage. We'll have two levels for the elite rooms. The highest will be ten-thousand a month, with games once every two weeks for them alone."

"That's a hefty sum."

"Henry Daugherty and Parker Krenshaw are both already signed on."

"You got Henry?" Mike's brows rose. "That's quite a feat. He'll bring in more names. Parker surprises me."

"Apparently he's better with money than Jackson was. He had his own wealth that wasn't decimated by Jackson's debt."

"Are we trusting him now?"

"Not in the slightest, but we'll still take his money."

Mike laughed. "At ten-thousand a month, I can't blame you there."

"Those select few will be allowed to partake in our lower tier, set at thirty-five-hundred a month. Graham has hinted he might be interested in that one. A few others on the hill are asking about both levels, and there's been a few inquiries from Denver and Pueblo."

"I am impressed, dear one."

A pleased flush of heat settled in her cheeks at the compliment.

"I'm still trying to figure out how Cole managed it." Mike glanced at her with a crooked grin. "Getting approval for a full casino like he did."

Jane smiled and shrugged. "You were at the town meeting. You heard just how Cole convinced the Council." Truth was, she was very proud of how he'd managed. Cole had managed to come up with some great arguments on his own, with very little input from her. Even Tom said he'd had little to do with the ideas Cole had come up with.

"He's been around you too long. "I've never heard him so long-winded as I did at that meeting. Did you coach him? Or wait, did Tom?"

"Surprisingly, we helped him very little. I was willing to live without the gambling tables if we had to, but without the whores he was insistent, as were our investors. So, I made him build his own arguments. Tom and I only added a couple of points and helped him make at least one of them less confrontational."

"Then he has been around you too long. His argument was impressive."

"When you feel passionate about something, you tend to be more involved. The casino aspect, and the burlesque, really helps keep much of the saloon aspect of the hotel—and that's where he feels more at home."

"The bar will go there?" Mike pointed to the empty area.

"Yes. I wish we could have made this area a little bigger but we had to work with what we've got."

"And you didn't want to give up any more space in your apartment."

"We really couldn't. With Alma moving in, taking in Sally, not to mention the baby, we needed the room. The only thing I didn't bother to waste space on was a kitchen."

"Thank heavens. I don't know what happened when you hit your head, but you lost all ability to cook. Clara wasn't the best, but at least she managed to make more than a really bad stew."

She offered him a glare, then pushed off the railing. As she headed for the stairs behind the stage meant for staff only, she shook her head. "You aren't funny, Mike. I'm sorry I can't cook like your sister could, but I have no desire to. I'm perfectly happy eating Cora's delicious meals."

"Can't say I blame you. My chef is good, but when it comes to filling and comforting food, no one can compare to Cora." He followed her upstairs, then stopped right at the top. "What about the sounds from downstairs?"

"Double floors. We're about three feet higher on this floor than we were in our old second floor." The hallway stretched before them. Three doors lined the hall in front of them, another sat in the corner. On the wall to the left were two doors. The hallway wrapped around with more rooms on the other side.

To their right sat a door for a bathroom, and another for a water closet, both already clearly marked. Mirroring them on the opposite wall sat another bathroom and water closet. Mike nodded as he took it all in. "Impressive."

"Thank you."

When she started up the next set of stairs, he followed close behind. "So tell me about the rooms."

"Tommy has about a third of this end of the building above our apartment. The rest is for Sally and Alma's sizable rooms, plus two extras for company, one that Jesse has claimed as his own. Tommy has agood-sizedd apartment. Two rooms and he has a bathroom of his own. Every other room on each floor, with the exception of the staff quarters, is a two room suite. Two bathrooms on the second floor."

"What about the third floor?"

"Two water closets and one bathroom, on each side near the stairs, just like this floor. The logistics of getting water pumped up to that level were more difficult, and we have fewer guest rooms on this floor." Jane heaved herself up the final few steps, regretting agreeing to the tour.

"Lady Jane!" Hammy's surprised voice wasn't any less happy. He bowed to her.

"Hello, Mr. Hamm." Jane smiled and tried to catch her breath. "I was just giving Mike a tour, showing him what your fine craftsmanship has accomplished so far."

"Aww, it ain't nothin'." Hammy cleared his throat. "Cole's down at that end. Ain't got much left on this floor 'cept the furniture."

"Thank you. We'll go see what Cole's up to." After a deep breath, she pushed forward and started down the hall. "Like I was saying. Every room on the level below us is a two room suite. We've got nine guest rooms on that floor, Tom's room, plus the bathrooms and water closets."

"That's a lot of plumbing you're putting in this place."

"I know. I was worried, but Hammy hired someone that's worked in some of the bigger cities to help." Jane paused halfway down the hall to rest. "On this floor we have six guest rooms. They are each three room suites, although the bedrooms are just a smidge smaller than those below. This is our only completely finished guest room, so you can get a feel for what they'll look like when they're all done."

Mike stepped into the room she pointed to. "This is a good amount of space. Even better, I like what you've done with it. The decor is comfortable, nothing too fancy. Some of your more elite visitors might not appreciate the lack of gilding, but I think many will. I sure would."

"Too bad you've subjected yourself to the lap of luxury, what with your health spa being for those elite." Jane grinned and laced her arm through his. As they headed down the hall, she pointed toward the door set behind the stairs. "We've also got eight staff rooms. They're all just one room, and a little on the small side, but not all of our staff will need them and we're hoping they'll only be temporary homes for anyone on our staff."

"What's going on here?" Cole stepped out of a room, hammer in hand. He grinned. "Couldn't wait for the place to reopen before you started snooping, Mike?"

Jane smirked, but ignored Mike's reply as she took in Cole's half-dressed form. More than ever she was grateful for the unseasonably warm day and the hard work he was doing. She sighed and leaned against the wall, but then realized both men were looking at her expectantly. "I'm sorry. What?"

Mike groaned and shook his head. "Jane. Really."

"What? I would have to be on death's door not to look—and even then I still would." She stepped closer to Cole and set her hand on his sweat-damp chest. "If it weren't so difficult to get up all those stairs I'd be up here every single day watching the show."

"She's not kidding, neither." Cole winked and tugged her close. "I'm just about done. How long until your appointment with Daisy?"

"Who cares?"

"On that note," Mike interrupted. "I think I'm going to get out of here before I'm witness to something I'd rather not be. Thank you for the tour."

"Sure." She waved in Mike's general direction before she slipped that hand along Cole's chest as well. "You've been working hard."

"All day. I think I deserve a reward."

"You want free beer like Hammy?"

Cole laughed. He brushed his lips across hers. "Not exactly."

"Hmmm." She let her fingers dance along the muscles in his shoulders. "Maybe a good hearty lunch at Cora's?"

"Oh, I'm hungry, but it ain't for meatloaf."

"No?"

"No."

She sighed and leaned into him. "Whatever could you want, then? Certainly not the elephant."

"I don't see no elephant."

"No?"

"Just you." He leaned close to her ear. When his lips brushed her neck, she trembled. His low chuckle warmed her ear. "My wife."

"You definitely deserve a reward now."

"Downstairs?"

"Fast as we can."

*The legacy of heroes is the memory of a
great name and the inheritance
of a great example.
-Benjamin Disraeli*

The candlelight flickered across the paper, giving just enough illumination for Jane to write without being too bright. Instead of wasting the fuel of the lamp, she'd been happy to settle with a simple candle.

A strong movement within caused her to flinch and she stopped writing. With a sigh, Jane sat back and rubbed her side in an attempt to ease the discomfort. She tilted her head to stretch her neck and fought off a yawn. Once the aches had eased, she dipped her pen back in the ink and resumed her letter.

The bedroom door creaked open, but Jane didn't pause. Cole cleared his throat, but his voice remained gruff from sleep, "Jane? What are you doing up?"

"Just writing a few letters." She shrugged. "I couldn't find a comfortable position to sleep in tonight. I'm sorry, I tried to be quiet so as not to wake you."

"You didn't wake me by writing. I just went to grab ya and you weren't there."

She smiled at the sentiment, but kept writing. When he brushed aside her hair, she automatically tilted her head to welcome the kiss to her neck. "I'm sorry I wasn't there."

"You should be." He let out a great yawn. After a big stretch, he grabbed another chair and straddled it. "Why don't you light the lamp?"

"I don't need that much light to write, there's no reason to waste the fuel."

"Who are you writing?"

"Clara's parents. I've already written to Al—"

"What? Why are ya writing to soldier boy?"

Jane sighed. Here she sat married and great with his child, yet Cole still couldn't rein in his jealousy of the man. "You are so pitiful sometimes."

"Just asking."

She pursed her lips and cast him a half-hearted glare. "I was filling him in on what's happening, just as I've done every month for two years. I also told him just how happy you are that he's found someone else."

"Long as he's not trying to pursue you no more, that's all that matters."

"Brute."

"Yeah."

"Well, he seems to be rather appreciative of the widow Eades all the way out there in North Carolina. I don't think you have anything to worry about. Not that you ever did."

He leaned forward. "You let me think I did."

"Of course I did. I'm no fool. Half the fun in the beginning was the challenge. It wouldn't have been any fun for you if I just fell at your feet."

"You still don't."

"True." She winced and set her hand to her side when one of the babies gave her another sound kick in her ribs. "Oh."

"You feeling okay?"

"Yes."

When she winced again, he snorted. "Wanna try again?"

"I'm all right—I just believe these two are recreating the civil war right here in my belly, so I've been more comfortable."

"What battle they on now?"

"The way they're killing me at the moment, I think they're burning Atlanta."

"Ouch."

"Now you know why I couldn't sleep."

"Still isn't an excuse.

She set down her quill and peered at him. "What else would I have done?"

"Could've woke me up." He laughed when she smacked him. When she tried to grab her quill again, he gripped her chair and pulled it toward him. "Even if you just wanted to make me as miserable as you are right now."

"I'm not entirely miserable. Just uncomforta-ow…"

He set her hand over hers when she pressed on her belly. "So what are you telling your parents—sorry, Clara's parents."

Grateful for his attempt at distraction, she took another bracing breath. "That I'm looking forward to their visit this summer. They've decided on July, by the way. I've told them that we'll have a room saved for them."

"Sure. We'll keep the one closest to Tom's open around that time."

The babies both moved at once and so fast she jolted half out of her chair. She exhaled slowly and let him help her the rest of the way to her feet.

"Why don't you come back and try to get some sleep?"

"Not yet. I want to walk and see if I can't get them to settle down." At his frown, she sighed. "Just for a few minutes. I won't overdo it, I'm just feeling restless."

"Just a few minutes," he allowed. With a supportive hand around her waist, he walked her the length of the living room. "Saw Kathy today."

"Oh dear. What on earth was she pestering you about this time?" Jane loved Kat with all her heart, but the closer it came to the babies being born the more Kat pestered them for details. Worse, she'd remind them of things Jane had already thought of. Jane had taken to pretending she'd forgotten everything and faking panic.

"She kept trying to get me to tell her what you were thinking of for names. Wouldn't believe that you haven't told me."

"I hadn't thought about it much." It was a half-truth. She'd thought about names, but nothing felt right.

"Bull."

"Well, I know what names I don't want." Jane smirked. "No Johnny, Alan, or Joe."

"Hell no."

"It's more difficult with twins. I should pick two boys names and two girls."

When they got to the sofa and she went to sit, he helped her down. He settled next to her and pulled her against him. One of his hands ran over the swell of her belly in a soothing circle. "I think you just need boy's names."

"You're that certain it's two boys?"

"I done had two girls already. This time it's gonna be boys. And you got six boys to one girl in your family."

"Too bad. I'm preparing girls names, too."

"Like what?"

She frowned. "I'm not entirely sure. I think for one of the boy's names we should use yours."

"Cole?"

"Colton."

"Well then for that matter, maybe you should keep Clara in mind."

"Not such a bad idea."

His hand stopped its lazy circle. "What? I thought you hated the name."

"I did. Possibly because I hated her, but…" For the first year of her existence Jane had fought against Clara in a never ending battle. Meeting Nick, and the rest of Clara's family, plus how Jane's own life had changed had made her start to think different.

Cole's hand ran along her arm, pulling her from her thoughts. "But what?"

"I can't hate her anymore."

"Why?"

"If it wasn't for Clara—even for her stupidity—I wouldn't be here. I wouldn't have what I have. I wouldn't have found you." She tilted her head to meet his gaze. "I owe her my life."

"Then I guess Clara is in the running."

"And Colton."

"I dunno."

"Or Christopher for Nick. That is his middle name."

"Colton's better."

"Well I like them both. Christopher George and Colton Thomas."

He squeezed her hand and laughed. "You got your mind set."

"Of course then there's the girls. Clara. I would like to honor Katherine in some way. Either her name, or Marie, her middle name."

"You'll figure it out, just like you did with the boys."

"I guess so." She settled back against him content. "I think it's time to get to bed."

"Good idea." He propped her up while he stood, then helped her to her feet. The whole way back to the room he remained silent. Once she was settled he leaned on the edge of the bed. "I'm not getting in there until I know you don't want nothing else."

"I am kind of hungry," she admitted sheepishly.

"I'm not surprised. I'll get that basket you brought home from Cora's."

She returned his kiss and grinned. When he left to get the food, she settled back against the headboard with her hands on her stomach.

The scent of her orange tea pulled her eyes back open and she took the cup from Cole gratefully. "Thank you. It's so nice to be able to drink this over that other brew I had to drink all those months."

"Thought you started to like it there for a while."

She pursed her lips. "I got used to it. I never liked it."

He settled into the bed next to her with the basket between them. When she sat up to dig through it, he leaned back. He didn't speak until she pulled out a plate of cookies. "That's what you're eating?"

"Is there a problem?" She grinned and nestled in next to him. "I don't have to be pregnant to want Cora's cookies. They're good to pass up."

He picked one off the plate and popped it in his mouth. "Can't argue with that. I just figured you were after the ham."

"Oooh, ham?" She shoved the plate at him and dug back into the basket. The ham was hiding on the bottom, and she pulled it out. "I didn't see that."

"There's no way you're gonna be able to function tomorrow."

"At least I won't be alone. I take you into misery with me."

"That dance is tomorrow night, you know."

"I most certainly do." Jane pulled a piece of ham off with her fingers. "I'll make it to that. Maybe then I'll sleep for a change."

"I got better ways of making you sleepy."

"You do?"

"Yup."

"The ham can wait."

"Good."

*Children are the hands
by which we take hold of heaven.
–Henry Ward Beecher*

"You made us late," Jane chided.

Cole laughed as she took his offered arm. They walked toward the meadow where the dance was already in full swing. "Don't go blaming me. You started it."

"But you were the one that got intent on finishing." She winked, her mood considerably bright despite how tired she was, and the fact that they'd closed the saloon the day before.

While the dance had been planned all along as a winter affair, the continuing fair weather had brought quite a crowd to the party. The platform they used for dances was overflowing, and some people gathered in the meadow to dance despite the mud.

When they stepped over the railroad tracks, a sharp pull in her side made her stop. She gasped and set her hand at her side, taking a few deep breaths.

"Jane?"

"It's all right." She straightened and let out a long breath of air. "Just a little pull. I think someone was stretching."

Cole frowned, his doubt etched into his face. When she dragged him toward the dance, he didn't argue aloud, but she figured there was an argument in there. Still, the moment they hit the dance floor, he swept her into the crowd.

She grinned as he spun her around the floor. "By all rights I should be too tired to do this. You really do give me energy."

"How much?"

"How much do you think?"

He spun her away and then back. Once she was back in his arms he pulled her closer than propriety allowed. "Bet it'll be enough."

"I do hope so." She laughed and curtsied as best as her body would allow when the song ended. When he led her from the floor, she sighed and leaned against the railing. "We just can't stay too long."

"Never planned on it."

"Jane!" Nick walked up and kissed her cheek.

She returned the kiss and smiled. "Good evening, Nicholas. I'm surprised to see you here. Dances don't seem like your type of activity."

"Mike suggested I invite Cora to attend, as she had considered forgoing the party." Nick quirked a brow. "I believe he is trying to meddle."

"I can't say as I blame him. You need some meddling." Jane giggled.

"Haven't you meddled enough?" Cole shook his head. "Leanne is already moving to Dominion Falls. Mike and Daisy are courting. What else are you planning?"

"Happiness, of course. For all—oh." Jane gasped and gripped Cole's arm at the renewed stretch of pain in her abdomen. This time it shot across her back, and she winced. "Oh, goodness."

"Jane?" Nick looked down and jumped backward. "Hell. *Daisy!*"

"What's going on?" Cole wrapped his arm around her waist.

"I, um." Jane took a few deep breaths. When Daisy ran up, Jane met her gaze. "I think something happened. What was that you said about water?"

Daisy moved to Jane's other side when she doubled over in pain again. "All right. I think it's time to get to the clinic."

Cole scooped Jane up fast and raced toward the clinic.

Each bouncing step rattled through her, but Jane held on and didn't dare whimper. At least not until they were already in the clinic and halfway up the stairs where another wave of pain hit. She dug her nails into his neck and whimpered into his shoulder.

He stopped in the middle of the stairs, waiting there until she'd relaxed.

"Go. It's all right." She nodded, closing her eyes when he moved again. Once he'd set her on the bed she took his hand. As the room began to fill up she pulled him into a deep kiss. After a few minutes she released him and smiled. "Now get the hell out of here."

Cole frowned. "I'm not gonna."

"You'll drive me crazy. You'll be—oh." She groaned and clutched the bedding as a wave of pain raced across her back again. Daisy said something, but with the doctor on her right side, she couldn't understand. As the wave passed, she took a shaky breath and met Cole's panicked gaze. "I'll be fine."

"Cole." Charlie set his hand on Cole's shoulder. "You'll be in the way. She's got us and Kat here with her."

Jane smiled, though she felt her lip tremble, and cupped his cheek. "I'll be fine. We'll all be fine. I promise."

When she winced again, Cole leaned in and pressed his forehead to hers. "You can't promise."

"I just did." Jane gave him a gentle kiss. "We'll be all right. All of us are going to come through this. I promise."

"I'll be right outside." Cole's fingers laced into her hair.

"I know. I love you."

Cole kissed her again, gentle and slow. When he stood up, he only took a step back.

Jane smiled. "Go, so Charlie can annoy me." She closed her eyes and lay back with a shaky breath. Once she was sure Cole was gone, she opened her eyes again. "Charlie."

"Yes, Jane?"

"Switch with Daisy—I can't hear her. I'd rather not be able to hear you."

Quiet laughter filled the room as Charlie did as she asked and Daisy came to sit on her left side. "How are you feeling?"

"You've been present at many births. How do you think?" Jane frowned.

Kat laughed as she moved closer to the bed behind Daisy. "Be nice. She's the one that's going to get you through this."

Jane managed a smile, but it faded when another contraction hit. This time the intensity was even greater and she grasped onto the closest thing, which happened to be Charlie's wrist. Even though he was on her right side, even she heard his shout of surprise and pain.

Before she could take the time to catch a breath, another intense contraction hit so strong she screamed.

Kat sat next to her the second Daisy moved away and took Jane's hand. A cool sponge pressed to Jane's forehead and Kat smiled. "You aren't going to take your time with this one are you?"

"I never do." Jane managed to laugh. "When it's time, it's time."

"One of your little ones is ready, Jane," Daisy said. "Are you?"

"No." Jane's body jerked at the next contraction. This time her scream was primal as her body instinctively sat. For the next half hour the only sounds where Daisy's instructions and Jane's screams.

Then Daisy told Jane to stop, and she gasped. Tears slipped down Jane's cheeks and she held Kat's hand tight while Daisy worked.

"All right, Jane. One more time and this little one will be here." Daisy gave her an encouraging nod.

Jane did as instructed, and with a final push Daisy pronounced the baby a boy. When his cries rang loud through the room, the tension seeped away. With a sob of relief, Jane sank back to the pillows and tried to catch her breath. She knew there was another baby, but for now her body was giving her respite.

Charlie walked over with the baby and set him in her arms. "He appears to be healthy as can be."

"Tell Cole," Jane whispered. A new rush of pain stretched across her abdomen and she winced. "Oh. Charlie."

"I've got him." Charlie took the baby back. "Get back to work."

"I'll tell Cole," Kat murmured.

"Tell him I hate him." Jane groaned, but held back knowing what she felt now could get much worse.

"I will." Kat laughed and crossed the room. She opened the doors to the balcony, leaving them wide open. Even from where Jane was in the bed she could hear the murmurs of a gathered crowd. Kat shouted over them, "It's a boy, and he's strong and healthy."

A cheer went up, calls for celebration and congratulations echoing through the room.

Kat's voice cut through it all, "But she's not done!"

"She chuffed yet?" Cole's laughing shout easily carried over the suddenly silent crowd outside.

"As a March hare! Be glad you're down there." Kat guffawed. "I think she'd even make you blush with the names she's calling you."

Jane wanted nothing more than to smile at the good cheer, and the laughter, and the fact that her son sat across the room healthy as a horse. However, the waves of pain were becoming constant, but something felt wrong. "Daisy."

"I know." Daisy stepped up closer to meet Jane's gaze levelly. "This one is backwards. I need to try to turn it."

When another contraction hit, Jane thought she might rip open. An intense scream rang in her ear so loud, she was shocked to realize it was her own. When she gasped for air, she sobbed, "No."

"Close the door, Katherine." Daisy moved back so she could work.

Kat did as instructed and rushed back to Jane's side. She clutched Jane's hands to her chest. "What is it? What's wrong?"

"The baby is presenting backwards. I wanted to turn it around, but she had other ideas." Daisy took a deep breath. "Jane. This is going to be difficult, but it isn't impossible. We have to try. If she becomes stuck, we're going to have to cut."

Jane sobbed, but couldn't respond as another contraction hit. She whimpered and shook her head. "No."

"Jane." Kat squeezed her hand. "You can do this. Just be as stubborn as you always are and Daisy won't need to cut."

Charlie touched Jane's shoulder. "You've got a strong, healthy boy here, let's go for two, all right?"

"I don't have much choice." Jane couldn't even scream when the next wave hit, her body jerked again and she gripped Kat's hands until she couldn't even feel her hand. With a sob, she sagged back against the pillow when it subsided. "Cole."

"He's outside out of the way. If he was in here you know what he'd be doing. The whole time he'd be fretting and getting mad at your doctor's." Katherine smiled and dabbed the sponge on Jane's forehead again. "He'll be in soon as this little one stops being so stubborn."

Jane's lip trembled and she managed a nod before the next wave hit. Each contraction grew closer together until she lost track of time. The concerned murmurs around her barely cut through, and she rarely had a chance to catch her breath.

On one brief break, she settled back against the pillows. Kat mopped her brow, but sweat soaked Jane's dress and hair.

Daisy squeezed Jane's knee. "She hasn't moved. I think we have to help her out."

"No." Jane wiped at her tears and tried to sit up again. "No cutting."

"Jane," Daisy said softly. "We may have to."

"No." Jane braced for the next contraction she could feel coming. "No."

Kat gasped when Jane gripped her hand tight.

Over her own scream, Jane hear Daisy's exclamation. Daisy grinned. "That's it, Jane. Be more stubborn than the baby."

Charlie rushed over to help. When it came time for Jane to stop, he gripped her shoulders at her argument. "You need to stop. Let Daisy take her time. I know it hurts."

"You have *no* idea," Jane shrieked at him. Just when she thought she couldn't bear the pain any longer it eased. A sob escaped, but then her breaths fell shallow and fast as she sank back into the bad.

"It's a girl!" Charlie laughed. "You got one of each."

"She's not crying." Jane whimpered and tried to see for herself, but the doctors were huddled around the baby.

"Just a minute," Charlie soothed.

When the soft cries filled the air moments later, Jane sagged in relief.

Kat brushed the sponge along Jane's forehead and chest. "You did it Jane. Now you need to rest."

Jane smiled and sighed. "Cole."

"Daisy will get him when she's done." Kat set aside the sponge. "I'm going to see those babies now. You rest."

"He is healthy as an ox, Jane," Charlie declared. "Your girl looks good, too. Not as boisterous yet, but her journey was a little more difficult."

Daisy leaned over Jane. "I'll go get Cole."

Jane could barely nod in response, her body caving to the exhaustion and pain, pulling her into the safety of the darkness of sleep. Cole's voice pulled her back slowly, and she woke to find him stretched out beside her. She didn't bother to open her eyes when she nestled against him. "I hate you."

"I know," his low chuckle rumbled against her ear.

"Are they all right?"

"Daisy says they are." He ran his hand along her back. "You did good."

"I did good? That is what you have to say?"

He tucked his finger under her chin and pulled her lips to hers in a slow searching kiss. When he pulled back, he smirked. "Actions. Not words."

She pursed her lips. "That's becoming far too convenient an excuse for you."

"You never had any complaints before."

"After today I do."

"You'll forget."

She snorted, wincing at the pain that rang through her body. "Don't count on it."

He kissed her forehead and then her lips before leaning in close to her ear. "I'm proud of you."

With her cheek pressed to his, she sighed. "I still hate you."

"I love you too."

She smiled and pulled back to meet his eyes. "And I love you."

"Did ya decide on names?"

"Colton Thomas and Clara Marie Mitchell."

With a brief glance to make sure everyone else in the room remained distracted, he squeezed her hand. He whispered in her ear again, "When is their Ma gonna start using the name, since it's hers too?"

She giggled. "That's a secret I want to keep."
"Forever?"
"Maybe."

We find a delight in the beauty and happiness of children, that makes the heart too big for the body.
—Ralph Waldo Emerson

Cole's voice filtered through Jane's subconscious, stirring her awake. He spoke low, "This is new to me."

Jane's eyes fluttered open as she was keenly aware he wasn't talking to her, he wasn't even in bed. She smiled as she remembered where she was, and the aching pain in her body reminded her what had happened the day before. A tiny cry reached her ears, but as much as instinct told her to get up, she lay still to listen.

"I ain't got any idea what I'm doing. You gotta be nice to your Pa."

She bit her lip to cover her laughter, but couldn't resist lifting her head to find him. Across the room she found him hovering over the bassinet. Tears filled her eyes when she realized he was holding one, and touching the other. She wasn't sure which he was talking to.

"Your ma, she can handle anything you throw at her. You gotta be nicer to me. I'm gonna be the one that lets you get away with mischief."

Her jaw dropped, but her protest died on her lips when he cast a wicked look over his shoulder. "You brute."

"Heard you moving around, I knew you was up."

"Ingrate."

"Wanna see them?"

"More than anything." Her heart picked up its pace in eagerness. She tried to sit, and was grateful to have him at her side helping her in moments. "They must be hungry."

"Clara's been fussing." Cole nodded. "That's why I had her, but I know you haven't slept much."

"Just give me that baby." Jane laughed and held out her arms for the baby he held. "You were spending time with them, and I love that. You can make pitiful excuses around Daisy—however I have no need or desire for them."

He chuckled and leaned in to give her a kiss before she got comfortable with Clara. "Glad you're feeling better."

"No you're not. You're annoyed by my tone."

"Just a little."

"Brute." She winked and turned her attention to Clara. Once she was latched on and feeding, Jane had to wipe another tear away. "She's so much smaller than Colton."

Cole settled next to her with Colton in his arms. "Charlie says she's gonna be fine, just needs a little extra feeding is all."

"Charlie doesn't know everything."

"Daisy says the same."

"She doesn't know everything either."

"Ain't no one that does."

"I do." She grinned at his chuckle. "I know everything."

"You think so, do you?"

"Sure do. I can even read minds."

"That so?"

"I know what you're thinking right now."

He bumped his shoulder against hers. "Then what am I thinking?"

"You're thinking…" She managed to pull her gaze away from Clara to meet his eyes. "That you love me, and that you'd like nothing more than to kiss me."

"Well I'll be. You can read my mind."

"Then what are you waiting for?"

He cupped her cheek and closed the distance between them. His lips danced along hers, slowly pulling her deeper into the kiss.

She melted into the kiss, reveling in the moment and the rush of emotion. A sharp pain startled her out of the kiss, and she grunted. She looked down at the feeding baby. "Ow."

"Problem?" He snickered as she readjusted the baby.

"Don't laugh. That hurt." When he started laughing louder she reached out and twisted his nipple between her thumb and finger. She grinned at his protest and looked back down at Clara as she latched on again. "Your pa should know better than to laugh at me by this point."

"You do know that any minute we're gonna have a bunch of visitors wanting to see the babies."

"They'll have to wait." Jane lifted Clara when she finished eating. "I'm spending some quiet time with my husband, and two of my children, to whom he's already proving to be an amazing father."

"I think I like the sound of that." Cole set Colton down next to her and took Clara from her arms. Once she had Colton feeding, Cole settled back down beside her.

"I'll be sure not to tell anyone you said that."

"I think you already done ruined my reputation."

"And you've ruined mine, so we're even." She leaned against him when he wrapped his arm around her shoulder. Contentment filled her soul in the simple moment. The way Cole couldn't stop staring at Clara added to her joy until she thought she might burst.

Cole smiled and kissed the top of her head. "Yes, Mrs. Mitchell?"

"I knew you had no reason to worry—Pa."

"Same back at you, Ma."

She leaned up and was happy he closed the distance. The kiss was brief, but sweet, and when they separated she had to wipe a tear from her cheek. "I didn't know it was possible."

"What?"

"To love you more than I already did."

"Yesterday you hated me, and were cursing certain former favorite parts of my body. Now you love me more?"

"Yes. That's exactly right. Also, I wasn't cursing those body parts. I still appreciate them very much."

"Good."

As Colton finished feeding, she lifted him to her shoulder. She sighed and nuzzled him gently, reveling in his smell. "Soon we'll be able to take them home, and our family will all be together."

"We're gonna have a week to adjust before Alma gets here. Then we'll be together. All six of us."

"Good for you."

"How so?"

"You included Sally in that number."

He smirked. "Kinda have to. She's living in our place, and calling you ma."

She hummed in disbelief, but rather than protest she yawned. When she woke to a quiet knock, an hour had passed and the babies were back in their bassinet.

After Daisy finished checking on everyone, the influx of visitors began. First Kat, Norman, Cindy and Lizzie stopped by. Then her brothers made their appearances. In between naps and feedings, Jane managed to spend some time with them all.

Toward the end of the day a bundle of energy burst into the room and leapt onto the bed. Cole laughed as he scooped Jesse off the bed before he could pounce on Jane, who was in the middle of feeding Colton. "Easy there. You don't wanna squash your brother."

"Sorry." David stopped at the door, breathless. "Minute we hit the door he took off. He's too quick for me."

"He's too quick for us all." Jane grinned, and adjusted the blanket she'd used to cover up at Jesse's appearance. "Jesse, if you promise not to jump again you can come back over. Or you can ask Cole nicely to take you to see Clara."

"Can I, Cole?" Jesse bounced in Cole's grasp. "She's my sister."

David walked over to the bed when Cole took Jesse to the bassinet. As he pulled the chair closer and sat next to the bed, David smiled. "So you named her Clara?"

"Yes." Jane shrugged. "I've made peace with the name. If it wasn't for her, I wouldn't have any of this."

"I think it's a good name. I always favored it." David squeezed her hand when she reached for his. "You look good."

"I look exhausted, but thank you." She shifted Colton when he finished feeding and brought him out from under the blanket. Once she'd resituated herself she caught David staring at the baby settled against her shoulder. "Would you like to hold him?"

"What?" David's eyes widened, but a smile broke his features. "I'd love to."

Jane handed him the baby, and used the moment of freedom to sit up straighter. While her body protested the action, she was still glad to sit straighter after sinking further into the bed every second.

David sighed. "He's perfect."

"Funny you say that." Jane chuckled and leaned in to brush her fingers over Colton's thick, light brown hair. "I think he looks just like his pa."

"Well then." David shot her a glance. "He wouldn't be perfect."

"I heard that," Cole piped up. "We are still in the room."

Jane giggled. "Doesn't always mean you're listening."

"Can I see, Pa?" Jesse climbed onto the bed and crawled over. He peeked over David's shoulder, but only sighed. "They don't look like much fun."

Cole snorted as he carried Clara over to the bed. "Well they aren't gonna be playing games any time soon. Just doing a lot of crying and sleeping right now."

Jesse gave a dramatic sigh. "But they're my brother and sister. We're supposed to play, right?"

"They'll get more interesting, you just have to be patient." Jane ruffled Jesse's hair. "Besides, you have plenty of people to cause havoc with. You want to drag these two sweet children into that too?"

"Yeah!"

Laughter filled the room and David gave Jane a pointed look. "I think you're in trouble. You got two kids that, well—they came from you and Cole—and Jesse's going to be working to make them more difficult."

"Too bad, Clara got a head start on that." Jane winced at the memory. "Stubborn and backwards is how she joined us, so she's already a trouble maker."

"Just like her ma," Cole pointed out.

Jane tried to hide her smile, but failed. She sighed and set her hand on the sleeping Clara. "Wouldn't have it any other way."

"Ma? Why are you crying?"

"Just tired." Jane wiped at her tears and pulled Jesse into a hug. "Maybe I should try to get some rest while Clara sleeps, hm?"

Jesse hugged her back tight. "Can I come back tomorrow?"

"I really hope you do." Jane didn't let him go while the two men carried the babies back to the bassinet. When she finally released him, Jesse scrambled away. "And maybe once we're settled back in our home, you can come stay a night just like we talked about. Then I'll have my whole family together."

"Yeah. Can I, Pa?" Jesse leapt off the bed.

"Once your ma is up to handling your energy, I'm sure it'll be fine." David laughed. He leaned down and kissed Jane on the cheek. "Congratulations."

Jane squeezed his hand and waved goodbye as they left. She sniffled and wiped at her tears when Cole settled on the bed next to her.

He pulled her close and muttered, "I still think it's crazy."

"What?"

"That we got them two kids sitting over there."

She chuckled. "I know. It certainly wasn't planned."

"Do that know what they're doing?"

"What? Who?"

"Colton and Clara. Trusting us with their lives?"

"I don't think they do. They should be afraid."

"Very afraid."

*There is nothing like a dream
to create the future.
–Victor Hugo*

Jane gripped the footboard and braced her feet. "Pull!"

"You sure?" Cole didn't move, despite her order.

She growled and nodded. "Just do it."

"Fine. On three. One…two…three."

She exhaled deeply, a small yelp escaping when he yanked the corset laces tight.

"You said pull."

"It's fine." She took short, sharp gasps. "Tie it off. Keep it tight."

"You trying to kill yourself?"

"No. I'm just trying to get my clothes on. It's been two months and I've lazed about for enough of it."

"Uh-huh. You did carry two babies, you know." Cole finished tying off the corset. His fingers slipped along her waist and pulled her close. "Just how much longer are you gonna laze around?"

"Why would you ever ask such a thing?" Jane turned in his arms. After a wink, she pulled out of his arms. She stepped into her petticoats and reached down to pull them up. When he grabbed her around the waist, she dropped them in surprise.

He spun her around and crushed his lips to hers eagerly, pushing her back toward the wall. His hands slipped down along her hips to pull her against him, and she trembled at the intimate touch.

"Cole," she managed to whisper, their lips barely parting.

"Yeah?" He trailed his lips along her neck. "Ain't too soon, is it?"

"No," she whispered. Her brain told her to pull away, but she laced her fingers into his hair. "But Cole…"

Her words were lost in another kiss as they clung to each other eagerly, anxious to make up for lost time. He lifted her, pressing her into the wall as her legs went around his waist.

"What?" He finally managed to ask, though he never stopped his touch or kisses.

"Nothing."

Pounding on the door pulled them both out of the moment and Tommy's voice bellowed out, "You two ready yet? We've got a crowd of people waiting and the train will be here in twenty minutes!"

Jane sighed. "We really do need to do this."

"That's what I'm trying to do," he muttered against her neck.

"No. Not *this*." She laughed and tried to push him off her. "The hotel. It's our grand re-opening, remember?"

"But you finally stopped—"

"The timing is horrendous, I know." She sighed and kissed his neck. "Once we come back here tonight and the twins are fed and asleep, you'll have at least two hours to see just how much I've missed you."

"Two hours?"

"And then we start the process over until we have another two hours."

"And then we start over again?"

"You're getting the idea." She laughed and gave him a quick kiss. "Now let me finish getting dressed."

"If I gotta."

"You do." She released the hold her legs hand on his waist and pushed him back so she could stand. "But trust me when I say it's no easier for me."

"Five minutes."

"Oh no. We may be able to, but after this drought there is no way I'm going to let you get away with a quick five minute romp the first time around." She stepped back into her petticoats and rushed through getting dressed. "I plan to use every minute the twins let us have."

"You don't play fair."

"I know." She gave him a quick kiss as she passed. Soon as she opened their door, she wrapped her arm around Tom's waist. They both made a beeline for the exit to the rest of the hotel. "Are you ready Tom?"

"Been ready since we shut this place down." Tom draped his arm across her shoulder. "Although I think you two are a little more willing to wait today."

"No, I'm ready to get these doors open and start making a profit again. Although Hammy has earned himself a lifetime of free beer with how quick and wonderful he handled all this work."

Cole fell into step beside them. "Definitely. I didn't think we'd made your best guess, and we came in ahead of schedule."

"Three weeks early." Jane stopped when they got to the casino and took in the staff already set up in the pit. She smiled. "Edgar, do you have Hammy's beer ready?"

"Ready and waiting." Edgar nodded. "Got glasses lined up for whoever comes. Seth's at Faro, Anne's at roulette, Chauncey has blackjack and Tony's got poker. Sally's gonna be on at seven with the burlesque set up for nine, until then we got Carl playing the piano."

Tommy nodded. "Just how we planned it. Best part, I can smell Cora's cooking from here so we know the restaurant is ready. I think we're all set."

"I think so." Jane laced her arm with Cole's, unable to stop smiling thanks to the excited jumping of her stomach. In the lobby she took a deep breath to take in Cora's cooking. "If nothing else we should have a full restaurant today."

"You've been advertising for weeks. It isn't just gonna be the restaurant that'll see business." Cole laughed. "You ready?"

"Not quite yet." She left his side to head to the table where Sally sat with the twins. After Jane had given both of the twins a kiss, she squeezed Sally's shoulder. "Thank you for keeping an eye on them while we get this place opened."

"You know I don't mind, Ma." Sally smiled. "Alma is staying at the library with Arthur until the worst of the craziness passes. She says she wants to watch me sing, though."

"We'll be watching from a premium seat, and she'll be with us so she's not on the crowded floor." Jane nodded. "None of us would miss it."

"Jane, it's time," Cole called.

Jane straightened and went to his side. They pulled the front doors open together and stepped onto the porch. The restless crowd grew silent and Jane winked at Cole.

Cole stepped forward. "It took a lot of doing, but Jane agreed no long speeches today. So we're just gonna say, welcome to the new Hangman's Inn! Come on in!"

Jane happily greeted their regular saloon crowd, and the group of people waiting to eat at Cora's. Once they were all taken care of, she turned her attention to those curious about the hotel.

She led them inside and passed them off to members of the staff to give them a full tour; all with instructions to end those tours at the casino, and if anyone wanted to see the hot springs they were to get charged. At the same time as the crowd was separated and taken care of she heard the first strains of the train whistle.

Cole wrapped his arm around her waist. "Ready?"

"I'm always ready." Together they walked to the depot and met the train. They secured guests and met Mr. Cutler for his promised return visit. By the time all the guests were settled and Alma had returned to the hotel, Jane was back in their apartment with the twins.

Alma touched Jane's shoulder as she fed Clara.

Jane smiled and followed Alma's gaze to the bassinet. "Colton is in there if you want to hold him. He's already eaten. Clara did too, but decided she wasn't done yet."

Alma stood over the bassinet for a few minutes before she lifted him carefully. She stared intently at the baby before turning back to Jane. Alma's brows creased in concern, "Don't want to hurt."

"I know," Jane whispered. "They seem so small, don't they? Don't worry. Come sit next to me, you won't break him."

Alma walked very slow to the sofa, and sank down next to Jane. "He will like stories."

"I bet he will. We'll have to make sure Cole reads to him, too. All of the adventures you like to read. And you can read to him too."

"Is everyone ready for supper?" Cole stepped into the apartment. His eyes looked as tired as Jane felt, but he wore a huge grin. "I asked Sally and Tom to help keep a table for us. I figured you were hungry."

"I am," Jane confirmed. "And there isn't much time until the show. I know Alma wants to be sure we get to see Sally on time."

"Then let's get them in the carriage." Cole helped Alma get Colton to the carriage.

While they got Colton settled, Jane made sure Clara was done eating. By the time Cole reached over Jane's head to get Clara, Jane was doing her best not to laugh over what he'd discover when he took the baby. She got to her feet and halfway to the bedroom before Cole grunted.

"You did that on purpose, didn't you?"

"Just change her diaper for me. She got my dress wet and I need to change." Jane pulled her shawl closer. "It won't kill you to change it."

By the time Jane emerged five minutes later, Cole had Clara changed and in the carriage, but he didn't look very amused.

Jane laughed and took the handle of the carriage. "Please. I've made you change five whole diapers in the past month. I'm letting you off easy."

"Sure you are."

Still laughing, she shook her head at him and dragged them along to dinner. The rest of the evening went by too fast. The shows met with great success and by the end of their evening, Jane was worn out, but happy. Once the twins were sleeping peacefully, she sighed happily.

The bedroom door closed and her smile grew. She leaned back into him when his arms went around her waist, "How are things in the casino?"

"Still hot. Tom's collecting the winning's from today now."

"The ten percent?"

"He ain't gonna forget to set aside the town's funds. It's Tom we're talking about. He got Cora's receipts for today too. Looks like real good business for the first day."

"It'll only get better...at least until our next catastrophe."

He kissed her neck. "You think there will be one?"

"We can't seem to avoid them. Hopefully we'll be catastrophe free for a while. I think we've had quite enough to last us a long time." She turned around to face him.

"And ya thought I'd be bored. Ain't happened yet."

"Any regrets?"

"Nah. Why would I?"

She tilted her head to meet his eyes. "Until I came along you had a nice quiet life...comfortable for you. Maybe you want to go back to the simple life you had."

"Not a chance." He turned her toward him and kissed her deeply, "I kinda like complicated. No chance of boredom—which I did have in that 'simple' life you say I had."

She slipped her hands up his chest and around his neck. "Well, Mr. Mitchell."

"Yes, Mrs. Mitchell?"

"The children are all asleep. I do believe we had plans."

"Yeah, we did."

"Those two had better behave."

Chuckling as he started to unhook her bodice, he nodded. "They'd better."

"Because if they don't—"

"Jane."

"Yes?"

"Shut up, you're wasting time."

"Yes sir."

To Be

Continued...

In Book 7 of the
Dominion Falls Series

Dust

Raiser

About the Author

Sarah Cass, author of over twenty novels in 4 series, is devoted to giving her readers well-crafted, emotional stories, with depth to even her secondary characters—to give readers a full world to explore. Stories that explore not only the labyrinths of the heart, but the nightmares of the soul. A RONE finalist, she is also owner and creator of Redefining Perfect. By day, she's a nurse, a mother, wife and cat-mom to 4 mischievous beasts. By night she crafts stories that take her across centuries. From the old west of Dominion Falls, to the small town of Lake Point for the holidays, and even into the paranormal land of Shifters and Magic in The Tribe. She loves hearing from her readers. Visit her at www.authorsarahcass.com

Other Books in
The Dominion Falls Series

Independent Brake
Changing Tracks
Derailed
Dark Territory
Green Eye
Runaway Train
Red Zone

Coming Soon in
The Dominion Falls Series

Dust Raiser
Chase the Red
Blizzard Lights
Dead Man's Switch
Bird Cage
A Highball Arrangement
Douse the Glim
Blood
Grave Digger
Bad Order

Books by Sarah Cass
The Tribe Series
The Tribe
The Wolf
The Chief
The Raven
The Lake Point Series
Santa, Maybe
Deep-Fried Sweethearts
Stalled Independence
Witch Way
A Thorough Thanksgiving
Eve's New Year
Heartstrings & Hockey Pucks
Luck of the Cowgirl
Stars, Stripes & Motorbikes
Free Falling
Love for Hire
Haunted Hearts
Stand Alone Novels
Masked Hearts
Leap